# The Good Side

**BOOK TWO**
of the Besser Trilogy

A novel within the Midnight Series

Dan Kovacs

THIS STORY IS ENTIRELY **TRUE**
(except for the parts *you* think are made up)

# prologue

## THE THING **BEFORE** THE THING

If pain ever became a physical manifestation of itself, what would *it* look like? Maybe a shabby roller bag that gets dragged through the airport by an old lady with no destination in mind. Each moment of pain gets another brick tossed in. Some people cap out at five bricks, while others power through with a few hundred. Checking the bag at the gate isn't an option.

Or, maybe pain looks like a half dead entity starting to creep up on you. Its hair is mangled; the clothes are tattered. Words and reason cannot persuade it. The look in its eyes is one of torment and longing to devour you fully. Every event makes you slower as it picks up speed until the day it latches on and forces you to a crawl. Eventually, you stop moving altogether as you are picked apart.

Or, maybe pain is a puppy. Sweet and innocent and entirely shaped by its environment. At first, the pain is small: the bumps and scraps from playing with the neighborhood kids or the innocent joke from a friend. Then, it begins to expand. The names become more hurtful, the loss of those around you becomes unavoidable, the sins of your past begin to plague the present. Your placid puppy grows into a vicious, snarling beast. It waits for a command to rip you apart.

Or, maybe pain is more literal. It's the otherworldly stare you have at a crowded party. You are surrounded by endless opportunities for social interaction, but none are appealing in the slightest. It could be the person that laughs the loudest in the room to make it seem like they are functioning normally. It could be untimely weight gain. It could be the dramatic shift in lifestyle: the newfound wanderlust that spurs a cross country move or the sudden end to a long-term relationship.

Or, maybe pain looks like losing the person you love to the ebbs and flows of life. You got pulled in one direction while they sought out another.

Or, maybe pain is the disease that gnaws away at you. Degrading you at a faster rate than modern medicine can cure.

It could be all of it or none of it.

You try to get better, but you don't know how.

You try to free yourself from the pain, but you don't know how.

So, you let it wash over as it defines and consumes you.

There's no warning to when, or if, it will ever happen, but you cling onto the idea that you *will* get better.

One day it does. Even the most undeserving get some opportunities to thrive.

The pain rushes from your body the moment you see him, and you realize for a short time that you are free.

The burdens fizzle out. The insecurities, doubts, and mental destruction you've put yourself through all disappear in an instant.

In hindsight, it all seems so trivial to the point where you question whether any of the feelings were real.

You realize how the pain was the thing before the thing.

What now?

part one

----------

# ANOTHER NIGHT ON MARS

# one

## UP, **UP**, AND AWAY

Midnight. As always.
    I was staring at the window, contemplating how it functioned.

In the far crevices of my brain, I knew how a window worked. Generally, when the latch was undone, you needed to lift upward in a motion that resembled a free weight curl at the gym. You continued in this motion until the window creaked open to a desirable position. So easy a caveman could do it. The crux of my problem resided in the edible I consumed an hour ago. It finally caught up to me and inhibited my ability to do much. The darkness in the room shrouded me in its embrace; the muffled sound of traffic outside the window passed by in an unrecognizable pattern; the sweat pouring off me kept distorting my vision. I needed fresh air. I continued my stare at the object in front of me. I was perplexed by the . . . uh . . . you know, the things that cover a window . . . blinds! That's right. The haze dispersed briefly, and I was able to pinpoint that blinds were the current source of my problem. I snuck my hand in-between two of the slats and struggled to lift the window. It budged slightly. I pulled harder, fearful I'd break the blind or shatter the window or piss off the creatures that watched me intently from behind the kitchen chair. I devolved into paranoia, but the window inched skyward. The sound of traffic, along with the harsh January air, rushed into the apartment. I continued down my path until the window reached a satisfactory height. Pleased with the work, I leaned my head against the blinds and heard a deafening *crunch* as they bent and squeezed against the force of my head. I panicked and backed away. My eyes darted to the kitchen chair. Nothing. I moved to the couch and covered myself with the blanket.

My head pounded incessantly. The headaches had kicked into motion over the past month, but it was hard to know if the current one was due to my tilted situation. I slammed my eyes shut and muttered some incoherent words. It likely wouldn't pass without—

An unignorable sensation took over and grew at an exorbitant pace. I whipped off the blanket and drifted to the bathroom. I stood there swaying before the toilet and realized any attempt to make a single drop into the desired location was futile. I spun around, dropped my boxers to the floor, and plopped myself down. Nothing came out.

*What the fuck is wrong with you?*

A simple thought with an overly complex answer. In this given situation though, the fuck wrong with me was being crossfaded. The alcohol from the concert did not mix well with an edible and caused a concoction of terrible results in my brain. You see, this was the first time I smoked or consumed pot since my days of walking around North Philadelphia as a lowly freshman at Temple University. Sure, I snorted drugs that one time with Dylan to limited success, but this was different. Apparently. I needed to take advantage of spending the weekend in a city where pot was as common as corrupt politicians.

But let's backtrack slightly.

We parted ways on New Year's Eve less than a month ago. Yeah, this isn't one of those novels where the time jump is so large that I've reinvented myself as a robotic and masculine camel, and life has magically realigned itself from the shit storm I created. Nah, we shall pick up nearly where we left off, but with the promise that this tale will be different. No person should suffer through the same debilitating story twice.

Also, I'm going to dial back the fourth wall breaks, self-deprecation, and other parlor tricks. I am older and minimally wiser while writing this, so I understand that interruptions such as this lose their appeal faster than a woman with a foot fetish after seeing her lover with an unsightly bunion.

Anyways, back to the backtrack.

We parted ways at midnight on New Year's Eve. The ending was rather bleak, but life trudges on and I found myself on a flight to SEA the second weekend of January. I really should have stayed home and packed, but what was life without a bit of adventure and total procrastination?

SEA was a bit of a bitch to get to from DAL. Thankfully, I had that Friday off. It would be the last since the policy of every other Friday off was determined "to not be strategically strategic in the strategical initiative to be more strategic." Their words, not mine, as indicated by the quotation marks. I took a flight from DAL to SAN, encountered a mild layover, and then pushed onward to SEA. I arrived in the City of Perpetual Rain and moved through the quiet airport.

I took the regional rail up to the Stadium stop. The ride was uneventful with the train car scattered with a few people who looked to be escaping work or heading out to ring in some weekend chaos.

Once I exited the train, I pulled out my phone and found the number for the individual I was meeting up with. It had been far too long since we saw each other. I eventually ran out of excuses as to why I hadn't made it up there, but the most prolific reason was that I had been trying to get myself better for a long while. The jury is still in deliberation as to where I stand, as it's something that doesn't happen in a flash, but a small, lurking voice in my head kept telling me that maybe I wasn't so bad to begin with. That voice was bullshit, probably.

They answered on the second ring. "BESSER! What the fuck? Where the *fuck* are you?"

"Always a way with words . . . I just got off the train and heading toward the stadium," I responded lazily. We had been texting sporadically throughout the day with me giving updates on my whereabouts, so my arrival shouldn't have been a shock.

"Okay . . . okay. I'll meet you at the end. I'm crossing the street rig—I SEE YOU!" The line went dead. The occasional lighting on the platform made it hard to see into the distance. I squinted and saw a figure running toward me. It was more of a shuffle than an all-out run. In most other scenarios I would have been alarmed. The figure closed the gap and arms flew out, embracing me in a hug.

"Hey, stranger," I said after we broke apart.

She stepped back into the light and I could finally tell that Lan hadn't changed at all. The same haircut, the same toothy grin, the same always-on-the-edge-of-rage look that sat beyond the eyes. She stared up and was likely processing the same about me.

"You look great!" she managed to say.

"Thanks. Just living life and all that fun stuff."

"I want to hear about everything that's going on. Especially the gossip from work," she said with a smirk. Lan left [REDACTED] in late 2016. She loved the company but quickly discovered how the pace and severity of work was not what she needed at the time. She wanted to work sixty hours a week and claw her way up the corporate ladder. No thank you. The thought was that she should do it now, at a young age, so when she meets someone and starts the next phase of her life, at least one portion of it would be figured out. With a previous internship at Google and the year and a half experience at [REDACTED], it was a no-brainer when Amazon hired her for a position in their corporate office in Seattle.

"So, what's the deal with this party?" I asked as we crossed the street. The stadium revealed itself from behind the parking garage and was depressingly generic from the outside.

"Obviously, that is our final destination," she pointed over to CenturyLink Field. "Well, actually, that is sort of where we are heading. There is an events center attached to the stadium, which is where the holiday party will be. Apparently, the food is insane and like a ton of different options. I think we can get a few drinks. But all that is secondary to the reason you are here." She was several paces ahead of me, stopped, and turned back. "Motherfucking Lorde. She comes on after Bishop Briggs."

"Do you want to get a good spot for Lorde?"

"Besser, besides Florence, this is the one artist I have wanted to see for years. So, yes, I want to be so close that I can tell her if she has a boogie in her nose." Amused with herself, she let out a cackle that reverberated down the empty street as she began to walk again.

"Don't sell yourself short. I came here to see you too, but Lorde is certainly a top priority. Did I tell you I am seeing her in March when she comes to Dallas?" I asked.

"What? No! Who are you going with?"

"Athena, Anders, and . . . Arturo," I barely muttered the last name, hoping she wouldn't catch it.

"How many goddamn people do you know with a name that starts with an A? Jeez."

"I think that's it." *There was one more, we don't speak of that any longer though. But we certainly think about it every day, isn't that right?*

We started our walk up a winding ramp that led us to civilization. We passed a few scattered people, but it was oddly quiet considering the nearby venue was about to be flooded by rabid Amazon employees.

Halfway up, Lan stopped as realization spread across her face. "Fucking Arturo!?! Besser, what the FUCK? Why are you going to a concert with him?"

"I plead the fifth," I said and threw my hands up in surrender.

"He is a piece of shit." She was wrong. Arturo wasn't inherently evil or what I would even consider a crappy person, he was just never present. I didn't hear from him unless I made the effort to reach out. The few times I did see him after the Bleachers concert, the conversation always drifted toward dangerous territory where he seemed detached from reality. He was entirely absorbed in his own life and struggles. I felt slightly jaded that he never wanted to hear what was going on with me. He had zero confidence in his music and was still hooking up with guys while continually making excuses for it. I was scared for him and wanted to keep him close. The romantic vibes fizzled out long ago, but the idea of being constantly available for Arturo did not. So, I forced him into interactions with me. Lorde would be the first one and Foo Fighters would be the other. They were checkpoints that allowed me to make sure he was okay because maybe I could still fix him.

"Lan, it's complicated. I have told you the story, but there are plenty of emotions tied up in it. I have a hard time letting go and I make poor choices because of that," I said evenly.

"You're better than that."

"Sometimes I wonder if that's actually true."

The conversation paused there as she continued up the ramp. The several minutes of silence between us faded out when we hit the top of the ramp and were blasted by a wave of people, weaving out in a multitude of directions.

From there, the night scattered into a series of distinct moments. We first went to an overly crowded bar to grab a couple of free drinks. I met her friend, Lucy, who happened to be dating Jag's best friend from college. The world shrank at odd times. Following that introduction, we left the bar and waited in line to get into the venue. We chatted about how her work was going. I caught her up on the parts of my life that she was unfamiliar with, which was mainly all of the details beyond September of the year prior. I didn't necessarily enjoy talking about it, but it made the situation easier each time I told it. Once inside, we crept about and snatched up all the food we could find. Without a doubt, we sampled over ninety percent of the available options. Filled to the brim on fried foods and with a drink in hand, we snaked between the crowd that stood in place after the Bishop Briggs show ended and found ourselves in the third row from the stage. It took Lorde a while to saunter out, but once she did, the crowd was more into it than I would have expected for a company holiday party. I drifted back and forth between being there and somewhere else entirely. Her songs conjured up feelings about my time in Dallas I wanted to forget.

Time continued on. Past the moment when I was handed a tiny edible. Past the moment when Lan said goodnight and went off to bed. Past the moment when I decided the lack of air in the apartment was going to suffocate me and I needed a release. Past the moment when all the thoughts were threatening to spiral me down toward the pits.

Back to the present.

After my excursion to the bathroom, I walked carefully down the dark hallway and laid myself back out on the couch. I popped open the Netflix app and listened to an episode of a show I didn't care about. The idea of falling asleep in silence weirded me out, but really it was a futile attempt to distract myself from the thoughts. I barely made it ten minutes before . . .

. . . I woke up the next morning. The mangled blinds brought in sunlight that beamed directly into my face. I felt groggy, but most of the uneasiness of the previous night was a distant memory. I pulled myself up from the couch and walked over to fix the blinds. Outside, I caught sight of a ragged man who was trudging down the street. His destination seemed undetermined with a pace that made me wonder if he found pain in each step.

I stepped away from the window and heard the bathroom door open. Lan strolled into the living room and let out a massive yawn.

"Jesus Christ. Why is it so cold in here?" she asked.

"Sorry, I needed some air last night and left it open way longer than I should have." I walked back over to the window and closed it, bringing finality to the saga with the inanimate object.

Lan didn't seem to mind too much. She was already in the kitchen working on a cup of coffee for herself. "You want one?"

"I'll pass. Hey, did that brownie hit you at all last night?"

She let out a long laugh. "No, it didn't. But maybe that's because I fell asleep before it had a chance to work its wonders. What about you?"

I thought about telling her my tale, but it didn't seem worth the effort. "Same with me. Oh well, there's always next time," I said with a shrug. The lie came off easy, as if I had practiced it in my dressing room before the cameras rolled. *Why do you lie about inconsequential things?* I rationalized that everyone did, so there was no harm in me doing it too. I also lie about consequential things, but I'm sure everyone else does that too.

It took us an hour to get presentable enough to leave the apartment and start our exploration of the city. Given more than one full day, I would have opted to go on a hike outside the city, but, instead, we decided that sticking to Seattle proper was the best bet. Following breakfast, our day started with a trip to the Amazon corporate offices, which was a scattered mess across several blocks. The buildings didn't mesh in a cohesive way and nothing stood out to indicate that Amazon was the ruling law of those buildings, but that was likely by design. We passed by a spherical structure deemed Bezos's Balls (oddly, the plan was for three overlapping balls) that housed a multi-level garden only available for the employees to go into. After her bragging was over, we spent the next couple of hours exploring the Pop Culture museum.

As we exited the Jimi Hendrix exhibit, I leaned over and asked Lan about her love life. It was a well-intended question that I waited until the proper moment to execute.

We continued to walk absentmindedly, past the school kids who were setting up a performance for their mariachi band. Eventually, she let out a massive sigh. "It is nonexistent. I had a couple of dates, but they didn't turn into anything serious. I'm getting to the point where I feel like I am never going to find someone."

"There are plenty of—"

"Save it," she said sternly. "I'm aware that there are plenty of people out there for me. I just haven't had the luck to stumble upon any of them yet—"

"Oh c'mon—" I complained.

"Will you stop interrupting me? I'm trying to be honest here," she said with mild frustration. "I see friends around me getting married and popping out kids like it's nothing. I think about how if I went back home to Korea that my parents would set me up on dates and I'd likely find someone to be with, but I really don't want that. Who would? I want someone who is driven and adventurous and laughs in uncomfortable situations and knows how to balance a checkbook and has a passport and can cook a meal instead of just shoving one into the microwave. My point is: it's the little things I'm looking for. The intimate details you don't put into your Tinder profile or describe to someone on the first date. I'm looking for that person you watch from the other side of room and wonder to yourself how you got so lucky. When I say that out loud, it sounds impossible to find, but it isn't. I just haven't found the right place to look yet . . ."

She continued on for a while as I tried to dig in more. It was an abnormal sight to see Lan vulnerable, so it was worth exploring.

We were halfway through the Star Trek exhibit when she flipped the question around.

"You know I was going to ask. What about you? What is the state of your love life?" she asked in a way where she was looking for an answer but didn't want it to spurn into a massive conversation.

I stared over at the Terminator model on display and considered if I shared any lineage with the robot. We had ventured into another sci-fi wing of the museum. Relics and costumes from numerous films lined the walls as curious people peeked to look at them in extreme detail.

I was immensely tired of that question. I wrote a book on the deteriorated state of my love life and she knew most it, so I wasn't sure what she was expecting. Still, though, I gave her one: "It's the same as always."

"Cryptic," she grumbled. "What are you looking for then?"

My mind flashed to the numerous times I had been asked that question before on Grindr. My usual answer was quite explicit, but that was then.

"I'm looking for something that doesn't exist and a person you'd only find in a place similar to this one."

I pushed forward, leaving her behind to contemplate my obscure answer that didn't make sense in retrospect.

## two

## PARADISE IS **WAITING**

"You don't realize how much useless shit you have until you pack and move it ten minutes across town just to immediately unpack it again," I proclaimed after our tenth trip to the moving van.

Daniel's answer took the form of him grabbing another box and repeating the familiar process. I fell in behind. Through the concrete lined hallway, past the apartment doors where I didn't know the creatures that laid in waiting behind them, down the elongated set of stairs, out the tall, slotted door that was tied back with a bungee cord to minimize hassle, and to the moving van and truck that were eagerly waiting to be stuffed with my junk.

The heavy objects—couch, mattress, dresser, your mom's ass—were the first things we took. Now, we were down to the miscellaneous items thrown into various boxes for ease of travel. Kitchen utensils were mixed with video games. Bath towels hung out with the books covered in dust. None of it made sense, but it didn't have to. I was overly eager to get my shit and go. The demons of apartment 1215 were about to be left behind with the intention that I'd be paving a new path. The nameless faces, the faceless names, the feelings of regret, the feelings of pity, the guilt, the shame, and any other memory I could pull from that apartment would be left behind.

Daniel pulled me from my thoughts.

". . . this bed frame?" he asked.

"What about the bed frame?"

"Where do you want it?"

"The back of your truck is fine."

"Okay then," he said in a cheerful manner. He hoisted the rectangular frame into the truck bed and laid it up against the side as he rearranged the current contents. I watched from a distance as the frame toppled over the side and landed with a loud crack against the truck, the grass alongside it, and the concrete sidewalk toward the building. Daniel had attempted to make a quick jolt toward the direction of the fall, but at the old age of thirty-one, he was unable to alter the course of events. I did nothing to prevent the situation from happening, and as a result, I let out a howl of laughter.

"If that's the worst thing that happens during this move, I'll consider us very lucky," I said as Daniel hopped off the back of the truck. "Any dings?"

He ran his hand against the metal frame above the rear passenger wheel and shook his head. "No damage to report."

"That feels like payback for the time you tried to crush me with your motorized couch."

"Oh yeah, but the couch looks great and I have taken plenty of worthwhile naps on it."

We grabbed the bed frame and secured it in a more stable manner. No chance of it falling out during the short ride across town.

Our trek up and down the stairs continued for another half hour until the tiniest remnants of my life lingered. Several boxes were scattered throughout the apartment, but a majority of my belongings were piled into the two vehicles.

The only thing to not make the journey was the dreadful **COWBOY** sign that hung in the kitchen. An unfortunate accident happened where it just got up and ran to the dump.

I stood in the doorway, on the cusp between old and new. The old was a drab sight in front of me. The walls were bare with the cheap white paint finally evident. Random dings, dents, and scuffs could be seen. The carpet on the edge of the living room and kitchen still had a long strip of black duct tape to hide all the chewing Rigby had done during her reign. The mysterious bite mark on the blinds I never discovered the origin of. All of the warts were out in the open, but it was still my home, and, to a certain extent, I would miss it. It was hard to picture how I had spent over two years of my life in that apartment. *The things you did in that apartment. Don't forget the people you hurt. The strangers you fucked . . .*

I pushed the downward trail of thoughts away. I needed the cycle to end; the idea that I had to continually carry the burden of all the things I'd done. I didn't commit a murder or scam the IRS from my money. No, I decided to live my life. I wasn't the best version of myself during my time in Dallas yet, but it was sure to change. It had to. Because if it didn't, I wasn't sure what I would do.

I'd make one final trip back to get the rest of my stuff and drop off the keys, but that was later.

Now, I took one last look and stepped out into the new.

# three

## SEVENTEEN

The drive over to the new apartment was essentially a straight shot. You would take Fitzhugh Avenue across US-75, which brought you over to west Dallas. (While not official, I always found that the highway was a good separation point between east and west Dallas, but who honestly cares, right?) You continued on Fitzhugh, past several lights, and down a hill. At some point, it turns into Wycliff Avenue. Once you see the tollway up ahead, make a left and my new apartment complex was tucked in right next to the overpass. Dominated by homes from the 1950s and shinier architecture, the area was not much of a change with the exception of a steep number of gay folks living nearby. The Strip was right down the street, which was the go-to area for the gay population of Dallas.

Daniel followed behind as I attempted to steer the moving van. I had zero experience driving anything half that size, but I knew which pedals did what and how to use my blinker, so I was already more qualified than a majority of drivers in Dallas.

We made it there without incident and pulled into two spots around the side of the complex.

"That wasn't so bad," Daniel said as he got out of his truck.

"Agreed. I'm going to find the leasing office and grab the keys. I think my apartment is on this side of the building, so we can probably unload the stuff here and walk around to the door."

"Whatever you say, boss."

"Last time I checked, you were the only boss around."

"Maybe so, but sometimes I like to take the weekends off. Pass me the keys. I'll start unpacking." I threw the keys over and turned toward the direction of the leasing office.

It was a short walk around to the other side of the building. I didn't pass by anyone as the lull of Saturday morning still had its spell on the area.

Inside the office, I felt a rush of warm air, which helped to dull the chill of the Dallas weather.

"Hello?" I announced to no one in particular as I scanned the room for any signs of life.

"Hi! How can I help you?" said a voice from the back room. There was the shuffle of shoes and eventually a woman walked into the lobby from the office.

"I am here to pick up my keys. I'm supposed to be moving into the apartment complex today."

"Oh perfect, what's your name?"

"Vin Besser."

We shook hands. "I'm Amanda. Welcome to Axis! Give me a second to find your paperwork." She returned to the other room and came back with an oversized envelope. She opened it and out slid a pair of keys and a door fob. "Here we go. You will be in apartment 134. I can show you where it is if you like?"

"Let's do it."

A strange feeling of déjà vu swept through me as we left the office and moved through the hallways toward the apartment.

Once there, she fumbled with one of the keys. "You know what? Why don't you do the honors?" she said to me as she stepped aside and motioned her arm out as if she was unveiling the grand prize.

"Is it this one?" I asked and held up the fatter of the keys.

"That's the one! The other is for your mailbox."

I nodded and unlocked the door. We stepped into the apartment. On the kitchen island, there was a small bottle of wine and a few pieces of paperwork.

"You can fill this out at some point today and bring it back to the office," she grabbed the papers and handed them to me. "Just take a look around the apartment and see if you find something worth noting."

"Will do."

"Need anything else?"

"I think I'm good. Thanks."

She gave me one last smile and left in a flash.

I gave myself a tour of the place. The apartment was bigger than the one I had just left, which is the only thing worth mentioning. You're not reading this for the superfluous details if I had to guess. Now, if the apartment had something sweet like a spiral staircase or a false wall that led to a sex dungeon, I'd be preaching about it to the congregation.

I opened up the balcony door on the far end of the living room. Technically, it wasn't much of a balcony since the apartment was on the first floor but calling it a patio felt cheap. Outside, Daniel was leaned up against his truck and staring off into the distance.

"Doesn't look like you did much unpacking," I said with a chuckle.

"I reconsidered and determined you should contribute to the fun."

I hoisted myself up and over the railing and landed in a pile of shrubs. "We should really just bring everything through the balcony, huh?"

"That would probably be smart. Do you think we can?"

"Yeah. For the big items, we can unload them together and once we hit the railing, we can prop up one side on top while you hop over the railing and can grab it. When you have a handle on it, I will jump over and then we can move it inside. Sound good? For everything else, I'll just carry it over and hand it off to you," I explained, in explicit detail. Talk about superfluous, sheesh.

He blinked several times and finally responded. "Wow, you have thought this out."

"Hardly. I just want this shit over with," I said with a sigh.

We set off to work.

The plan went flawlessly. We were stuck in several awkward situations with the bigger objects, but we shoved them through the door, setting them down with a huff and a heave. Things moved quicker once we got to the pieces I could carry by myself over to the railing. By the end, the living room was piled high with boxes and a smattering of furniture that was yet to be put into its rightful place.

Following the unloading of my life, we returned the U-Haul to its home. Daniel and I parted ways as I thanked him for his faithful service to the cause. He cautioned me that I owed him for when he and Danielle finally got a house. Saying goodbye to him was always a formality since I'd see him at work on Monday morning.

After he left, I walked around the perimeter of the complex several times.

The building was separated into two sides with the entrance to the garage, and subsequent path to the upper levels, being the divider. I lived on the side opposite of the pool and leasing office, directly in the middle between the two entrances on either side. I soaked in the sights and eventually went back to my apartment where I was met by a mountain of responsibility. As much I would have loved to leave the mess for another day, I began my trek to methodically put everything into its place.

The bookshelf was assembled, and the three boxes of books were arranged in an ordered fashion. My empire was growing at a steady pace.

The bed frame was set into place and I flopped the mattress on top. The sheets and pillows were added.

The couch was lined up in the center of the living room with the television stand on the opposite wall. The coffee table stood in-between the two, decorated with stains and dents that only the finest IKEA furniture could show.

The kitchen became stocked with various pans, utensils, cups, plates, spices, and other non-essential items to fill out the cabinets.

The clothes were unloaded from a multitude of duffle bags and stuffed into the dresser and onto hangers in the closet.

Several hours later, the apartment took shape. I sat on the couch and fought off the urge to take an extended nap. Instead, my gaze drifted to the scrapbook on the coffee table in front of me. The cover was a light tan color that housed a picture of me when I was four, which was proven by me holding up the correct number of fingers. It was a scrapbook I had created during my senior year of high school. I didn't do it by choice, instead, it was an assignment given to me by my psychology teacher on the first day of school. Naturally, I waited to do any work on it until less than a month before it was due, and my teacher had little faith that what I'd turn in would be more than a slapstick effort.

I have no explanation for it, but I took the assignment seriously. I mean super seriously. I spent more time crafting each page, cultivating all of the necessary pictures, and thinking through the mandatory documents I had to write than any other assignment I had been given (because I always found school so goddamn boring). I knew I would look back upon it and didn't want to disappoint my future self.

I opened up the scrapbook and thumbed through the pages. I was met by pictures of friends and families and moments that were etched into my brain. I wasn't interested in reexamining the entire thing and skipped toward the end. I turned to the page where I wrote a letter about my five-year goals. I pulled it out of the sleeve and skimmed through it.

> I would love to tell you that in five years I want to be filthy rich and not have to work a day in my life, but I am supposed to "be real" when I come up with these goals. How is it unrealistic for me to want to be rich in five years? I could win the lottery, win a lawsuit against Bill Gates and take all of his money, or I could invent the next Facebook. Becoming rich in five years isn't impossible, but personally, I do have more realistic goals than that.
> I will be attending Temple University in the fall, and though I am undecided about what my major will be at the moment, I hope that whatever I decide upon will create plenty of job opportunities for myself when I enter the work force. To sum it up, my major five-year goal would be to graduate college and find myself a job that I love and can also be successful in. Some may see that as being unrealistic to have a job that you both love and can make decent money in, but I think otherwise. I believe that I can have the best of both worlds. It is just a matter of picking and choosing the right career path. On top of that, hopefully within the next five years the economy will become more stable than it has been so that there will actually be jobs out there for me to compete for. I know that college will be a lot of hard work. I hear people talk about how college is so much different than high school, and it seems like they are trying to intimidate you. The thing is, I know what I am capable of, and I know that I will put in the work needed to succeed in my five-year goal, so I am not worried. The hardest part about college will not be the schoolwork (even though that will just absolutely suck most of the time), but it will be how to budget my time. Do I go out and have fun with friends or do I stay in and study for a big test? The decisions won't be easy to make considering my friends will try to peer pressure me, but once again I am more than positive that I will make the right choices.
> There is absolutely no doubt in my mind that I can complete my five-year goal, but for me it is also important to think about further than that. Over the course of my lifetime, I want to be a great father and husband while continuing to be a good friend and son. It is hard to imagine myself with kids and a wife at this age, but it is bound to happen and when it does I want it to be the best time of my life. So, the goals for my life when I get older will be significantly different than they are now, but regardless of what goals I have, I will strive to achieve them to the best of my ability.
> I feel that life is too spontaneous and unpredictable to set specific goals and wants for you a majority of the time, so that is why it would be

difficult for me to create a bucket list as suggested. For example, I never thought in a million years that I would ever want to go on a canoeing trip in Canada, hours and hours away from civilization, but when Mr. Muntazar talked about the trip, I knew right then that I wanted to do it. I still have slight hesitation about going because of my bum knee, but besides that I am looking forward to this trip very much. I know other opportunities will come along that I would never have thought about doing and I hope I will have the chance to take advantage of them. I want to do stuff in my life, but to create a bucket list would only seem to confine me to those certain ideas and I do not want that. I want to have a set path, but also at the same time, have room to stray off the path and do something incredible.

I reread it twice and considered how I could have possibly submitted that for the project. The writing was contrived and silly, but at seventeen, I poured out all the insight I had onto the page. Amazingly though, I still felt the same. There was still the opportunity to be incredible and experience unique things, so I never wanted to define a set path for myself. But my goodness, I do not enjoy my job as much as I thought I would.

It got worse. I put back the papers and flipped to the next page where I had written a letter to my future child. I removed it from the plastic cover.

To _____,

How do you write a letter to your future child whom you know nothing about? On top of that I am only 17 years old at the time of this writing. I am going to try my best to write a coherent letter, but I don't know how well that will be (especially since I am writing this the day after prom, so I am a little sleep deprived).

To start off, I am your father (well at least I think, the DNA tests were inconclusive). Depending upon how old you are when you actually read this, I hope that you see me as a role model. I hope I have been a part of your life. I hope I have attended all of your sporting events, band concerts, or anything else you may possibly do. But more important than that, I hope you are doing what you love regardless of what that is. You should find a passion and stick with it for as long as you can. If I have not told you already, my passion was football. I played it all my life, at least until high school ended, and I have so many memories from that. Memories of friends, awesome games we won, heartbreaking defeats, and so on. The best thing about having a passion is the memories that it brings, whether good or bad. I hope you have found your passion and that you stick with it for however long you can, and I will always support you one hundred percent.

I hope that a major ideal that I have instilled in you was determination. When I say determination, I mean that you strive to be the best you can be in everything you do, whether it is in school, sports, or relationships with friends and significant others. My mother taught me to try hard in school and sports, and eventually all of my hard work paid off. I hope the same will happen to you.

In life you will be faced with a lot of choices, and whatever you choose, people will take notice. Sometimes you will not make the right choices, as you know no one is perfect, but remember that your mother and I will be there to catch you every time you fall. When you do get back up, you will be stronger than you were before. I know you may think that I am being cliché, but it is the truth. You can always count on us, but I know that you will make the right choices.

I hope you read this letter with an open mind. I will not have touched this letter after initially writing it, so everything that I said may not apply to you, but I hope you realize that I love you very much, and that I will always be there for you.

Love,
Dad

That was tough to get through. I don't think I've ever hoped as much as I have than in that letter. Let's leave alone how my sexuality was still a mess back then. Can you blame me though? That shit takes time and I had no one to talk to.

I took a second to consider why I felt the urge to reread it in the first place. *You wanted to remind yourself of the family you'd never have.*

I shook my head to brush away the thought.

I returned the letter to its plastic barricade and closed the scrapbook. I took one last fleeting glance at the photo on the cover. *Remember when you used to be* that *happy? What happened to you?*

I was still that happy, and to prove it to someone, I absentmindedly hopped on Grindr and quickly found a nameless face to hang out with that night.

I had to christen the apartment in some way, right?

# four

## PEOPLE'S CHAMP

I woke up with a startle the next morning. I laid in bed trying to recall a half-remembered dream, but it sat on the fringes of my mind until evaporating from thought.

What I did recall, from the night before, was the rhythmic motion of me moving in and out of the stranger sprawled on my bed. The pulsing seemed to match the pace of a popular song, but my mind was too preoccupied to narrow in on it. His moans of pleasure indicated I was doing a better job than I probably was. There was a squishing sound as the lube worked its way around the crevices of his ass. From an outsider's perspective, it was not a picturesque sight—certainly not how it looks in the movies. We ended up on top of each other in a heap when everything was all said and done. The usual wave of regret did not come, unlike me.

I heard the sounds of "Ain't It The Life" by Foo Fighters drift into the bedroom. What a life indeed! I grabbed a towel from beside the bed and wiped myself off. The large poster of a wooden dock leading to endless waters stared back at me. I'm sure the picture was a metaphor for something momentous or maybe it was just cheap artwork. Who's to say?

I pushed my mind back to the present, not needing to rehash the final minutes of that encounter.

I sat up, shook my head, and forced the sleep from my eyes. I wandered into the bathroom where several towels were spread out on the vanity with the stains of the night before. I threw them onto the floor to deal with later. *Out of sight, out of mind, right?*

After a long shower, I emerged from the bathroom with a solid idea of what I wanted to accomplish for the day: meet up with Lee and tell him that we would be better off as friends.

Upon Lee's return from Philly after New Year's, we hung out a few times and things escalated. It was confusing to understand what he wanted, which was odd considering the brutal honesty he liberally conveyed. When we were hooking up, it seemed like he wanted something more real, something more in line with a conventional relationship. When we were apart, it felt like we were just old friends catching up at the local dive bar. A tired war raged on in my brain until I concluded that it would never work between us. There wasn't even a definitive reason why—it just was.

I was so over finding myself in the same situation over and over again. When would I stop stumbling across someone just to grow weary of them and determine we aren't a good fit? When would I stop finding people who lie about their feelings or their most fundamental traits? When would I rationalize that I was the problem and everyone else was just variables?

Until that point, it was just another night on mars.

Lee responded to the text I had fired off by mid-afternoon while I was knee deep in traversing ancient Greece in the newest Assassin's Creed game. I had fallen off from my gaming obsession over the last few months, so it was a relief to get back into it. The escape from reality was always welcome.

Besides studying for his steady stream of exams, Lee had no plans for the day and said I could come over at any time.

An hour later, I hopped in my car and ventured over to Cedar Springs and moved north toward Canada. I wouldn't be traveling that far north, so after the third light, I swung a left into his apartment complex. I typed in the code and the gate agreed as it began to open.

I found a spot within sneezing distance of his apartment. I considered bringing some sort of booze, but that would have required extra effort. I knocked on the door and immediately heard a cautious bark—the natural reaction to when a stranger decides to encroach on a dog's territory. The patter of feet followed, and the door eventually flung open.

"Do I know you?" he said with a curious look and furrowed brow.

"Fuck off," I spat back and pushed my way into the apartment.

He blocked my path and stared up at me. I leaned down and kissed him, assuming that was what he wanted. Lee took a sidestep and let me pass.

Down at my feet was Biscuit, his ten-week-old Cavalier King Charles Spaniel. The dog jumped up, trying desperately to get my attention. I couldn't deny him of the simple ask, so I bent down and gave him all the pets he deserved. Satisfied that the stranger wasn't there to harm him, he eventually wandered off to find another source of entertainment.

"What are you up to?" I asked. I scanned the room in front of me. It was largely empty. The normal furniture was there, but swatches of space were barren. The walls were cold and in need of some artwork to spruce it up. He always told me that it was a work in progress, so I decided I wouldn't bug him about it again.

"Like I mentioned earlier, just doing schoolwork today," Lee said with a smile. His teeth shined brightly in the fluorescent glow. His eyes scrunched up and hid behind the glasses that were twice the size of his head, but perfectly conveyed the look of a sleepy hipster. The stumble on his face was a few days old. He was attractive in the traditional way where you'd look at him and assume he never had any trouble approaching someone and getting what he wanted. Lee would absolutely disagree with that assessment, but he isn't here to defend himself.

"Oh cool," I finally returned with. I fell back onto the couch and wondered when I should tell him. There was no rush.

"The way I see it there are two options right now: I can either keep making flashcards or I could whoop your ass at Mario Kart."

"Bitch . . . how dare you? Do you know who I am? I have been playing Mario Kart since you were in diapers. I mastered the N64 by the time I was eight months old. The disrespect . . ." I said.

". . . We are the same age."

"What? I thought you were forty-five."

"Just stop talking." He threw me a controller and turned on the television.

He destroyed me. Every single lap of every single race. He hit me with blue shells and lightening and those stupid sound boxes. He knew every shortcut and got first place by a mile. I was mentally exhausted and visibly frustrated by the end of our second set of races.

"Why don't we do something else?" he offered.

"Why? I am having a total blast and certainly not annoyed in the slighted."

"You hide it well."

"I'm just trying to prove my dominance."

"Try harder next time."

I tossed the controller in front of me and collapsed backward. Lee moved my way and laid his head on my stomach, staring up toward my butt chin.

"I'm writing a book," I muttered as if I was afraid of the words.

"Huh?"

"I'm writing a book," I repeated. "I started about a month ago now. You're the first person I've mentioned it to."

"Why are you telling me?"

"Because I actually think I will follow through with it. A lot of people claim they are writing a book or have the intention to, but how many actually finish? I have been itching to tell someone and you happen to be the lucky recipient of the information."

"Oh cool. Okay, I'll ask . . . what is it about?"

"I haven't really thought of a way to describe it yet. It's . . . it's about this guy who doesn't know what he wants. He moves somewhere new and floats around through life, making bad choices and screwing over any opportunity. I don't anticipate a happy ending, but we will have to see how it goes."

"This is clearly about you, right?"

"Yeah," I said, without hesitation.

"Pretty narcissistic of you, huh?"

"Maybe."

"Will any of it be true?"

"The whole thing." The lie came easy like the way a knife glides through warm butter.

"Huh. How will anyone know if it is true?"

"Why would I lie?"

"Sometimes I feel like the people you have talked about can't possibly be real. A closeted, religious twink? A guy that dumps you because of his fear of commitment? And then you go and stay at his place, just to run out during the middle of the night? It's like a shitty soap opera."

"Believe what you want. I'm not smart enough to make it up."

"But you are smart enough to write a book apparently. Doesn't that require you to make stuff up?" He moved up onto his elbow to get a better view.

"Yeah, if I was writing about things that didn't happen in my life."

"Do you think anyone will care about what you have to say?"

"Nope, but I'm doing it for myself."

"Why?"

"Because I'm tired of carrying around shit I shouldn't continue to worry about."

"That's deep. Well, good luck with the writing. Make sure you change my name to something fun like Mordecai or Nosferatu or Craig or Lee or . . ." The suggestions continued to flow until he tired himself out.

A few beats passed between us. *No time like the present.*

"Lee?"

"Yeah?"

"I don't think this is going to work out."

"Obviously."

"Wait, what?"

"This was never going to be more than us fooling around. I want to be friends with you. Not your boyfriend."

"Oh. That's refreshing." I thought a moment longer and dipped into my overflowing vat of sarcasm. "You wouldn't date me? I'm perfect in every way."

"Vinny Boy, you've got lots of work to do. You need to love yourself before you could ever love someone else," he said, patting his hand against my chest.

"You don't think I love myself?"

"The answer to that is quite clear. Don't force yourself into something unless you really think it'll work out."

Biscuit gave a whimper to announce his presence. Lee gave him a look and a slight sigh.

"I need to let the dog out. I'm going to study when I get back. You can stick around, but it may be boring."

"No, it's okay. I can head out," I paused. "Are you sure we're good?"

"Yes. Don't bring it up again."

We both moved to the door and he gave me a quick hug. "Shut the door behind you please." He walked out and disappeared around the corner.

Back at my apartment, I tried to digest what happened. I was relieved to tell someone about the book, but what the shit had just transpired at the end? Was he really okay to part ways like that? I was expecting anger or disappointment . . . or any sort of emotion to show that I meant something to him. Instead, there was nothing behind his eyes. For a second, I was convinced he was more fucked than I was.

And, dammit, I did love myself. Right? Maybe in an unconventional way, but I still did.

More concerning than his lack of emotion and my denial of self-love was his notion that I made up any of the stories I told him. There was nothing to prove to Lee, but it was a cruddy feeling I couldn't shake. I could show him pictures of each person to prove their existence, but I doubted he cared to see any evidence. Sometimes I did wonder if those people were real. As time continued to slip by, their faces became more twisted with the features becoming less recognizable. The mannerisms that defined them became an afterthought. The sounds of their voices became muffled.

I tried to think of his face and couldn't. A panic surged through me. It was the one face I wasn't ready to forget.

I dug for my phone and pulled up Facebook. I avoided the nonsense, clicked on the search bar, and quickly typed in the name. It was there. The top result. I selected it and the screen popped over to show me his face. Relief spread through me like a shot of morphine.

A steady calm took over.

I needed to forget him, but I didn't know how.

I needed to forget the dimples when he smiled. Or the bright flash of teeth that covered too much of his face.

I needed to forget how he would roll his eyes at my lame jokes.

I needed to forget the layout of his apartment and how I dreamed I would share one with him someday.

I needed to forget the amount of complaining he did about his job, but how it never bothered me.

I wanted to forget his existence.

I wanted to forget what he did.

I wanted to write the book, so I could leave him behind on the pages.

I put my phone down and stared up at the ceiling. His image was burned into my retinas. It would get easier I told myself. The love I thought I had for him would eventually fade.

It wouldn't be long before he was just another faceless name.

# five

## DANCING ON GLASS

The greatest benefit of moving was the shorter commute. Remember the twenty-six-minute commute I had at the old apartment? No more! I was free from its eternal grasp. My new and drastically improved commute consisted of the same route as before except now it was half the time. That's the sort of stuff that gets me thrilled to be alive.

On that first Monday morning with the substantially better commute, I sang each word to the songs that came through my Spotify playlist. I was in a cheery mood, but I figured it would be soured before lunch. While the commute was enhanced, my job was not.

As I entered the building fifteen minutes later, I climbed the four flights of stairs and was dumped out into a long hallway. I had a choice. Making a left would take me on an amazing adventure of wonderment and peril, while making a right would lead me to my desk for the same ho-hum busy work I had been plagued with for months. I decided to go right, only because that option involved me getting paid.

I vowed to travel left one day and never look back.

I passed by the massive collection of memorabilia that clung to all the free space on the wall, past the conference rooms that always had five too many chairs than needed, and eventually ducked down a side alleyway to reach my desk.

Mine was the first one that anyone would see when you entered the area. It was adorned with coffee mugs I didn't use, a *New York Times* crossword puzzle calendar I was too stupid to finish on any given day, and other miscellaneous merchandise from various popular franchises. The signs still hung on my cubicle that I received on my first day—sometimes you weren't ready to let the good memories associated with a piece of paper go.

I shared pleasantries with the few people who were already at their desks and I settled into my seat to check the meetings I had. It would be a light day. It was the end of our iteration, so we had a sprint review and retrospective, but they wouldn't be until the afternoon.

Time skipped.

I was still at my desk when I felt a *tap tap tap* on my shoulder. I spun around and looked up at Athena Hall. She glanced down at me like a librarian getting ready to scold noisy students.

"Hello," she began in her typically calming voice.

"Hello."

"Do you plan on having lunch today?"

"I do."

"As am I."

"Did you bring your lunch?"

"Yes. You?"

"No. I need to run upstairs."

She checked the watch that she wasn't wearing. "Want to meet in the culture center in approximately twelve minutes?"

"I'll be there."

"Great." She turned and walked back to her desk.

Our conversations had a twinge of strangeness attached to them. I didn't mind. She was a good friend and made me laugh more than anyone else at work. She was goofy and constantly proved that her mind was an unsolvable Rubik's cube.

Athena started at [REDACTED] the previous July. It was around the time that I shifted teams and moved all my stuff down the hall. We sat next to each other and worked on the same project. I tried to mentor her to the best of my ability, but it was a slight case of the one-eyed man leading the blind. We spent an incredible amount of time together. Going to the same meetings, eating lunch together nearly every day, and having the casual conversation you do when you sit next to someone for forty hours a week. From an outsider's perspective, it may have looked like we were interested in each other. There was no doubt I was attracted to her personality—the spontaneity, the random quips, the generally upbeat demeanor—but there was nothing physical. Things became confusing when Anders told her I was gay. She wasn't quite sure what to believe since she assumed I was flirting sometimes, but after months of being vague about how I was spending my time on the weekends, I finally fessed up to the both of them. It was such a trivial matter by then that I wondered what took me so long in the first place.

Eventually, I switched pods and moved to my current seat, so we don't sit next to each other anymore, but we continue to grab lunch multiple times a week.

Okay, enough of that crap about context and character history.

I made my way out to the culture center and found a table in the corner. I put down my stuff and sat in silence until Athena showed up.

"What's up? What's happening? How was your weekend?" she started off with.

"It was moving weekend, which actually turned out to be non-eventful for the most part."

"Oh, that's right. Congrats on the new place! When are you having a party?"

"Sometime soon. I need to fill out the space a bit more." It would take me months, but I got a rug for the living room and a new coffee table, television stand, bookshelves, and a massive 4K TV. When it was all done, the apartment looked more established than my old place ever did.

"Also," I continued, "I christened the apartment this weekend."

"What do you mean?" She picked at her salad and stared across at me.

"I hooked up with someone. The whole situation was strange. They came over on Saturday night and it was obvious the intention was to do stuff. We exchanged the bare minimum of pleasantries and started going at it. I'll spare you the details of the middle section, but afterwards they asked if they could stay over. I wasn't really into that idea, so I said no. They broke into this long-winded rant about how they thought I was different, and I was nothing more than"—I suddenly paused as someone passed by close to the table—"okay, so yeah, they said I was an asshole and thought I cared since I seemingly asked a lot of questions about their life. Were they wrong about me sucking? Probably not, but what did they expect? I have just been so worn down over the past year that I don't really get bothered by people passing and going anymore, but I guess other people aren't quite the same."

She took a moment to digest the information. "Maybe you shouldn't keep hooking up with people?" she said as if it was the most obvious hint to give. "You are becoming desensitized to being unsafe and, quite frankly, being an asshole. That's not the person I see here at work—most times—so it is difficult for me to understand exactly how you act, but you certainly don't paint yourself in a positive light."

"You're right. It's a high though. The thrill of meeting someone new and hoping it'll be somewhat different. It's foolish, but my brain continually goes down that road."

"Just be patient. You went through a lot last year, so what's the rush?"

"I have a date set up for Friday," I said with a chuckle. I had been chatting with someone on and off for the past week, and we finally set up a time to meet.

"That's good though! Dates usually don't mean hook ups, right?"

"Honestly, who knows these days."

A few ticks of silence passed between us.

"How are you and Stavros doing?" I asked.

*Stavros* was the codename for Athena's actual boyfriend. Since it was a workplace romance, the two of them didn't want the entire company to know, so they kept it on the down low. I respected their decision, but I was highly suspect that anyone would give them a hard time.

What made the situation even better was that I knew the person she was dating. I even knew they were interested in each other before they did. Remember that Halloween party I went to last year and left in a huff due to being ghosted by the faceless name? Yeah, well, as I left that party, they were blocking the door due to the concern of me walking back home in a drunken stupor. I was upset and not in the mood for emotional support, so I yelled at them to just fuck already and get out of my way. Not a very good look for me, and they were super pissed about what I said, but in my defense, they did go on their first date the following week.

In reality, Stavros equaled Jag. Athena was dating Jag and I couldn't have been happier.

"We're good. He went home this past weekend, so I was just hanging around with roommates."

"So that means you spent a long time watching Netflix?" I questioned.

"Yeah, but you don't need to call me out on it," she said under her breath.

"My apologies. You know I don't do anything of significance most nights, so there is nothing to be ashamed of."

"Uh huh—"

We were interrupted by a new arrival. "Hello to my two favorite people," Anders said as he walked toward the table. He's the shitbag that told people how I was gay. While once a friend, I view him more cautiously now. I have tried to forgive him since he alluded to being out for a number of years. He likely didn't have to go through the change curve I did, or, if he did, it was a distant memory. He expected my life trajectory to be the same as his and for me to be comfortable to let the world know about my sexual preference. I wasn't at that point yet and not sure if I'd ever make it there.

"Hey," Athena and I said in unison.

"How was everyone's weekend?" he asked. It was tradition to inquire about every single person's weekend when you worked at [REDACTED] because you never knew where someone may have flown to or other shenanigans they were involved in. The interesting thing about Anders was that he had more ridiculous stories than I did. He was always under the impression that every straight guy was attracted to him and every guy who did show him attention, he tossed aside because he enjoyed the thrill of the chase rather than the actual relationship that followed. Enough shade about him though. For now at least.

Our conversation drifted to us rehashing our weekends (again) and I quietly reminded them about an obligation we had in another month and a half. They nodded in acknowledgement but didn't seem to care for the reminder.

Once Hurricane Anders left, Athena and I looked at each other, knew our conversation could not recover from the fragmentation, and figured we should head back to work.

I had to keep conning people into believing I was busy doing nothing while I secretly worked on my book.

# six

# KAMIKAZE

I was really looking forward to the date on Friday. The more I talked with Evan, the more he seemed like a massive anomaly to what was usually found on Grindr.

But, before that, let me give you a side story that happened leading up to then.

Moving over to Oak Lawn, as I previously mentioned, meant I was surrounded by a higher number of gay folks, many of whom were prowling on the digital wasteland. The closest person to me when I was in my apartment was fifteen feet. There was a slight concern they were hiding out in the shadows, but I made sure to check all the closets to debunk that theory.

Scrolling through the nearby folks, I discovered many oddities within the profiles. I found ones where people claimed to be deleting them, but it was an idle threat. They were just looking for an uptick in attention. I stumbled upon profiles where the specifications for who they were looking for was so out of touch with reality that I severely doubted that user HUNG WHORE was ever going to find someone between the age of 22–23 with a red, four-door Audi, who is the CEO of a Fortune 500 Company and likes to step on cracks to break their mother's back. The ungodly expectations that people set were baffling. The last set of profiles I came across were the ones where English was an afterthought. Beautiful sentences of "me want fuk now" or "suk & go" or "who lokin to parTy" sprouted up like a pesky weed.

Grindr was its own world and we were just the pawns.

With an odd amount of people in my complex on Grindr, I had a lot of conversations those first few days. The strangest example had to be with a guy named Kyle. He proceeded to tell me how he lived on my floor—just down the hall—and was in an open relationship. What a silly concept. You want to have the perks of being in a committed relationship with the flexibility to mess around with others. Anyways, Kyle was looking to hook up, so naturally we did. Following the less than memorable encounter, besides meeting his pug, he asked for my number and we began to chat. At one point I asked him why he's in an open relationship. Kyle explained that his sex drive was so high that his boyfriend just couldn't keep up. He had to resort to strangers like me to help fulfill his constant need. Okay fine. I didn't necessarily agree, but I could sympathize. I dug further though. I asked how long the relationship had been open and he said a couple of months. The follow up question I had of how it had been going spawned a multi text answer. He described how hard it was to let someone you love and care for be intimate with others and not know if it going to change the dynamic of the relationship. They didn't want to know when the other person was fooling around, and they tried to continue showing each other the same love and affection as before, but to mixed results.

I didn't know how to make sense of it all. Why do people force away others by doing something silly like an open relationship? Why don't people communicate their distastes to stop a negative cycle? I was certainly generalizing, but it was confusing, nonetheless.

Two days later, I met another guy from the building named Layton. He came over and we fucked the night before the date I was planning to go on. Afterwards, I asked him if he wanted to stick around for a bit since he seemed like a rational, sane individual. While interested, he insisted he needed to let the dog out. I was always curious to hear about dogs, so I inquired. It was a pug. Go figure. In less than a week, I managed to hook up with both halves of the couple without the other person knowing.

The plot thickened when Kyle was upset that Layton was attempting to text some guy from Grindr while they were at an event. Surprise! It was me. Once Kyle discovered that tidbit, he wasn't as annoyed until he grilled Layton with questions and felt like he was lying about what we did. Kyle didn't let his boyfriend know he hooked up with me as well, so that was somewhat hypocritical on his part. Kyle confronted me about what I did with Layton and I told him the truth.

And then they broke up.

Because of me, I think. Maybe that was a gross simplification of the situation, but holy fuck, what the shit was wrong with me? I couldn't even get my own life together, but I went around wrecking others. It made me feel as skeevy as when I had that threesome a few months back.

So yeah, I couldn't wait for the date, so I could wipe my mind of the whirlwind I caused, only to just cause a new one. My path of destruction knew no bounds.

## seven

## THE NIGHT WE **MET**

I stepped out of the Uber on Friday night and became aware of my surroundings. It was a different part of town than I was used to, but the abundance of snobby SMU students lurking around made me remember exactly where I was.

Uptown—where any diversity Dallas had died off.

I turned toward my destination. Bowen House was tucked down a side street, half a block away from the chaotic nature of Uptown. It was nothing more than a small, one room restaurant that specialized in serving unique cocktails at an outrageous price. I sidestepped the three Lime bikes that lay scattered on the curb. They were quickly taking over the city and no one seemed to mind.

As I entered the building, I scanned the room for Evan. I was looking for a tall, skinny guy, which was difficult to determine since everyone was sitting down and the lights were turned to the lowest possible setting. I continued to stand awkwardly near the door until I noticed a head perk up.

I turned left and found Evan at a table near the back.

"I'm so sorry I am late. Not the best first impression to make," I said with regret.

"It was only fifteen minutes, so I wasn't too worried," he said.

I extended a hand across the table. "Nice to meet you Evan."

"Likewise."

We both sat down.

The candle on the table bounced the shadows in a strobe-like fashion. He had a long face with evenly proportioned features that were accentuated by the bright smile he flashed toward me. He was clean shaven which showed off the sharp edges to his jawline. Much like half the male population, his hair was trimmed close on the sides with the top being considerably longer and laying neatly at a precise angle. A small scar was noticeable in the space between his eyebrows. The light caught his eyes and I could see the deep shade of brown behind the glasses. His lanky arms stretched their way onto my side of the small table and were covered with a floral print button-down.

He was staring over at me and likely performing the same critical analysis. I wondered briefly what his first thoughts were, but I'd never know.

"Did you order a drink already?" I asked.

"Just got a water." He picked up the glass and shook it.

"What looks good then? I am putting the pressure on you to decide for me."

"Oh wow. Hmmm . . . well, what do you like?"

"Anything. I am not picky when it comes to alcohol."

He grabbed the tiny menu, placed a hand on his forehead, and went to work in trying to find a drink.

"No pressure," I continued. "This will only make or break the date."

He glanced up briefly then returned to the menu.

The waitress eventually came over and asked what we wanted.

"I will have a Negroni and he will have the French 75. Also, could we get an order of the brie?" he questioned.

"Of course! I'll be right back with that. I'll leave the menu at the table in case you want anything else," the waitress said with a smile.

"Tell me more about what you do." It seemed like a logical place to start the conversation.

"I work in HR at a manufacturing company. Specifically, I have been transitioning into more of an HR manager role for a site with about two hundred employees. Previous to that, I was doing recruiting, but that was short lived due to someone leaving the company. Every day is slightly unique and overwhelming to say the least," he urged.

"I am involved with recruiting for new college hires at [REDACTED], so I deal a bit with the HR side of things. By far the best part of my job. Is the location anywhere near where you live?"

"That is one of the downsides: it's an hour commute."

"Yikes. I would die from heart failure from the massive road rage I'd experience."

"I don't think I am that bad, but I can't say I enjoy it."

"What part of town do you live in?"

"Downtown. Pretty close to Klyde Warren Park. I actually walked here since it was nice out."

"You are adventurous!"

Our drinks arrived. He stared at me as I took my first sip. I gave a nod of approval, showing how he chose wisely. If the drink sucked, I had every intention of making a major scene and leaving the bar.

He continued. "Your turn. Tell me about yourself."

I did. I told him about where I grew up and why I was in Dallas. I told him more about my job and how I had recently moved across town. He made me feel at ease. I could tell he absorbed every word and followed along as I bounced from topic to topic. I appreciated his attentiveness and ability to just listen. It was a highly underrated feature that a limited number of people possessed.

There were some things I kept to myself. You don't spoil the ending of a book in the first ten pages after all.

Without asking, he revealed how he had only been in Dallas for five months. He moved from Kalamazoo, where he left his first job out of grad school after a year. He was used to moving and seemed unfazed by the change, but he agreed that it had been difficult to meet people. Evan didn't strike me as the type to go out on dates with just anyone—they had to pass his sanity test. The proctor must have been out of town or dead because I certainly wouldn't have passed anything.

The more we talked, the more I enjoyed spending time with him, but I continued to caution myself. How many times had I been down this road before? How many more times would I get smitten with someone I didn't know just for them to rip my heart out and feed it to the gremlins? No, I couldn't allow that to happen again.

"Ask me a question," I suggested sometime after our second round of drinks arrived and the empty plate of brie was removed from the table.

"Worst date you have ever been on?"

"That is super easy considering that I haven't been on any dates," I laughed. "Okay, I have been on a few, but I could use an introductory course on how to start a relationship with someone. Anyways, to answer your question: there was one time I went out with someone and they convinced me to go with them to an event. He was vague on the details, but I was bored most nights after work, so I agreed to go. He picked me up and drove me thirty minutes north to this shitty Marriott hotel. We walk in to one of their conference rooms and it just reeks of cheap carpet and tackiness—"

"How does a place smell of cheap carpet?"

"If you don't know the answer to that question, then consider yourself lucky. He wandered off to mingle with some people he knew. I sat there and surveyed the room. Folks of all ages began to occupy the seats. There were even a few strollers. What the fuck had I gotten myself into? He eventually comes back—his name was Vincent too, oddly enough—and the event starts. Very quickly I can tell that this is an MLM scheme."

"MLM?"

"Multi-level marketing scheme. It is what pathetic people do to rope others into spending their money for absolutely no financial gain."

"Oh yeah. I have heard of that before."

"Yeah, so my anger just starts to skyrocket the longer I sit through the presentation. They bring up person after person who claim to have made $x$ amount of money from selling this coconut water that was cultivated from the beaches of Neptune or some outlandish crap like that. They kept trying to hype up the crowd and get everyone interested. The scary part was that people started to nod in agreement and seemed keen to the idea of getting in on this. I'll be generalizing for sure, but a sizable portion of the audience did not look wealthy, which meant that they were trying to find any way they could to scrape by and make a better living for themselves. That's what bothered me the most. The idea that these people were willing to sell a complete lie to individuals who were desperate. A capitalistic wet dream. I met a few of the speakers afterward, but once they caught a whiff of what I did, they immediately stopped badgering me. Con artists don't like to have the script rewritten on them.

"On the way home, I ripped into Vincent for the entire ride. He was adamant that it wasn't an MLM, but his argument was weak. I told him how he was a disgrace to all the Vincent's out there and I was embarrassed to share the same name."

Evan laughed.

"He dropped me off and we never spoke again. Thank Christ."

"Quite the story," he chimed in. "I don't think I can compete with that."

"What a shame. You are missing out."

We hit a moment of stalled conversation. I wanted to ask him, but I was nervous. I finished the last dregs of my drink and the liquid courage amped up.

"Would you want to go somewhere else?"

"Yes. That would be great," he said without hesitation. "Any suggestions?"

"We can go to The Strip. It'll be quiet down there this early and easy to keep talking."

We split the check and called an Uber. Evan gathered his coat and we moved outside. He didn't tower over me, but I still felt like a hobbit standing next to him.

Fifteen minutes later, we were in the upstairs portion of JR's. A few guys lingered around the bar, but we were able to hide out in a corner and continue our conversation. It was there that I told him everything. I lied. I did spoil the book within the first ten pages. I told him about my sketchy past with meeting people and how I had a number I wasn't proud of. I divulged the details of how I was afraid to get into an actual relationship due to my complete lack of experience and self-doubt that I would muck it up.

At that point, the truth was blurred in my head, but I told a convincing story anyways. Maybe Lee was right about some of them being lies.

He soaked in the information and didn't pass judgement. It was likely a lot for him to process, but he was not disgusted by anything I said.

I couldn't tell you why I spilled my guts out onto that table. Maybe it was being tired of running away from my mistakes. Maybe it was wanting to start out on the right foot with someone. Maybe it was a multitude of things my brain couldn't connect.

My speech was interrupted when a guy dressed as a nun walked over to our table.

"Hello ladies," he started off. "How are y'all doing tonight?"

We told him.

"Glad to hear it. I am a part of The Nuns of Perpetual Indulgence. We go out around Dallas and promote safe sex. I could tell from across the room that y'all would need some materials for later on," he said with a wink. "Take one of these." He dropped a small bag onto the table. Inside were two condoms, a small package of lube, some mints, and other miscellaneous items.

We were both blushing.

"This is actually our first date. I don't think we will be needing that tonight," I stressed.

"Save it for the second date then," the nun stressed.

We chatted for a few more minutes until he moved on to the other group of people sitting near us.

"I . . . I am not used to such a friendly presence from the church in a gay bar," I said.

"That's not an actual nun," Evan chuckled.

"News to me." The sarcasm was undeniable.

Evan held onto the bag when we ventured out of JR's sometime later and across the street to Round Up. The bar had a moderate amount of people loitering on the dance floor. We grabbed one last drink and went to join them.

We danced and moved closer to each other. It stretched into a series of awkward movements as we tried to sync our rhythms. I was never known for my dancing ability, so I let Evan lead.

After the third song, we leaned into each other and kissed. It was brief. A momentary spike in pleasure. That was all I wanted. I didn't need it to go further.

"Ask me a question," he smiled down at me.

"Would you want to go on a second date? This has been really shitty, but I'm willing to give it another shot."

He gave me a shove. "I'd be disappointed if we didn't go out again."

We exchanged numbers. No need to continue using that dreaded app.

We shuffled off the dance floor and went outside. He called an Uber and we kissed one last time as his ride pulled up.

I walked back to my apartment and enjoyed the time to reflect on what happened. I was elated. I was nervous. I was a muddy mix of emotions.

A headache crept its way in. I ignored it

When I made it home, my head soon hit the pillow, and, for once, I fell asleep in an instant, knowing that this time would be different.

And better.

part two

# HELP ME **RUN** AWAY

# eight

## WHEN THE **CURTAIN** FALLS

The feeling of elation I had the night before didn't last long on Saturday morning. As with most things for me, the wave crashed and scattered out into unrecognizable form. I could have attempted to chase after the feeling, but it would sneak away like a child playing hide and seek. Instead, I let it go. I'd return to the neutral emotional state I often found myself in. Neutral was an overly kind and false word to use.

I went to the mall to escape. No need to shroud myself in feelings of inadequacy and doubt by myself when I could just do it in a public space.

NorthPark was a massive epicenter of activity on the northeast side of Dallas. The somewhat square building was home to every store you've never heard of. The artwork within ranged from creepy to undistinguishable in its purpose. It was always packed with lazy shoppers slowly weaving in and out of random storefronts. If you valued your life, you didn't go anywhere near there after Thanksgiving and through New Year's.

I parked in front of the entrance closest to the movie theater and made my way inside. I went toward one of the generic clothing stores to see if there was anything that would fit my regular look of jeans and a T-shirt. Within moments, I determined my overweight stature would not yield any clothes. Most of the stores catered to the clientele that was in shape or just shaped like a brittle twig. Any item I would have tried on would accentuate my moderately sized tits, which would have put me into a spiral I was not ready to face that day.

To be frank, I had no reason to feel the way I did. No one went out of their way to criticize my appearance. No one even tended to look in my direction. The burdens I had, I put on myself. It probably stemmed from the years of subtle pushing from my mom that I should drop a few pounds even though I was force fed fast food as a kid. Or, it could have been the countless times in high school where I was referenced as the fat one by my friends. Whatever the underlying reason may be, I have never been able to move past it. A mental block occurs each time I try to tell myself I am good enough or that I look okay. It's just not that simple.

After the disappointment of the mall, I went across the highway to a bookstore. I searched around for the perfect book. It would sit on my shelf for months, since I had an overwhelming backlog to read, but I was determined to walk away with something.

As I stared at the selection in front of me, a thought crept through me.

*There is no way that anything you write will end up here. Look at how many people write books. Yours will be nothing special. It won't stand out. Just stop trying . . .*

For a fraction of a fraction of a nanosecond, my brain processed a scenario where someone would walk into that bookstore with a gun and calmly stroll over to where I was standing. The woman would lift the weapon, placing the end of the barrel snuggly against my left eye, and before I could give any protest, she would pull the trigger. My head would snap back. The blood would douse all the books behind me, effectively ruining them. My body would collapse haphazardly onto the floor with one final twitch before I went completely still. Bits of my brain would be a real bitch to get out of the carpet. All she would repeat was that she saved me from being a failure and from doing it myself one day.

After that brief separation with sanity, I settled on a sci-fi trilogy that involved the main character being re-sleeved into a new body each time he died. If real life worked that way, maybe I'd just start over.

I saved ten dollars at checkout since I was a member of the bookstore, so that was nice.

✦

Evan texted me in the early afternoon and ripped me from my funk. He said it was short notice but wanted to see if I was down to get dinner that night. I happily agreed. I offered to pick him up at his place.

It was nearly dark out when I pulled into the parking garage attached to his complex. I found a spot in the visitor area and moved into the building.

"Welcome to Skyhouse! How can I help you?" the guy at the concierge desk asked.

"I'm visiting my friend. I wanted to see if I could get a parking pass," I said while leaning my arms against the counter.

"Sure. What's the apartment number?"

"Uhhh. Hold on." I pulled out my phone to find the text.

"I can look it up by the name too," he suggested.

"His name is Evan. I don't know his last name."

The guy gave me a curious look. "Okay. Let's see if you can find the number then."

I did.

He then asked for my license plate number, which I surprisingly knew for no reason in particular. He wanted to know the make and model and why strawberries were the gravestone of fruit.

I must have answered correctly because the printer fired up, triumphant music played, and he soon handed me the golden ticket.

I returned to my car and stuck it on the dashboard.

I walked back into the building and the concierge led me to the elevators.

Up, up, up I went to the fourteenth floor. My ears popped as the elevator came to a halt.

The doors opened and I stepped out, wondering if each floor had the same dull look to it. A sign to my right indicated that I was headed in the right direction. I found my target (apartment 1413) and knocked on it three times. I heard a distressing bark and a quick scolding from Evan.

The locks disengaged, and I was greeted with a big smile.

"Hi. Come in!"

It was a studio apartment that overlooked the highway and the great expanse of west Dallas. The lights from Reunion Tower flashed to signal that SMU won their basketball game.

In the apartment itself, his bed was situated off to the right, underneath a row of LED lights that stretched to the opposite wall. He managed to cram in a couch, dresser, and miscellaneous tables that held his record player and vintage cameras. The concrete walls and ceiling gave off a cold vibe.

The barking continued and pulled me back into the current reality.

"Izzie! Chill out!" he yelled.

The chihuahua and Maltese mix gave an annoyed huff and growled several more times before cautiously approaching me.

"She just wants to make sure you won't eat her."

"She's in luck. I only eat dog on Sundays," I confessed.

Evan glared over at me.

I bent down to get somewhat eye level with Izzie. I stuck my hand out as she inched closer. She hesitated, gathered some more courage, and trotted over to sniff my peace offering. Her tail was tucked tight between her legs, but I sensed we would be friends in no time.

I stood back up. "I like the apartment. I always thought it would be cool to live in a studio."

"Thanks. It's not much, but good enough for the moment. I am itching to move into a house."

I moved toward the floor to ceiling windows and stared down at the House of Blues. It was teeming with people. *Arturo.*

I shook my head and turned my attention back to Evan. "You seem like the type who would want to live in a house."

"What does that mean?"

"I meant that it looks like you got your shit together. Good job, nice apartment right in downtown. From what I can tell, you are methodical. Everything is in order here and has its place. So it wouldn't surprise me if you have been saving up for a house and checking the listings every day."

"Guilty," he said, somewhat embarrassed.

"Nothing to be ashamed of. But anyways, I have a plan for dinner. Do you want to hang out here or head there?"

"My vote is for dinner."

"Same with me. Let's do it."

He told Alexa to stop the music and dim the lights. Izzie watched us from the couch as we left the apartment and immediately started to bark as soon as the door closed.

I decided on a restaurant in Lower Greenville. It was the area of town where the mid- to late twenties crowd went when they graduated from the dirty streets of Uptown.

"By the way," I said as we stepped out of the car, a few blocks from the main drag, "what is your last name? The guy from the front desk was not pleased that I didn't know. Probably thought I was a stripper or something."

"Eaton."

"Small world. I grew up in a town called Easton. Please tell me your middle name starts with an E."

"It does."

"Oh wow. That is hitting the E jackpot."

"What is it?"

"My middle name?"

"Yeah."

"Ethan."

"Evan Ethan Eaton—has a nice flow to it."

We walked over toward the noise and lights. Lower Greenville was a stretch of two and a half blocks of bars, restaurants, and businesses. Our destination was in the middle: HG SPLY CO.

"I didn't make a reservation," I said as we pushed our way through the crowd that spilled out onto the patio.

We were presented with two options: we could either wait forty-five minutes for a table or grab the two empty seats by the windows that had limited room. We elected for the latter.

A waiter came over to present us with two menus and a drink list. We gladly accepted. As Evan scanned the menu held up close to his face, I asked him how his day was. He divulged a large dump of information and got into specifics about the inner workings of HR at his company. I didn't question how he got stuck doing work on Saturdays, but I sent him all the thoughts and prayers I could muster to make up for his rotten luck, I digested as much as I could, but most of it passed through one ear and seeped out the other. I nodded and stared, still captured and confused how I found myself sitting next to him twice in twenty-four hours.

He spoke in a reserved and hushed tone as if he was telling you a secret he didn't want the neighbor to know. He was strait-laced compared to my self-described looser demeanor. He didn't laugh at all of my jokes, which was okay since not all of them were funny. I operated moment to moment, so it was hard to predict what would stick.

In just the limited time I had known Evan, I could surmise that we were complete opposites. The fact didn't bother me then.

Once he finished with his rehash, he flipped the question around and asked me. I gave him a canned answer and avoided details. It wasn't worth diving into or, rather, it never *seemed* worth diving into.

"Tell me a fact about yourself that no one knows . . . or only a few know," Evan said after it was clear he wasn't going to get me to chronicle my day.

I contemplated whether I should tell him about the fact that had been brewing in my head for a while. It was a simple one: I knew one day I would kill myself. I put my faith in people too much and they were a constant disappointment. The excuses they gave about being too busy to meet up or even send a text or the inability to ask questions to see if you were the one that needed help. There's a reason I still thought about Arturo and Dylan and Red and Xander and the Nameless Face. Especially the Nameless Face. I wished they would reach out to pull me from the massive grave of darkness that I felt myself in. They never did, so I keep burying myself deeper. What little light is left continues to fade. I knew one day I would kill myself because I'd be tired of the failed relationships and the thoughts of not being a good enough friend or son or boyfriend. The pain was overwhelming. I wanted to disclose that to Evan, but it was only our second date.

"I have weird eyes," I managed to say.

"I don't understand."

"Let me help you out." I pulled out my phone and turned on the flashlight. A glow burst out from the top and I held it in the direction of my eye. I tilted the phone, so the light caught it at the right angle.

"Whoa. What the heck."

"I was born with this condition where my iris never fully formed, so, instead, it is like a semi-circle that continues all the way down under my eye."

"You have this in both?"

"Yeah."

"That is certainly unique."

"I consider myself lucky. I don't think anyone would look me in the eyes if it was more noticeable. For once, it is good to have boring brown eyes."

"I cheated on the SATs," he said flatly.

"No! Not you! You are too . . . even to do that."

"It's true. I guess it isn't a big deal now, but I bombed the test the first time I took it and I really wanted to get into USC—"

"The USC?"

"University of South Carolina."

"Ahhh. The ugly stepchild."

"Shut it. Anyways, I wrote all these notes and possible answers onto a piece of paper and glued it to the inside of my leg. I was wearing pants so when I needed some inspiration, I would put my foot up on my knee—sit all fancy like—and roll up the pants. The teacher was barely in the room and the classroom was half empty, so it wasn't hard to cheat. I probably could have picked a simpler way," he finished with a shrug.

"I have so many questions. How could you possibly think that notes would help on the SATs? All that crap is random. And why glue it?! Did you get a better score? Were you worried about getting caught? I'm on overload right now," I said.

"I scored a lot higher, but I think it was more psychological than the notes. I studied more as well, so that had to be a factor."

"Evan the Cheater. The first of your name. Congrats on ruining the education system."

He smiled over at me and took a long sip of his beer.

I quickly fell in love with the honest smile he had, the one that didn't show up as often as time went by.

# nine

## MY MY MY!

This is the part in a movie where the glorious montage would play. Let me set the scene for you.

It starts with me sitting at a similar table from the previous week. Athena moves into frame. She mumbles something about it being a Monday. More like mundane, am I right? I agree with her and, unprovoked, I spill the beans about my weekend with Evan. (I have to move the plot forward somehow! I can't be waiting for the secondary characters to ask me all the necessary questions.) She processes the information and asks me if I plan on seeing him again. I say that I do. She asks me how long it'll take before I royally fuck it up, before I get tired of him, before I realize that living a loner life is what all the cool kids should be doing. I tell her that I don't know. The camera lingers on my face. The audience swoons over how good looking I am. The dramatic music quiets to a lull.

Hard cut! To our third date. It's at a fancy restaurant within walking distance of his apartment.

The music is upbeat and signifies the happiness that's spread between us. It's a smokescreen.

Hard cut! To our fourth date. We go bowling and drink. Evan slips, and I catch him. He tells me how I am his hero and that he's lucky to have found such a charming stud like me. Everyone at the bowling alley claps in praise of my heroics.

Hard cut! To us laughing and not acting like human beings. Like any good movie, we don't notice the flaws in each other to build up the emotion and tension. There's always a breaking point, right?.

Hard cut! To our fifth date. We are down at White Rock Lake. He brings me a sandwich and we walk awhile. The montage slows momentarily to capture the occasion. We look at the elaborate houses that sit nearby. We ponder what it takes to have all that. He asks me if we are in a relationship. I say yes. It's official.

The music picks up again as the camera pans wide to show us resuming our walk and reveals the twinkle of the skyline in the distance.

End of montage. End of dream.

***

While exaggerated, that montage is still accurate. We continued to go on dates and made it official after a month. I was happy in that moment. Thoughts raced through my head, but I quieted them for as long as I could.

It is pointless to capture every moment, but honestly, I wouldn't want to. Some of them were meant for just me and you and not any of the prying eyes who may ever see this.

When we think back to the beginning of any relationship, there is a glow that surrounds it all. Everything is shiny. The desire to dig in deeper and learn the most trivial material drives each conversation. The hope to impress the other person on each date is apparent. But at some point that changes. You get complacent with hanging out at the apartment instead of exploring. The conversations turn more serious as you fixate on the flaws. You let the outside pressures dictate your mood and take it out on each other. We got to that point quickly.

Lee's words still echoed in my head . . .

If I didn't love myself, how could I possibly love another person?

If there is one thing I learned during those first few months, it was that relationships are fucking hard.

# ten

# MADNESS

I picked my mom up from Love Field to commence our third annual Let's Go on a Trip Somewhere: An Excuse to Check in on Vinny to Make Sure His Life isn't a Complete Dumpster Fire (trademark pending). I enjoyed having my mom in town, but with me having a new apartment and boyfriend, I knew she was going to be more critical than normal.

She had already asked me truckloads of questions about Evan, and while I could sense apprehension, it was undeniable that she was happy for me.

As we entered into the complex, she said, "Oh, I remember this place. You must be excited to have air-conditioned hallways now!"

"It is certainly worth the extra money I'm spending," I said without a hint of sarcasm.

"Looks like one of your neighbors is moving out," she keenly observed. Up ahead, one of the apartment doors was propped open with a hand truck sitting halfway into the hallway. I quickly peered into the apartment. I remembered the Marilyn Monroe picture hanging near the entrance. I remembered the crate where the pug stayed when they weren't home that sat toward the living room. I guess it was official that I ruined that relationship.

"I imagine people are moving in and out of here all the time. Anyways, here we are. 134."

My mom spent the next ten minutes rummaging inside the apartment and making tiny comments about the state of things.

"Are you still good with the dinner plans tonight?" I asked after she investigated the apartment.

"I'm nervous, but yes, I'd like to meet him."

"Nothing to be nervous about. He is a nice person and not very intimidating."

"I suppose."

"Can you be ready in an hour?"

"Yeah."

I sent Evan a text to relay the plans.

✦

Dinner was at a restaurant in the Design District. We settled into a booth in the back corner. The introductions that took place twenty minutes earlier went well and only had a minimal amount of awkwardness. Evan went for the handshake while my mom went for the hug. They compromised and did a chest pump, which was an interesting sight.

Honestly, the conversation during dinner was boring. Evan rehashed all of the previous material he had told me in relation to his job, his upbringing, and his fondness to eat the lint from his bellybutton. My mom gave away all my childhood secrets. I was particularly peeved when she told Evan about how I would eat the knotted yellow blanket I had and proceed to poop out long strings of it. I shit you knot. I mean, like why does anyone need to know that?

The lighthearted tone of their back and forth indicated that both were comfortable, especially my mom.

The isolated beach from Provincetown popped into my head. *You two have come a long way. She always loved you, even more so after you told her . . .*

I hoped that was true.

"Vin?"

"Uh huh," I droned back. Both of them were staring at me.

"Did you want another drink?"

"No, I'm good," I said, finally noticing the waiter also staring at me.

Evan and my mom both ordered another round and carried on talking like I wasn't even there.

✦

Over the course of dinner and the ride home, my mom mentioned to Evan the short trip we were going on the next day. While not overly saying it, she hinted at the idea of him tagging along. Once we parted ways with him, we continued the discussion.

"I wish I hadn't said anything about the trip to him. He is probably expecting an invite now and if he doesn't join then I look like I don't want him around. I just really look forward to these trips and I want to spend time with you," she said.

"It's not a big deal. I can assure you that he won't care—"

"Just invite him. I need to get another hotel room though . . ." she trailed off and walked away to find her iPad.

It was the second time that evening I texted Evan with plans. I gave him an out if he wasn't interested, but he assured me he was.

Wonderful.

✦

Let me give you the high level: The trip did not go well. Seeing the city was great, Hamilton Pool was a secluded paradise, and the time away from Dallas was always welcome, but there was tension the entire time. It started when my mom was delegated to the backseat. She complained for most of the drive down south that she couldn't hear any of the conversation happening in the front because the music was so loud. No matter how low I turned the volume, it never solved the problem. It got to the point where she disengaged in talking completely and stared out the window. I knew I needed to partake in damage control, but I was never good at public relations, so I fudged up any attempt at reconciliation. Everything boiled over when my mom made a backhanded comment about how we should have taken an Uber to go see the Greetings from Austin graffiti. I snapped back saying I had asked her ten minutes earlier if she wanted one, but she said no. It was a moment that makes me cringe in how swiftly the anger and nastiness took me over. I felt a rush of adrenaline . . . at yelling at my own mother. What? It was pathetic. The air went stale between us and didn't recover until after we returned to Dallas.

It was embarrassing for Evan to witness the collapse of my patience with my mom, but he reassured me several times he could only tolerate a certain amount of time with his mom before they started to degrade. But it wasn't that for me. I loved my mom deeply. She was the only person I felt comfortable saying that too. I was tragically flawed in gut punching those closest to me over the tiniest things.

We were all tired by the time we returned to my apartment. The usual three-hour drive turned into nearly five with a combination of traffic and random bursts of severe thunderstorms causing delay. I wanted to sleep, but I had one last event that weekend.

The concert.

# eleven

## BUZZCUT SEASON

Arturo Yanez was always late. There was no plausible deniability. In a future time, when roses are blue and violets are red, historians will stumble upon Mr. Yanez and wonder to themselves about the inability for a sentient creature to end up in a desired location at the appropriate time. The historians will have a meeting in a bombed-out building where the main item on the agenda will be to scratch their heads at the actions of Mr. Yanez. After the scratching was completed, they would move to rubbing their chins. There would be more free time in the future.

I sent him several increasingly annoyed texts and demanded to know where he was. His lackadaisical responses were clear indication of his level of caring.

In the meantime, Athena and Anders showed up and came into the apartment until Arturo arrived. My mom was excited to meet more friends of mine and quickly kept them busy while I continued to harass Arturo.

Fifteen minutes later, he texted saying he was outside.

I found him waiting at one of the doors on Congress. The situation felt eerily similar to the times he came over when I lived across town.

A smile spread across his face.

"Howdy."

"You're late," I spat out.

"Nothing I can do about it now," he said with a shrug.

I opened the door and he gave me a hug.

How long had it been since I'd seen him? Five, six months probably. He looked largely the same. His hair was a constant evolution, which was currently in the style of a buzzcut, but the skinny frame and retro wardrobe were consistent to what I remembered.

"You look good. How is everything?" I asked as we wound our way through the hallway.

"I'm about as good as I could be right now. I am getting ready to move out of my place and into an apartment with a couple of friends. I'm hoping that they will be able to help me out with—"

"Right here," I said, pointing to the door. "Hopefully this won't be system overload for you."

We stepped inside, and I introduced Arturo to Athena, Anders, and my mom. Athena was cautiously optimistic about meeting him as she certainly had preconceived notions based on things I told her. Anders knew less about Arturo and was likely to make several comments about how he was surprised Evan wasn't upset I was going to a concert with "an ex." My mom knew the bare minimum about Arturo, but that would eventually change.

My mom drove us to the venue, which was downtown near Evan's apartment. We did a duck and roll out of my car as she turned back to spend her last evening in Dallas by herself.

The four of us maneuvered through security and each got a drink.

Our seats were technically on the floor, but they were way in the back. I didn't mind since it was my third time seeing Lorde in a year, so I likely could have performed her setlist for the crowd.

As we walked onto the floor, I saw him. The Q-tip shaped head with the pinned-up eyebrows that made him look like he wanted to talk to a manager. A shiver went through my body.

That was the only guy I ever bottomed for (besides the failed attempts with Benji) and the worst sexual experience I'd had. It was the usual talk-for-half-a-day-then-come-over-and-hook-up type encounter and I felt a compelling need to try out bottoming. He slowly moved his way in and pushed my head against the pillow in a romantic way (apparently). He started a rhythmic motion and grunted like a savage animal. The pace picked up significantly as he soon turned into an uncontrollable jackhammer, hellbent on destroying my internal organs. He put his minimal body weight against my back and continued his forceful thrusts into me. (Remember that scene from *The Two Towers* where the orcs are using that sharpened log to break into Helm's Deep? His movements felt similar to each time that log slammed against the door, splintering it marginally until it burst open.) He whispered unpleasant things in my ear about how I was enjoying his cock and that I was his bitch. I wasn't sure how to respond so I didn't. I removed myself from the situation. My body was in that room, but my mind tried to escape. The unpleasantness of it scarred me for a long time. The hesitation to try it again has followed me around ever since. After he was done with the task at hand, he quickly put on his clothes and left. The used condom was tossed aside on the bed for me to clean up. And for once, I understood what it was like to be on the receiving end. I deserved it.

It wasn't a rare occurrence to see someone I hooked up with out in public. It was an entirely avoidable scenario, but I was a massive people watcher. My eyes would constantly drift over to watch the couple at the table two rows down that hadn't uttered a word for the past ten minutes or stare at the disheveled passerby who had no idea where they were going. Most times though, I was looking at other guys. My mind would instantly think about the idea of hooking up with people again. Evan would be sitting right across from me, telling me about his day or admiring my presence and I would be thinking about how one person wasn't enough for me. The irrational thoughts would pile on. How could someone spend their life with the same person? Didn't you get bored of each other? Would there ever be a moment where the silence that spread between you both not feel uncomfortable? I'd take a breath and refocus my attention back to Evan. I'd remind myself that the one night stands didn't allow for someone to help meal prep because they wanted to see you reach your goal or for the lazy Saturday mornings where getting out of bed wasn't a priority and you'd roll over just to get another look at their face or how you knew which people were the crappy coworkers even though you have never met Mullet Todd or the inside jokes you had built up with each other. That pulled me back to Evan. That leveled me out. That made me realize how important a relationship was for me and how I couldn't fuck it up.

Lorde took the stage and sang her heart out, as did Athena, Arturo, me, and sometimes Anders. Arturo let out a primal, inhuman yell six times at the most random moments. Each time, people turned back to stare at him and wondered if they should call animal control.

"Vincent, this is the best show ever," he told me. "Well, only after

Paramore and Bleachers," he corrected himself. That was the extent of the dialogue that passed between us during the concert.

This story is no longer about him, which is why the details have been scarce, but I will give my final say on the matter below. Let me reiterate that I kept reaching out to him because I felt bad. This is not a new feeling for me. He was a pathetic person that thrived off of making belittling comments at unexpected times. Case in point was later that night when he told Athena about how me and him would have never hooked up if he was better. Athena was livid to hear that, and it pushed her into the total idea that he sucked (which was the meanest thing she would ever say about anyone), but I told her he had said that to me before, so it didn't come as a surprise.

Anyways.

Lorde finished her set and we left, which is usually how those things work.

Arturo and I walked home since any transportation back was outrageously priced. During the walk, he gave me more insight into how December Sun was becoming a thing of the past and he would be kickstarting another project. Cool. He told me about how he hadn't used Grindr in several months and said it as if we were sitting across from each other at a Grindr's Anonymous meeting and I was supposed to hand him a sobriety coin. Awesome. He mentioned he was going on Warped Tour again. Wonderful. HAGS.

Not once did he ask about me during that walk. Not once did he dig in for details. It wasn't that he was incapable or inept, he just couldn't be bothered. He just didn't give a fuck.

How do you know when it's the last time you will see a person? It's rhetorical because I don't know. Unfortunately, many times it isn't by choice. In this case though it was. The Lorde concert was a long-winded experiment to see if Arturo had the capacity to care about someone that he didn't need to. I'd find someone else to go to the Foo Fighters concert with; it's not like he would even remember I had invited him at some point. He failed the single-blind study, so when we got close to my complex and he splintered off to his car, I knew, with certainty, that I would never see Arturo Yanez again.

I had no need to dwell on the past when my future begged for attention.

And for once, I was happy to have someone out of my life.

## twelve

## TURN! TURN! TURN!

It took a couple days to unwind from the events of the weekend, but I persevered. My mom made it back home safely and we talked through how she was feeling about it all. We came to an agreement not to let something like that spiral out of control again.

Evan came over on Tuesday evening for a quiet hang out. He had a particularly long day at work (someone had keyed another employee's car after they parked in their spot) and my day was as bland as a salad without dressing.

He brought over Izzie and the three of us squeezed onto the couch. I flipped open my laptop to try and find a movie for us to watch.

"Wait, what is that? Or I should say, what are those?" he asked, pointing to the left corner of the screen.

"Ahhh. Those are slideshows I made for special birthdays. When my grandmother turned eighty, when my mom turned fifty, and when my dad turned sixty. They were a pain in the ass to make. All of the photos needed to be scanned into the computer and put in chronological order and then there was the music and timing to figure out. I spent a long time on each, but I got pretty good by the last one."

"Show me."

"Why?"

"Because I want to see it."

"But why? It is just full of random people you don't know."

"Because you made it and I'll take any opportunity to get a glimpse into your life since you are oddly uptight about it."

"I just don't like to talk about work. I'm an open book about everything else."

"Prove it then."

"Which one?"

"The most recent."

I clicked on my dad's slideshow and it popped into full screen mode.

"Shit. I forgot how long this is," I said, looking down at the timer which clocked in at over forty minutes.

"I don't mind. Play it."

I did. Naturally, it started with pictures of my dad as a kid set to the tune of a song by The Byrds. When creating the slideshow, it was the first time I ever stumbled upon pictures of him that young. He looked drastically different. An unburdened smile. Large, obtuse glasses that covered his face. Blonde hair that fully covered his head. I tried to find any semblance in how I looked but it was a useless task. It was hard to see him as the same person I knew. He didn't smile much anymore. His hair was clinging onto its last warriors until they died off in battle. Mainly though, it was because he didn't have a mustache, which is something I'd never seen him without.

The years passed by and he morphed from a kid to a teenager and then an adult who was slinging a guitar in many of the pictures. Suddenly, my mom showed up. Wedding photos, pictures of their litter of puppies, and then my sister showed in rapid flashes.

And then me. The star of the show.

At no point did any of the pictures capture the pain he went through of having a kid at sixteen and signing away his parental rights. Or the fucked-up childhood he had. Or the failed engagement he had before my mom. A picture may be worth a thousand words, but the story is always longer than that.

"That's you!" Evan pointed out.

"Good call. My fat head was recognizable from a young age."

Partway through *Times Like These*, the pictures stopped, and it cut to a video clip. My mom had grabbed the cam recorder and was walking from the kitchen into the living room, where my dad had fallen asleep with me curled up on his chest. He woke up and gave a long stretch. Leigh came over and started bugging him about getting her chocolate milk. A brief flash of annoyance passed through him, but it faded as quickly as it appeared.

My mom laughed at him for falling asleep and—

The clip ended.

I paused the slideshow.

"Have you ever seen the movie *Philadelphia*?" I turned and asked Evan.

"No."

"It's a movie with Tom Hanks and he is a lawyer that gets AIDS and the firm fires him. Stuff happens, but the ending is what I'm driving at here. Tom Hanks's character dies—sorry, spoiler—and the film ends with his funeral. The last shot is home video of him as a child. I think it is meant to highlight the innocence of who he was at that age. He was a *normal* kid, if you believe that being gay is abnormal.

"I bring it up because watching that clip now of my family, I can't help but think about the same thing. They had no clue I was gay at that age. How could they? I couldn't even talk yet. I was the son they wanted to raise as best they could and try to give the world to if it was possible. And now, I shattered their dreams. I don't fault them for being upset or caught off guard when I told them, but I wonder if they still look at me that way. Am I still the baby in that video? I think that's the case. The love my parents have for me is virtually endless. I have certainly questioned how my dad views me now, but moments like that, moments I wouldn't even remember if it wasn't for my mom recording, remind me that I am still his son. I'm still that little guy asleep on his chest. I just hope I've made him proud."

Evan avoided eye contact with me. He was the type that either showed no emotion or an overabundance of it. He was on the verge of the floodgates bursting.

"He loves you very much. You know that. You are lucky to have two parents that are supportive of you," he eventually said.

"I am. I just need to remember that sometimes."

"I . . . now that you have me in a heightened emotional state, I want to tell you about Kieran. Maybe it's an odd time to bring it up—or to bring it up at all—but it's a large piece of me that I've alluded to but have avoided telling."

Ah, yes. Kieran. Evan's long-term ex-boyfriend that he only mentioned in passing. I showed him my fake scars, so it was only fair for him to pull out his real ones. Something told me his stories wouldn't be made up.

"If you are comfortable . . ."

"It's certainly not a pleasant experience to rehash, mostly because I'm worried you won't believe me, but I'm willing to take the risk."

He shifted and moved himself to the other end of the couch. We were apart, but it was the closest I'd felt to him in our time together.

"You know I moved around a lot while growing up, but my mom and I settled in South Carolina. I spent my high school years there. I went to a school where it was just me and one other guy who were officially out. It wasn't easy. It's not that I got made fun of, but I just didn't have anyone to relate to.

"When I started my sophomore year, I had an English teacher. I mean, duh. Obviously, I had one. I'll spare the theatrics: it was Kieran. I gravitated toward him. I went to get help from him, and we just started spending more time together. I couldn't tell you the exact moment we crossed over from that student-teacher relationship. You'd think that memory would be vivid. At the time, it didn't feel weird that I was seeing him more than normal, and, quite frankly, it still doesn't. I needed someone to help get me through that time in my life and often times you attach yourself to the first person who shows interest.

"We started dating, but obviously kept it a secret. This continued through the remainder of my time in high school. I was always cautious whenever I went to his house or spent time with him at school. We did our best to hide it, but rumblings started to happen. People began to ask questions and we both lied."

"How much older was he?" I cut in.

"Ten years."

I nodded.

"Once I graduated high school and went off to college, our relationship became a bit strained. The distance was problematic, but it was more so his flirtatious attitude. He was quietly talking with a couple other students on the side, and while nothing physical ever happened, the school essentially ran him out of town. Without a job, he moved closer to me where I helped support him for a short time. I was in school and working and doing the dance stuff on the side. It was chaotic, but it leveled out when he got a job and we moved in together.

"He bought a house close enough to campus so that I was able to easily commute. At first it was great. We settled into the rhythm any couple would when they take that next step. Kieran let me make all of the design choices and the house rapidly turned into a home. But this wouldn't be a worthwhile story if things didn't go south.

"I could spend all night chronicling the ups and downs of our relationship and the dynamic between us, but the short answer is this: Kieran suffered from mental illnesses. He tried to kill himself by overdosing on pills. He had severe anxiety and depression. He was my boyfriend though and I helped him work through that. I don't think he ever got better though. He just pushed it down until it boiled over.

"About six months into living at the house, we had a party. Kieran's friends became my friends and vice versa, so we knew everyone there really well. We all had a great time—you know I love to host small gatherings like that—and while we were cleaning up the kitchen, we noticed that one of the pictures on the fridge looked weird. We moved closer and saw that Kieran's face was scratched out. It was as if someone had repeatedly scraped a coin across it. We didn't understand who would have done that since no one at the party had a grudge against him. We shook it off and replaced the picture.

"It happened again a week later. The same picture, the same scratching."

"What the fuck . . ."

"I don't really have an explanation for it, but my mind started to race. We didn't know the history of the house. There could have been a number of things that happened. I am moving into the part of the story where I lose people. I know it sounds crazy, and I know that's something everyone says when they are telling a story like this. I'm not asking you to believe me. I just need you to know why."

"Why what?"

"Why I still get nightmares. Why I haven't been in a serious relationship since."

I was fully absorbed. I trusted every word he told me.

"There was one time in particular where Kieran woke up in the middle of the night. I heard him sit up and stay there. I woke up enough to ask him what was wrong. He didn't respond. Instead, he turned to me and stared with a look I will never forget. I knew Kieran for five years at that point and I have never seen him with a look so devoid of emotion . . . of life. I was scared and quickly got out of bed and moved out into the living room. By the time he came out of the bedroom, he asked me why I was out there. I told him, and he said how he just woke up and didn't remember looking at me. The next morning, he was in the bedroom getting ready for the day when the door slammed shut. I ran over from the kitchen, and he started banging on the door. It wouldn't open. He was screaming, and I was yelling at him to let go of the door. We continued the back and forth until he pulled it open. Again, I have no idea what the cause of that was. It could have been Kieran thinking it would be funny, but by that point, he knew how on edge I was, so I doubt he would have purposely done that. Following those two events, I started to read up on ghosts and how to get rid of them from a house. Seems silly, right? I had convinced myself it was the only logical cause of what was happening. One of the suggestions I found was an old Japanese trick. You are supposed to spread rice out on the floor, and the ghost is supposed to get frustrated from trying to count each grain and leave. Wishful thinking, but I tried it out. Out in the kitchen, I tossed an entire box of rice across the floor. I wasn't sleeping much by then, but I decided to sleep in the bedroom for once. I woke up sometime during the night and the bedroom door was open with light trickling in from the kitchen. I felt the other side of the bed and it was empty. I walked out and found Kieran in the kitchen, staring back at me. He asked me if I did it and pointed to the floor. The rice was arranged into an upside-down cross. Not a single grain was out of place. It was meticulous as if someone—or something—spent hours perfecting it. I was numb by that point. I accused Kieran of doing it. Why else would he be up? I moved closer to the rice, fixated at the symbol. I turned back to see if Kieran was as freaked out as me, and I only saw the void in him again. He was gone, replaced by something else. This time, he lunged at me. I ran. Out the front door and hopped over the six-foot-high fence that surrounded the yard. I ran through the neighborhood until I got to a bar that was still open. I was only in my boxers, so they probably assumed I was some lunatic. I don't remember much about that. They must have called the police because they showed up there to drive me back. They searched the house and talked to Kieran to make sure it wasn't a domestic abuse issue. Kieran was flustered because he said he had woken up outside, laying in the grass and was worried about where I went."

He spoke with unparalleled calmness. He had retold this story to himself numerous times, trying to dispel any uncertainty. Evan continued:

"I couldn't do it anymore. I left after that. In a matter of days, I packed my stuff up and was gone. We had been on the fringe of breaking up for a while. I had caught him sexting other guys and the house stuff put a ton of strain on me. I had lost weight, was barely sleeping, and still trying to balance school and work.

"I came back a week later to get the last of my things and I found a used condom in the bathroom garbage. It was the closure I needed. I have barely spoken to him since. I moved on with my life the best I could, but I still get the nightmares occasionally. I had them every night for months after that. At some point, I couldn't help but wonder if I had gone crazy. Did I make it all up? Would anyone believe me if I told them? And I have told people, but they never respond in the way you'd hope. That's why I was hesitant to tell you. Between the circumstances of how I met Kieran to all the house stuff, I didn't want to freak you out. But here we are, and you listened to all of it," he finished.

"I believe every word." I moved over and gave him a hug. "I'm sorry it happened to you."

"I'm okay now."

He may have been, but I didn't sleep at all that night.

## thirteen

## COUGH SYRUP

The next day at work, during a particularly long stretch of time where I received no emails or had meetings to attend, my mind drifted to everything Evan had told me. Setting aside the unexplainable things that happened, it was fairly obvious how Kieran was a turd. How could I avoid the same fate? The clear and easy answer was to not cheat on Evan. Done. The thought never crossed my mind. But what about the stuff that takes more work? And what if we ever moved in . . .

I stopped it before it could gain traction.

. . . Okay, but what about the paranormal shit that happened? Did I actually believe him? I told him I did, but it all sounded very convenient. The classic ratcheting up of spooky stuff until a final crescendo that caused everything to crumble. I searched for upside down crosses and discovered that the Church of Satan had adopted the symbol back in the 1950s—not exactly a long history there. Of course, it is impossible to know if what Evan saw matched the pictures I was looking at. And what about the strange behavior Kieran exhibited on several occasions? Could it have been him slipping mentally or actually possessed? The questions swirled around, but quickly dissolved. Evan and I never spoke about the topic again. No sense in dwelling on stories with dead ends.

I've said it before (maybe), but it's worth repeating again with an addendum: This is not a love story as much as it isn't a scary story, which is why Evan's campfire tale never amounted to anything more than conjecture and smoke drifting away into the night sky.

We managed to squeeze onto the nonstop from DAL to GSP on Friday. The plan was to spend the weekend with Evan's friend Bryce, and then meet up with his mom for a few hours on Sunday. Just to recap: In the span of a week, he had met my mom and I would be meeting his. Needless to say, the relationship train was chugging along.

From the airport, we went to downtown Greenville. It was a quaint, medium sized city. The main drag lasted no more than six or seven blocks. A river passed through the middle, which was made the main attraction. A bridge was suspended high above it so you could walk across and take all the pictures you wanted.

That trip was the last time I remembered Evan having his camera. For the first month and a half of our relationship, he carried it around religiously. He would try to take unassuming photos of me, but I generally knew each time he did. I enjoyed the fact that someone was pining to take my picture, even though he constantly caught me in unflattering poses.

As expected, he whipped out the camera as we were walking across the bridge. He was explaining to me the parts of town he lived in during his time at USC, his friendship with Bryce, and the lack of a gay bar within the city in between his picture taking. I was enthralled to hear him speak about a topic not relating to work. He was an amazingly intelligent person with knowledge about a wide assortment of things, but he rarely dove into them. He bent down and snapped a few pictures in between the railing. He—

*Don't fuck this up. Don't fuck this up.*

I shook off the thought.

"Vin?"

"Yeah?"

"Thought I lost you there. Want to sit for a bit? We have some time to kill before Bryce is going to meet us for dinner," he said as he put the cap on the lens and slung the camera strap onto this shoulder. He must have noticed my distant look. "Is everything okay?"

"Yeah, of course. I'm just thinking about you."

"Well, I don't mind you doing that," Evan said as he moved closer and wrapped an arm around me.

We walked to the other side of the bridge. It dropped us out onto the main road, and we spotted a bench nearby to take refuge at. I sat down and watched the people who casually walked by. No one was in a hurry. It was Friday afternoon and anyone who wasn't at work was likely thinking about the weekend ahead.

"Ask me a question," Evan said, breaking up the silence between us.

"You with the questions!" I said jokingly. "I should have never started this trend on our first date. You know, it gets harder and harder to think of stuff."

"Isn't it your job to ask questions?"

"Well, yeah, but that doesn't mean I'm good at it."

"You are . . . I'm waiting," he raised his eyebrows and shook his head.

"Hypothetically speaking—of course—if you had the ability to take any painting and get away with it, which would you take? Added bonus if you tell me why," I said, proud of my off-the-cuff question.

"Easy," he said with no hesitation. "I would want the painting my grandmother created back in the 50s. It's not famous or anything, but she described it in a journal of hers my mom gave me after she died. The painting was lost in a fire a long time ago, so I'll never get the chance to see it. It would have been nice to have another memory of her. She had a lust for travel and lived a full life. I aspire to be like that."

"You got depressing with your answer."

"A majority of our conversations are depressing."

"Well, I was hoping for something more upbeat."

His look grew more serious. "I answered your question, Vin."

"Okay. Fine. I'll tell you mine. I would steal the panel in the Sistine Chapel of Adam and God doing that weird almost-touching-fingers thing. I wouldn't do it because of the religious component, but more so for the logistics behind it. How would I get in there to steal it? How could you possibly get it out of there? And then, where would you store it? Also, I could hold it ransom for lots of money. If that doesn't shine capitalism, then I don't know what to say. The absurd idea of it makes me laugh," I said.

"That's interesting," he said, likely not being interested in any of it.

"Welp, now I can see you are annoyed."

"Vin, just stop."

I did, ensuring that the cycle continued.

He grabbed the camera, got up, and walked across the street. He went toward the statue with a balloon hanging off it and took several more photos.

I watched him from the bench.

It bothered me how uptight he was. Every answer had a twinge of seriousness to it. I could only joke so much before I was condemned for my behavior. I didn't want to constantly live inside my own head where everything was serious and depressing, so I tended to be looser externally. If I couldn't be myself around Evan, then what was the point?

I paused. I didn't need to fall down another side path. If I did, I would shut down and not recover for hours. I shook off the pit that was forming and waited patiently for Evan to come back.

Once he did, we went to get chocolates and then to the restaurant to meet Bryce. I kept convincing myself I was fine.

I couldn't tell you the last time I was.

※

I discovered what it was like for my mom the previous week. I only contributed three times to the conversation during dinner. Bryce was nice enough, but I had nothing in common with him. He talked incessantly about work just as much as Evan did. Last time I checked, I didn't get paid enough for work to occupy my headspace all the time. After his long-winded introduction, Bryce and Evan reminisced about their time at USC. The classes, the bars, the housing, the random names that meant nothing to me. I didn't mind not being the center of attention, but I could tell from the sideway glances I periodically received from Evan that he assumed I was having a bad time.

Dinner passed by and Bryce drove us over to his house. He lived with three friends, none of whom we saw during the weekend. The house was three bedrooms with enough space for each to spread out. He gave us a tour and we got to meet his dog, Life—a greyhound rescue. She was shy, but an absolute sweetheart.

After the tour, Bryce went to take a shower as Evan and I set up our sleeping arrangements for the next two nights.

"Are you alright? You didn't talk much during dinner," he said as he took the pillows off the fold out couch.

"Yeah, I'm fine. I was absorbing all of the information between you two. I just didn't have much to say since I have no ties to this area."

"Okay. I'm sorry."

"For what?"

"That you didn't talk much."

"Are you still upset about earlier?"

"We can talk about it later."

That certainly didn't make me feel good to hear, but I brushed it off and helped him get the makeshift bed set up.

It took another hour for us to get ready to go barhopping, even though the weather was looking grim.

Bryce called an Uber and Evan decided on the bar. It was a twenty-minute ride that we got to take in a minivan, so the mood was immediately set.

Once there, Evan picked up the first round and we found a table toward the back. There was a light crowd inside, most of which were focused on the basketball games being shown on the televisions.

"So, Bryce, are you seeing anyone?" I asked from across the table.

"Sort of, I guess. I'm in a weird position with this one guy. We have been on a few dates and we get along pretty well, but I think he may have a screw loose. He gets clingy if I don't text him back fast enough and assumes I am out humping other people around town."

"Sounds like a massive red flag," Evan chimed in. (We live in a time where a slight negative is seen as an insurmountable red flag and immediate grounds for termination. The FEAR methodology was at play: Fuck Everything and Run. What happened to the good ole days where the husband could beat the wife and kids after a few sips of scotch without persecution? The morals in this country are slipping so much.)

"Agreed," I said.

"I feel the same way. I should call it quits with him, but I don't know how."

"Let's do it right now," I suggested.

Bryce was taken aback. "No! That would be terrible," he said with a laugh.

"I'm more of the rip off the Band-Aid type." That was a complete lie, but neither Evan nor Bryce would know that. I let things linger. I let relationships crumble to their lowest possible form even after it became obvious there was no salvation. I constantly clung onto the belief that things could change but repeat after me: PEOPLE. DON'T. CHANGE.

"Okay, so my love life is a bit muddied right now. This too shall pass. Tell me how you two met. Evan hasn't told me a single thing!" he said with a huff.

Evan and I looked at each other. "You can take this one," I said. I was always slightly embarrassed to admit when I met someone off a dating app, especially Grindr, but besides my friends from work, anybody I knew in Dallas was from one, so I really needed to face the music.

Evan broke off into a tale about how we got to being in that bar together. It was a take of intrigue and mystery and murder. That's not the case considering you have heard it already. I'm guessing part of you wishes you got to hear the condensed version he told Bryce instead of the unending monologue you had the divine pleasure of reading through.

Bryce repeated no less than four times about how we seemed like the perfect couple and that he was so happy for us. I appreciated the kind thoughts, but we had only been dating for a month and knew virtually nothing about each other.

The remainder of our time at the bar was a hodgepodge of conversation I no longer recall. I had been having trouble remembering things that happened after my second or third drink. It was never a problem for me in college, but maybe it had something to do with getting old? In any case, while I don't remember the chat the three of us had, I do remember running through the rain to hop in the Uber to be taken back to Bryce's place. Once there, Evan and I immediately fell into the couch/bed and sleep nipped at my feet. I fought through it because I needed to know.

"Can we talk about what happened earlier?" I asked, barely slurring my words.

We were plunged into total darkness, so I couldn't see his face even though it was inches from mine. I turned my head and stared up at the ceiling, briefly wondering if there were any balloons up there sitting and waiting to be released.

"Vin, I can't help but think you keep trying to change me. You have to understand I am the way I am. I don't think every joke you make is funny. Sometimes when you act weird it annoys me. But that's not even the point—you need to stop trying to morph me into this person you want me to be," he said, rather harshly.

"I don't understand. Where is this coming from?"

"On numerous occasions, you have told me to lighten up or to stop overthinking something. Obviously, I could say the same thing to you, but I don't. You need to realize I am finally happy with the way that I am. It took me a long time to be comfortable with how I look and act and am perceived by others. I don't need my boyfriend to think it isn't good enough."

"I . . . uh . . . I'm sorry. I didn't recognize I did that. But now that you mention it, I can see how it would be true. I have an issue with trying to get people to a better place than where they are now. I guess I do it to others because I can't seem to fix myself, but it comes from a place of compassion. I never want to see someone be complacent. I look at you and see this beautiful person; someone that deserves better than the hour-long commute to work each day or the mental gymnastics you put yourself through sometimes. I just want to help you."

"I don't need your help. Stop trying to change me. You're not my savior."

"Okay," I said, dejected. I rolled over to face the wall and tried to sleep. I knew I wouldn't find it easily like most nights. I wanted to say something and desperately willed myself to do so, but stubbornness and not knowing what wouldn't piss him off triumphed over me. Not another word passed between us until the morning.

---

The main goal of Saturday was to get to Tallulah Gorge. That wasn't a difficult task considering it was just a car ride away. We grabbed breakfast, dropped the dog off at Bryce's friend's house, and then set out.

Evan and I were on speaking terms, but neither of us brought up the conversation from the night before. I didn't want the day to go to shit before it even started.

The drive was dull, but I enjoyed the colors of spring making an appearance. Up in Pennsylvania during March, things would have been brown and dead or still bearing the weight of the last snowstorm. Down in Dallas, well, I can't remember what anything would look like because I never took the time to notice nor care.

Once there, we took some time in the welcome center and pretended to read all the information about the wildlife roaming around.

We ventured outside and followed one of the trails. Bryce had been to the gorge before, so he led the way. It gave me an opportunity to talk to Evan.

"How are you feeling about last night?"

"I know you mean well. I think we are still in the phase of our relationship—watch out for that rock—where we are feeling each other out."

"We don't do much of feeling each other out, if you catch my meaning."

"Not the right time," he shook his head. "Anyways, let's just have fun today. I think you are going to like this."

"Okay."

He turned to me, and as if the light flicked on in the attic, he said, "Are you mad?"

"No. Just disappointed."

'Why?"

*Why? WHY? Because I am trying to help! I am a failed experiment and the only thing I can possibly get right is to make someone else better. That's fucking why and the fact you aren't aware of that makes me wonder what else you can't see about me. . .*

"Nothing. I'll be fine."

"You always say you'll be fine or that you *are* fine. I'm starting to think you aren't."

*No shit.*

"Yeah, I've heard that before."

"Hey!" Bryce called up from ahead. "Here is the overlook."

We scrambled up the last few feet and out onto the platform.

"Wow! Do you think they call it a gorge because the sight is *gorge*ous?" I asked.

Bryce laughed, and Evan booed. Typical.

The view was striking. The park was massive, and the line of trees waved up and down along the cliff side like lazy brush strokes on a canvas. The gorge itself was at least two hundred feet below where we stood, and we could see the tiny shapes moving across the bridge to the right. The water was somewhat low and moved at a methodical pace. Several birds swooped in and out of the gorge with a destination beyond eyesight.

Both Evan and Bryce took out their cameras as I stood like Rose on the edge of the Titanic. I sensed a bit of rivalry—more so from Evan—because

Bryce was an established photographer that did gigs on the side. They blabbered on about what camera the other one was using.

After five minutes, we descended from the lookout point and forged our way back to the main path. The next area in mind was the bridge we saw in the distance. It took close to an hour to reach it, but that was due to none of us being a rush.

We had to walk down hundreds of steps to get to the bridge, which meant we'd have to walk the same amount to come back up. There was even resting points for those who needed a break.

We navigated to the bottom and stepped out onto the bridge. It swayed lazily with the added weight but seemed like it could hold a hundred more people. Everyone else must have had other plans at that time because it was empty.

"Quick! Take pictures! Mush! Before the crowd returns," I urged.

They both looked around, noticed the barrenness, and quickly swung their cameras into action.

"Vin, can you take a picture of me?" Bryce asked.

"Sure." I took five just in case.

"Vin, let's take one together," Evan said.

I walked over, pulled him in close, and put on a large grin. The only downside to the condition I have with my eyes is that standing out in the daylight makes me squint without the aid of sunglasses. I was fresh out of sunglasses, so squinting was what the sun gods demanded. Evan held out the camera with his lanky arm and snapped several photos. I looked like trash in all of them, but I was glad to have captured the moment. We were both (fake) happy. Happy to be at the gorge. Happy to be out of Texas. Happy to be with each other.

The rest of the expedition was centered around more walking and more stairs. We were all exhausted when we reached the car. Bryce mustered his will power and drove us back without falling asleep. The same couldn't be said for Evan and me.

We parted ways with Bryce early Sunday and thanked him profusely for the hospitality. Evan begged him to visit Dallas sometime and he promised to.

Evan's mom picked us up from the house. The plan was this: there was no chance we'd make it back to DAL from GSP on Sunday, so we decided to set up standby travel from CLT. It was less than a two-hour drive and gave Evan an excuse to see his mom. Even though it was out of her way, she was eager to see her son, and I couldn't blame her because my mom would have done the exact same thing.

I'm not sure if I was an added bonus or just more weight to transport.

She pulled up to the house, and Evan leaned over. "Are you nervous?"

"Nah. If she is anything like you, I have nothing to be nervous about."

"Awww," he said and kissed me on the cheek. Sometimes I knew the right thing to say.

His mom stepped out of the car and gave Evan a huge hug. "Mom, this is Vin. Vin, this is my mom."

"It's great to finally meet you!" I said. She also greeted me with a hug.

"You can call me Liz. Evan has told me everything about you, but I'd rather hear it from the source. Are y'all ready?"

"Yeah," we said in unison. We threw what luggage we had in the back.

Ten minutes into the ride, she looked at me through the rearview mirror and said, "So Vin, what do you do?"

"I work at [REDACTED] in the Technology Department. Currently, I am working on a project to help us fly to Hawaii."

"Oh really? I love flying [REDACTED]. I just flew [REDACTED] the other week. [REDACTED] has the funniest flight attendants! Tell me more about your role on the project."

I dove into the details. Evan stared back at me. Much of the information I shared with Liz was a first for him as well. He smiled and seemed genuinely interested in what I said. I guess that's what happens when someone really likes you. I also guess that the conversation we had on Friday night was not still hanging over him. I can't say I was completely over it yet, but it wasn't at the forefront of my mind either.

We stopped at a tiny diner for breakfast on the outskirts of Greenville. We each ordered huge plates of pancakes though none of us made it even halfway through the food. At one point, Evan got up from the table to use the restroom.

"He seems happy," she said. "I know the breakup was tough with Kieran, and he spoke about how hard it would be to date again. Quite frankly, you must be really special."

"I try to do my best every day, but I have learned that relationships are hard."

"Oh, I know sweetie. I've been married three times. It takes a village to get a relationship off the ground and takes an entire civilization to keep it going. Can I give you some advice?"

"Absolutely."

"Love him fiercely. It may take time for y'all to get there, but once you do, fight for each other every day. Never go to bed angry. You won't be able to sleep anyways. And continue to grow. You don't ever want to be bored with each other."

"Thanks Liz." On one hand, it felt strange to have that discussion with his mom since it sounded like she was talking to me in the back of a church before our wedding ceremony, but on the other hand, it was solid advice to keep in mind.

Evan came back to the table, asked what he missed, and we told him it was our secret.

Liz grabbed the check and we set out for the airport.

Hours later, we were high above the clouds heading west to our home. I told myself I had a great weekend and it didn't take much convincing. Out of sight, out of mind. A saying that always worked well for me. Evan was sitting in the aisle seat; I was at the window. I turned my attention from the passing scenery outside to him. I stared at him long enough until he noticed my gaze and pulled out his headphone.

"What's up?"

"Nothing. Just looking at ya."

"Oh yeah? If you stared any harder, you'd likely burn a whole in my cheek."

"I had fun this weekend, and I want you to know that the talk we had on Friday was important. Promise me you will always tell me when I am fucking up. Or when I am doing something good." I grabbed his hand. "This is a whole new life for me. I'm going to stumble, and I need you to guide me. Communication is the most vital resource we have."

"I will." He gave my hand an extra squeeze.

I returned to staring out the window. We were soaring above it all.

# fourteen

## NO TIME FOR CAUTION

May was going to be a motherfucker. Evan would be visiting family in Orlando, then I would be there at Universal Studios, then he was going to EDC, and then I was going home for Memorial Day. We wouldn't see each other for a month on the weekends and sparingly during the weeks.

That was going to be a radical shift to our dynamic, but I was hopeful it wouldn't be too much of a strain.

Before that though, let me recap the month or so in between then and where we last left off.

Evan and I continued down the path of trying to understand each other better. That led to very serious conversations. Up until the point of the Greenville trip, we hadn't had sex. It was not an expectation for me, but I couldn't wrap my brain around why we hadn't taken that next step. It was undeniable that I was the needier one. Evan was much more casual in his physical needs. Sex wasn't the ultimate goal for him. He enjoyed the cuddling and quiet moments of affection—the hand on the lower back, the unexpected kiss, the laying in his lap. I was atrocious that those things. My brain was too wrapped up in itself to realize his needs. On top of that, he still made me nervous. Each time I saw him, I felt as if we were meeting for the first time. I wouldn't know what to say or if I should kiss him or throw him a high five. I questioned every movement I made, every word I spoke in his direction. I was so fearful I wasn't doing something right that I didn't even bother to try at all.

So, we talked.

Many times, it was him on one end of my couch with me on the other, reminiscent to the night he told me about Kieran. We talked about why I was behaving a certain way or what his thoughts were on a topic. The conversations were hard. It was difficult to hear direct and honest feedback about yourself from someone you cared about. I didn't want him to think I was just trying to get in his pants all the time or that me putting up such a façade was wearing him down. There were instances when I became silent, stuck in a place of not knowing what to say or not wanting to say anything. I would shut myself off and kill the whole mood for the rest of the night. He was guilty of it too. I never viewed it as a negative thing because we were taking the time to understand each other more. I strived for better communication in my previous relationships, but people were never receptive.

We eventually began having sex, and I eventually started to bottom. He created such a safe environment for me that I was able to put aside that past experience and enjoy the moment with him. I don't see the need to go into further detail than that. I did in the first book because I wanted you to understand how much I cared about those people, but maybe that sentiment was misguided and not the right way to go about things. Live and learn.

During the midst of those in-depth conversations and our foray into the world of sex, I had a party at my apartment. He finally got to meet Athena, Jag, Anders, and the other people who magically showed up. I watched Evan from the other side of the kitchen as he interacted with each of them. I beamed with joy at how easily he fit in. Evan didn't have many friends in Dallas yet and I wanted him to discover that there were good people around.

I felt myself falling for him, ever so slightly more each day. The small gestures of kindness he showed me, his commitment to planning unique dates for us escape the tedium, and the thought that I finally found someone who mattered were all serious contributors to the growing feeling. Love doesn't happen at once. It takes time. The series of moments you build with someone creates a foundation you stand upon and keep reaching higher. Sometimes the sour moments bring you down, but you need to keep reaching.

I don't recall the first time we said it to each other, but if I had to guess, I likely struggled to say it even though I meant every word and he likely told me he wanted to say it long before he ever did.

Love—the disgustingly overused word that meant nothing anymore.

## fifteen

## TAKE YOUR TIME (COMING **HOME**)

Evan went to Orlando the first weekend of May to visit his aunt and uncle. On my end, nothing of note happened. I laid around in my boxers, ate pizza rolls, played Xbox, continued to write, and do other worthless activities. My brain tried hard to get me to slip, to focus on the endless possibilities of what Evan could be doing or who he could be with, but I stiff-armed that shit out the window.

I nearly forgot! The only joy of Evan being out of town was that I had the distinct honor of hosting Izzie. The bundle of mangled fur was my best new friend of 2018 and we were destined to become a power couple. She watched my every move from the couch when I would roam around the apartment and would sleep right up against me under the covers. It made me miss Rigby and how that big oaf was my shadow.

Anyways, to avoid sounding clingy, I'll stop myself from talking more about him being out of town that first weekend. I'll save the real story for when he went to Vegas.

❖

As I briefly spoke about in another life, my parents went nuts for Christmas. My sister and I always got a big gift at the end, usually something different for each of us. Last year, it was combined and her fiancé, Lorenzo, was also included in the madness.

My parents got us four day passes to Universal Studios in Orlando. Four days of rides, thrills, spills, and mediocre food at unaffordable prices. My mom was weary about how my sister and I would get along given our previous history, but I was confident that in our mid-twenties we would be civil around each other.

The trip logistics were as such: Lorenzo was graduating from Miami University with his doctorate earlier that week. His plan was to move himself, and his entire life, back up to New Jersey where he was hoping to find a job. My sister flew down for his graduation ceremony. Following that, they rented a U-Haul, shoved all his shit in it, and drove up to Orlando. That was on Thursday. I flew in on Thursday night.

MCO was a conundrum. On one end, you had a massive buildup of elderly folk who moved around at the pace of a dead snail, shuffling back and forth between their seat and the bathroom. Some would stop in the middle of the terminal, squint down at the boarding pass, and recognize how Terminal A did not equal Terminal B. Their intention was pure, but their execution was horribly slow. On the other end, there was the mob of families. Kids darting in and out between luggage, others screaming for no coherent reason, and a large portion of parents that looked defeated.

I arrived rather late when neither of those groups were out thriving in the wild. The elderly had been asleep for hours already and the families would likely be coming in on the morning flights. I hopped on the train to the main hub and then moved toward the ride share pickup.

Twenty minutes later, I was dropped off in front of Cabana Bay, the 50s-themed resort we were staying at for the next four days.

I walked into the main lobby and plopped down on one of the long rows of seats that were scattered throughout the area. A few people hung around the bar, likely ordering their last drink of the night. The final remnants of late check-ins were at the counter. I sent Lorenzo a text to let him know I was there, and he responded saying they were coming back from CityWalk.

A wave passed over me as I waited for them.

*You could do it. You could download Grindr, find someone here, and get away with it.*

It would have been impossible for Evan to ever find out. Why though? Why would I even entertain the idea of sabotaging my relationship? I firmly believed you could never stop someone from cheating. It was entirely their choice and something the guilty party would have to live with if the other person never found out. For me though, the answer was easy: I was constantly on a warpath to destroy—no, absolutely annihilate—anything that was good in my life. There was no way I could find anyone half as good as Evan in the Cabana Bay resort, but it didn't matter. The thrill of *potentially* finding someone half as good was enough to make my brain contemplate the idea. I had no way to run from it. The thought kept building, gaining mass with every passing second. I had nowhere to run to. I had no way to cope with it or push it from my mind. It sat next to me in that lobby and stared intently at me, waiting for any movement I made.

God, I was such a fucking joke. It wasn't even the self-deprecation talking; it was the harsh reality I needed to face. I was a waste. How many times did I think about killing myself that day alone? Worthless at my job, worthless in my relationship. Worthless, utterly wor—

"Vinny Boy!" a voice said in front of me.

I looked up and saw Lorenzo. My mind wiped itself of its current spiral.

I stood up and anticipated his movements. I predicted correctly, and we embraced successfully in a handshake/bro hug.

"Hey man. How's it going?"

"Pretty well. Your sister went to the bathroom. We can head to the room once she gets back if you want," he suggested.

"Yeah, I'm tired and I'm sure we will be up early to get to the park at a good time."

"We scoped it out tonight. We know where the bus is and how to get over there, so we should be all set."

"What is CityWalk?" I asked.

"It's this area full of restaurants and shops you have to walk through before getting into the park. We brought back some food. Do you want some?" he said, holding out a bag in my direction.

"I'm good right now," I said with a chuckle. "By the way, congrats on graduating! You must be glad it's finally over."

"You have no idea."

"How's the job hunt going?"

"No luck yet, but it was to be expected. Getting your doctorate doesn't guarantee a job, which I have been learning very much so over the past few months."

For the last three years, Lorenzo was living down in Miami, as previously mentioned. He met my sister during their freshman year of college. They started out as friends, but it eventually developed into a relationship. They stayed together throughout college as it became clear they were in it for the long haul. Lorenzo moved down to Miami while my sister stayed up at home to do a course correction with her career. She became a nurse. My sister wanted the commitment from him, even though they were hundreds of miles apart, so during the first winter I was down in Dallas they got engaged. Naturally, it was down at the beach where they went to school. He returned to Miami and forged ahead toward graduation. Time passed, as it usually did, and she would occasionally visit him, and he would try to make it up for holidays and summer break, but I imagine the strain was difficult at times. The wedding planning likely distracted my sister for the last year of Lozo being in Miami, which hopefully made the time go by faster. Leigh was itching to get out of the house and put some distance between her and my parents. They clashed about nonsensical things and all three agreed that some separation would benefit everyone.

The wedding was finally coming up in September. They would very shortly be jumpstarting their lives together. It was long overdue.

"I remember how painful it was during my senior year of college. I applied to what felt like hundreds of places. But I'm sure you don't feel like talking about that, so I won't bug you," I said.

With a shrug, he said, "No worries. It's nice to know so many people care."

Leigh walked over from the check-in counter. "Hi," she muttered.

"Hey. How's it going?" I asked, giving her a hug.

"Good. Had dinner over at CityWalk."

"Yeah, Lozo was telling me. Are you ready to go back to the room?"

"Yes," they said in unison.

They led the way out the lobby as I slung my backpack onto my shoulder and lifted up the handle for the rolling bag. I anticipated I would be bringing back a few souvenirs, so I packed light. Only one pair of boxers for me. I doubted anyone would notice the smell until the last day.

Our room was in another building at the backside of the resort. We snaked around the pool and multitude of lounging chairs between the buildings.

Leigh and Lozo were several paces ahead. I could feel the lightness she had around him. He had the key to the treasure chest that turned her cold, calculated demeanor into something more . . . real. She was relaxed around him. Her weird sense of humor shined. They argued, but it always seemed playful since Lozo was more laid back. My family and I wondered why she wasn't like that around us as often, but some mysteries were never meant to be solved.

"Here's yours," she said, handing me my key card while we were waiting for the elevator. My name was etched into the corner. I was royalty. The card had 727 on it.

Once in the room, there was shit everywhere. They brought in all the valuables from the U-Haul to make sure nothing important was taken. Outside, our room had a view of Volcano Bay, the new waterpark that was recently completed. The volcano was constantly changing colors and created a soothing reflection off the windows.

"Didn't Mom pay extra for this view?" I asked no one in particular.

"Yeah. I FaceTimed with her when we got in, so she could she see it," Leigh said. "She was paranoid it wasn't going to be as good as they claimed."

I shook my head. My mom went all out to make sure we had the perfect time.

I walked to my bed and tossed my backpack onto it. I was exhausted. Flying was a tiring chore even though the majority of it was spent exerting no energy.

I sent Evan a text to let him know I was there, and his response was almost immediate. He was glad I made it but was going to miss me terribly while I was gone. While I had the same thought, I rarely externalized it, so I sent him back some nonsense that didn't pertain to the conversation.

Without conversing with each other much, we all got ready for bed and fell asleep within the hour.

## Day 1

The mightiest perk of the Four Day Pass (yes, it will be capitalized) was that we would gain access an hour early. It came with a catch though—the only part that would be open was The Wizarding World of Harry Potter. All three of us were big fans of the series, so we were more than thrilled to get there before the Muggles overran us.

We stumbled downstairs and had a quick breakfast at the resort cafeteria.

That was an easy ten bucks tossed in the garbage for just a sandwich. Following breakfast, they booked it over to the buses. Sure enough, there was one ready and waiting.

Twenty minutes later, we pulled up to the security checkpoint outside of CityWalk. Up the escalator we went and emptied our pockets of anything that could resemble a bomb and quickly moved forward.

I deftly avoided the woman asking if I wanted to open a credit card. Not today! The walkway to get to CityWalk expanded for a quarter mile. Nothing much to see during that stretch. Once at the end though, there was stuff to see—shops, a movie theater, and endless food choices. It was excess to the nth degree. How many options of pizza could one person ever need? Three donut shops? Fifteen Starbucks? It was outrageous and each one was jam-packed with eager souls looking to spend however much money was required.

We came to a fork in the road and veered right. The park was split in two. Technically, it was two separate parks, but we had access to both. We moved closer to the entrance with the massive Universal globe spinning near the water. The crowd surged behind us, forcing us to pick up our pace.

At the gate, we had a moment to gather our surroundings as the line came to a standstill.

"Okay, so we know we are going to the Harry Potter stuff first. What's the plan after that? I downloaded the app and never bothered to look at it," I announced.

Leigh and Lozo looked over with blank stares.

"I think Harry Potter world is going to take most of the morning," my sister finally said.

She was right.

The next four hours were spent walking around Diagon Alley. We saw a fire-breathing dragon on top of Gringotts. We waited in line for a half hour to get to the ride inside the bank. I had the absolute pleasure of hearing Lorenzo scream like a banshee each time the ride whipped us in a new direction. We contemplated buying souvenirs at every shop we passed by. The pull of the wand shop was too great to ignore and we each walked out with one. Naturally, I got the largest one as it signified my masculinity and intense desire to be a size queen. We used the map that came along with the wands to find the locations where we could perform spells. We went into the Leaky Cauldron to get a round of butterbeers, slung them back in record time, and went right back for more.

By the time we walked out of Diagon Alley, the sun was reaching the peak of its arc and we felt the full force of the heat on our faces. We didn't have much of a plan since we'd be able to cover everything multiple times with our four days.

After consulting the app, we decided to go to the other park called Islands of Adventures. In that portion, they had Hogsmeade, the meeting place where Harry and the gang went to escape the confines of Hogwarts.

Instead of walking back to the entrance and circling around to get to Islands of Adventure, we hopped on the train in King's Station (also from *Harry Potter*) and finally had a chance to sit.

I sat down across from Leigh and Lorenzo as the attendant closed the door to our compartment.

"How is the wedding stuff going?" I asked as the train started to move. The screens on the windows and doors showed a changing scenery from Diagon Alley to the stormy hills of England.

They both looked at each other with a brief passing of weariness. "It has been a lot of work. Sometimes you just get stuck in the details. And of course, the price of everything skyrockets as soon as you mention it's for a wedding," Lorenzo said. "Your sister is handling everything," he finished with a pat on her leg.

Leigh laughed. "The big thing right now is the wedding invites. Mom and I have been clashing about that."

"Big surprise," I chimed in. "I think it'll be good for you two to get some space once you move out."

"I am ready," she said, staring back at the window.

I wanted to ask how they did it, how they could possibly keep a long-distance relationship going for as long as they did. There had to be moments of doubt or times when they questioned whether it was worth it. Or maybe they never did. It was possible they got up each and every day and the other person was the first thought that formed in their mind. Was there ever a day where they didn't love each other? What would happen if that day turned into a week, month, or lifetime? My brain started firing off the possibilities of how loving one person for your entire life was a sham. All those thoughts occupied me until the train came to a stop. I never got the chance to ask them what their secret was.

Once we ventured out of the station, we spent a few hours in Hogsmeade. We meandered around the area looking for places to practice our spells. I continued to chug butterbeer as if it would get me drunk.

Leigh and I waited in line for the ride that was embedded deep in the bowels of Hogwarts. Lorenzo decided his heart couldn't take another ride that jostled you around like a chew toy. It was probably a smart choice considering we got stuck on it for nearly ten minutes. It was the first of three rides Leigh and I would get stuck on during our time at Universal.

Following our time in Hogsmeade, we had no destination in mind . . .

(To be frank, this chapter has sucked. I have tried to write it for over a week and not an inkling of wisdom has poured onto the virtual page. I know the ending to this story. I know that sparing you from another sixty thousand words sounds like heaven right now, but I want to do this right. I want you to understand why. I want it all to make sense. I want each character to have their moment and feel like they have a purpose. This isn't a book about some grand adventure where the world—no, entire universe—hangs in the balance. Nah, this is about me, Vincent Besser. A lowly peon in the scheme of things. The reason I have been trying hard to write this chapter is because I need to show you how my relationship with my sister evolved. I lack the necessary skills and subtlety to tell you without actually telling you, which is what any descent writer would do, but I'm doing this for you. I know who *you* are, even if you don't. What a mind fuck! Instead of worrying about being descriptive and making you feel like you were on the trip with me, how about I just tell you the facts? I'm going to skip the rest of Day 1 and try to give this a fresh start. There will be plenty of other opportunities to dive deep into the well of thoughts I have. Also, I apologize. I promised I would cut down on the fourth wall breaks and I didn't make it very far before I did. Add it to the list of things I fucked up.)

Yada, yada, yada. Insert things that happened for the rest of Day 1.

Loading . . . Error 404 Not Found.

Executing Protocol 27.

## Day 2

Our second full day at Universal started similar to the first. An early wake up. Expensive breakfast. Bus ride. Security. Walking, walking, walking. Diagonal Alley. And finally, the train ride over to Island of Adventure.

It was an *if it ain't broke* type of situation.

Where the day strayed was the discovery of our favorite ride. It was an unlikely candidate. One that was tucked away behind the veil of monstrosities that surrounded it. It was a modest ride that relied on animatronics rather than computer gimmicks. The line was constantly short as if people forgot about the relic.

If you have been to Universal before, maybe you have a faint understanding of what I'm hinting at. No, it isn't the Fast and Furious ride. That piece of turd shit sucked ass through a straw.

Jurassic Park: River Adventure was the pinnacle of rides. Our first time we were in the front row with zero idea of what to expect. It started out casually enough. You entered into the park and saw dinosaurs frolicking around. It was a slow burn until you made it near the building. Ominous music and sounds echoed from all around. Debris was thrown about. The crate that hung above the entrance swung about as something tried to break free. Once inside the building, we began our ascent. The patches of light showcased where the dinosaurs had infiltrated. At the top of the climb, we began to hear the muffled sounds of the T-Rex. My pulse quickened as an impending doom shifted into place. We turned the corner as a silhouette appeared ahead of us. The T-Rex emerged from the shadows and made its presence known with a roar that singed my ears. The cart carrying us picked up pace. We needed to escape! We dodged the T-Rex and entered into a what felt like a free fall. Lorenzo let out a primal yell that rivaled the T-Rex's. Down we went and landed back in the water as it lapped up the sides and sprayed everyone sitting in the first few rows.

The three of us exchanged a look as the cart slowly returned to where we initially hopped on.

"That was epic," I said, wiping the water away from my face. I pressed my feet down into the floor and dribbles of water squished out.

"We need to get the picture!" Leigh demanded. Halfway down our descent, it was evident that our picture was taken. I didn't know what to expect from the outcome.

We moved out of the cart and navigated to the gift shop. The walls were lined with numerous shirts and other memorabilia, most of which were celebrating the new movie coming out. Leigh took the lead and walked over to where the pictures were propped up onto a screen. After a quick scan, we found ours.

We were the only idiots that didn't have a rain poncho on. My sister had an expression of shock. Lorenzo had a look of terror. And I looked like a fucking gerbil. My elbows were squeezed against my sides, my hands positioned closely together on the railing in front, and my mouth was contorted in a way that my front teeth protruded out prominently.

They thought it was hilarious. For me, I thought otherwise.

"What packages do you offer?" Lorenzo asked.

The lady explained.

"We will take it," he said. The lady punched in the order and moved to the printer. She gathered a bag and handed off the goods to Lorenzo.

For the record, I still have the magnetized photo hanging up on my fridge. Sometimes you need to embrace absurdity.

I ended up purchasing the shirt with the classic Jurassic Park logo on it.

Satisfied with my investment, we left the gift shop and continued to poke around the remainder of the park. Over the next few hours, we grabbed food, waited in line for the King Kong ride, waited in line for the Hulk ride, waited in line for the Spider-Man ride, and waited some more. The park wasn't stuffed like a sausage, but it seemed like the crowds kept following us, except for the last ride we went on.

The weather was beginning to turn sour. It didn't seem like a passing storm, so people began to scatter. We were unfazed. We were young, spry individuals. With a determined attitude, we went on Dudley Do-Right's Ripsaw Falls.

I didn't know who Dudley was or what his stance was on colonization of other planets, but the ride seemed fun enough. We weren't oblivious to the fact that the ride had water involved as evidenced by the log shaped transportation device you sat in was floating on water. We found a locker to stow our belongings in and stuffed three people's worth of crap into it.

"Do you think we should find out how wet we will get from this ride? I wouldn't say we are dressed for the occasion," I suggested, as Leigh repeatedly slammed the locker door shut. She moved the backpack strap that was caught on the edge and it finally closed with less resistance.

"We will be fine. Anyways, it looks like it's going to rain, so we'd probably get wet at some point before we made it back to the bus," a random individual said to us, but no one seemed to mind the stranger eavesdropping.

With our fate decided, we followed the path up and around to the ride.

Thirty minutes later, we returned, completely drenched. Ripsaw Falls turned out to be quite the water ride. From the moment we stepped into the log flume, the water licked up the sides and threatened to soak everything. It didn't take long until that happened, and since I was in the front, I experienced the brunt of the punishment. With every turn, I was met with a wall of water that doused me all over as if I was a house fire. By the end, I was dissatisfied with the situation even though, yet again, Leigh and Lorenzo were thrilled at my misery. It seemed that my sister enjoyed when unfortunate events happened to me. That's one way to build a bond!

It took a while to dry out, but once we hit the bus, we were tired and dry enough to not leave an imprint on the seat.

It never did rain that day, proving the two things in life you can't trust: people and the weather.

## **Day 3**

It did rain the next day. A significant amount. We spent the morning at the park, cleaning up on the few rides we hadn't had a chance to go on yet.

By the early afternoon we fled and went back to the resort. We settled at the bungalow bar hidden next to the pool. We ordered some food and drinks and sat down at a table in the corner.

The only sounds were the rain and bartender making drinks. The place was empty besides us and a couple of stragglers.

No one talked for a while. It wasn't a bad thing. The notion that you need to fill empty space with meaningless conversation is pointless. Beyond the timeline in this "book," I went to Maui with Jag and Athena. We are great friends who have a lot in common besides work, but there were long stretches of time where silence prevailed. We'd be driving to the next hiking location with the sound of passing cars and the wind slapping against the plastic Jeep windows being the only noises. There was no need to break the silence prematurely to force conversation. We talked enough at dinner, during the hikes, and all the other events we did. The car rides were opportunities to unwind and take in our surroundings. My point to this ramble is that silence with a group of people is okay. Sure, I was extremely uncomfortable to be silent around Evan (or any other significant other from days past), but hopefully that would pass. With that in mind and returning to a more present time, Leigh, Lorenzo, and I remained in silence for a while longer until I finally broke it up.

"Not the ideal afternoon," I said with remarkable insight.

"Could be worse," Lozo said, stirring his drink.

"So, what's the deal with the guy you are seeing?" Leigh asked from across the table. "What's his name?"

"Evan. Evan Eaton. Has a nice ring to it, right?"

The question went unanswered and replaced by another. "How did you two meet?"

I rehashed the series of events that began in February. I kept the details light but sprinkled in enough truth for them to stay invested.

Following my speech, Lorenzo chimed in.

"Sounds like everything is going well then."

"Yeah, I guess. It's always a work-in-progress, you know? I don't think you figure out someone completely in three months. It's going to take a long time for us to settle into a groove, but that's fine. This is just all very new for me so I'm overly conscious of everything I say and do."

"After eight years, I'm still learning new things about your sister."

"How did y'all do it?" I finally asked. "The long distance, I mean."

"I'm not sure there is a single, blanket answer," he said. "There has been a lot of trust between us and a huge amount of patience. We knew we'd make it to this point, so that was a driving force for a while, at least for me."

Leigh spoke. "For me, I've been distracted with the wedding and trying to make that day perfect, so time has passed by more quickly. Before we were engaged though, it was a big struggle. We always tried to see each other and utilize that time as best we could. You realize the tiny arguments don't matter. There were days we didn't talk much because I'd be at the hospital and he'd be in the lab, and for brief moments, you'd forget you were in a relationship because you were so busy and the person you cared for was never with you. But then you'd get one text and all the emotions rush back in. Or we'd finally see each other after months and the time apart didn't seem so hard in hindsight."

I nodded. It all made sense. I just didn't think I had the capacity to be successful at a long-distance relationship, but it wasn't a concern I needed to have.

"Does anyone want another drink?" I asked.

"Only if you're buying," Lozo said.

## Day 4

The end of the line.

The last day was reminiscent to the other three so I will spare you the details.

## Day 5

I was up early that last morning to catch my flight.

I nudged my sister to let her know I was leaving. She woke up briefly, threw an arm around me, and said she had a great time. Lorenzo muttered something from the other side of the bed in an unestablished language.

I'd be seeing them again in two weeks, so it wouldn't be a long goodbye.

I walked out the hotel and into the Uber, happy with the time I spent with my sister and her fiancé. It was difficult to pin exactly why I felt that way, but I believed our relationship was going to evolve. She was on the cusp of a major change and I was hellbent on not being a douche to her and everyone else in my life.

Maybe the idea would have stuck if people actually changed, if people were able to get better.

## sixteen

## WHAT A HEAVENLY **WAY TO DIE**

I settled back into Dallas on Tuesday. Evan left for EDC on Thursday.

He was always paranoid before traveling, so it took him two days to get everything in order, which meant the only time I saw him was when he dropped off Izzie for the weekend.

For the uninitiated, Electric Daisy Carnival (EDC) is a massive EDM (you can look that one up yourself) festival that takes place over three nights. The festival runs from 6 p.m. to 6 a.m. Similar to Coachella, or any other reputable music festival, EDC has numerous stages constantly showcasing different acts. Honestly, EDM isn't my scene so I didn't know too much about the festival, but I was excited for him . . . except he was going with someone he met off Grindr.

Did I mention this already? Sometimes I can't remember what I've told you. I have so much swimming in my head all the time. I want to tell you all of it. Even the bad parts and the things I made up.

Evan was not the hook up type. He wasn't interested in the quick and easy, but yet, I was still concerned about this guy he was going to EDC with.

They had met prior to us. They went to a few concerts together around Dallas and found common ground in that. At some point, the idea must have come up to go to the festival. I wasn't too in the know on the details.

I never said much to him about it because I would have been a massive hypocrite. I still stayed in contact with people I fooled around with, and I'm sure I'd spend one on one time with them eventually. The most outrageous part is that they never did anything sexual before, so there shouldn't have been any worry on my end.

I trusted him. I knew he loved me and wouldn't do anything to jeopardize our relationship. But my brain thought differently.

I theorized about how the EDC festival was just a front to go see his long-lost lover. I theorized about how the moment he saw Grindr guy they would embrace and laugh about how good they were at keeping secrets. I theorized how he would meet someone at the festival and realize they were a better match than me and him. I theorized he would come back to Dallas and that we would need to "talk."

I sat at work on Thursday and Friday with those theories beating away at me with a sizable stick. *Thwap, thwap, thwap.* Each smack put me into a worse mood. Each smack gave more life to the theories.

I want you to understand the sheer loneliness I felt. Imagine a room. There is nothing special about it. The walls are painted to hide the scars of previous visits. The ground is covered in dust that scatters about with every step. There is no furniture. There are no windows. You sit in the middle and observe, waiting for something to happen. You start talking to yourself to pass the time. You begin suggesting that you notice a slight change or a movement out of your periphery. The sane part of you dismisses it; you don't want to give it life. The irrational side fixates on it. You continue to imagine the impossible. The slight movements morph into creatures that dart out of sight. Eventually, the irrationality wins out. The walls start to close in. The floor gives way to a hellish underneath you never want to directly face. You run for the door, but it doesn't budge. How convenient. You can do nothing but stay there and endure the pain that washes through you. Time passes. You don't know how much and how you've been impacted, but when you hear the door click, you rush toward it. The door swings outward without much force and you're blended back into a staggering group of people who are shuffling along in the same direction with an unknown destination. You rejoin them without anyone noticing your absence, but you are different. The room changed you. You don't speak about it, but the thoughts swirl about what you saw, how you responded. You convince yourself it's okay to forget, that you didn't do anything wrong. No one battles you on this point because no one else knows what you went through, what you did. It won't be long until you stumble into that room again and repeat the process. You can't help yourself. The walls will be repainted. You will see the creatures again, even interact with them to try and understand. You quickly realize it is a futile effort. You want to be like the staggering group, but you always seem to wander off and ruin the status quo. Maybe you are trying to escape the loneliness. Maybe you are trying to run, only to end up in the same dead end. Maybe you are just too idiotic to realize that repeating the same thing over will never yield a different outcome.

I wanted to text him, but I didn't want to be a bother.

I wanted him to text me, but I knew it wouldn't happen.

I didn't want to download Grindr, but I did. I needed someone to talk to.

*You fucking moron. Someone is going to see you on there and it's going to ruin everything. All for what? A blowjob?*

I casted the thought aside. I downloaded the app and didn't provide a picture of myself. It would make conversation harder since people demanded it, but I'd survive.

The conversations flowed easily with total strangers. They knew nothing about me, but most seemed to be impressed with my job and the flight benefits that came along with it. At a certain point, the chat would shift to the sexual details. Sometimes it was quick; other times it took longer.

*You are nothing.*

By Saturday, I had multiple offers of people wanting to hang out and do various graphic activities.

I peered over to Izzie who was tucked into a corner of the couch. She sensed movement and woke up, quickly tracking where I was. She stared at me—more like through me. Guilt crept in about what I was doing.

*Do it.*

My head throbbed. They were becoming more frequent and severe. I felt the urge to ram my head through the wall to numb the pain or at least to knock me out for a bit. I probably should have considered going to a doctor, but that required effort, and that effort was not worth the effort. I popped some Advil and squeezed onto the couch next to Izzie.

*Do it.*

I put my hands on my forehead in an attempt to massage away the discomfort. I tried to sleep but it was useless. The headache was commandeering the ship and its intention was to ram us into the cliffside where the creature was perched up top, watching and smiling as the disaster unfolded.

I didn't understand how my mom handled the headaches she got. When I was younger, she would be out of service for days at a time, barely moving from the couch due to the intense pain. I thought it was silly how something unseen to the eye could be so debilitating. I got older and more experienced. My back was constantly tight and would ache if I sat for too long. Each time I returned to a routine at the gym, I'd experience a setback in the form of a pulled muscle or some other silly injury. Is this what I had to look forward to with getting older? The constant shifting of my body toward E. The gas tank would continue to leak and sputter fluid until there was nothing left. My body was one thing, but what about the speed of my mental degradation?

*DO IT.*

I had a text message from Evan I hadn't responded to for hours. He asked about how my weekend was going and how he missed us both. I didn't want to respond too fast because it would seem like I was clinging to my phone. Instead, I let it linger and get to the point where he eventually texted me again asking if everything was alright.

*DO IT.*

I had nothing to say to him. I was so dead inside. I had a total relapse to the person I was before I met him. It would have been foolish to think I magically moved past that portion of my life without some ramifications. I still craved the attention of others who didn't know or care about me. I still wanted to believe a hook up was key to deep satisfaction. I still thought I could get away with it and that Evan would never find out. The flaw was that I'd have to live with it. I'd be the one to know each time I looked at him that I had cheated. I was the scum you scraped off the haul of a boat, the shit you picked out of the sole of a shoe, the dregs of a warm beer you discarded.

*DO IT.*

On Sunday, I continued to fight the urge to hang out with someone.

*DO IT.*

**DO IT.**

*do it. do it. do it. DO IT. DO IT. DOIT.* **DOITDOITDOIT.**

By Sunday night, I gave up.

# seventeen

## SIMPLIFY

I flew into PHL the next weekend for Memorial Day. You know how this part of the story goes. I see my family. I see the dogs. I exchange pleasantries with every person I came across and lie to them about how happy I am in Dallas, how I'm still single, and how no woman has stolen my heart yet.

This time was different though.

I told Quinn I was gay. (Remember him? My best friend from college.) It was pretty unceremonious. He came up to visit Easton and we spent the night downtown going to bars and grabbing food. We ended up at a place with a massive oak tree dominating the room. It was exotic for a city as bland as Easton. As we sat up there, the conversation turned to more personal topics. He opened up about his luck with women in Philadelphia and the moment seemed right to tell him, so I did. No sense in continuing to hide behind my manufactured lie, seeing as the foundation collapsed almost a year ago. He didn't care at all and stressed how he wanted me to be happy.

I wish I could say I was happy at the time, but my mind kept drifting to Evan. *He must have noticed a change when he got back. Do you feel guilty? Was it worth it?*

After Quinn, the next person I was tasked to tell was my grandmother. My mom has been adamant that she needed to know. It was meant to set off the chain reaction. I'd tell my grandmother. She'd tell my aunts, uncles, and cousins. Then the neighbors would find out. Then the friends of friends of enemies of slight acquaintances of grave robbers of craftsmen of ore who swore allegiance to the Starks but found themselves fighting down south for the Lannister's in an effort to avoid that winter had come (ha) would shout the news in squawks and ravings across the Seven Kingdoms. The spider web of people who knew would expand rapidly, all because of the single source. That's real power right there.

The only problem: I sat in her and Walter's apartment for four hours on Sunday and never brought it up. I wanted to, I promise you I did, but I just couldn't find the words. Anytime I contemplated saying it, my palms would get sweaty and the threat of an incoming headache began to pulse behind my eyes. I distracted myself by playing Phase 10 with them, a game that Faceless Nameless (yeah, I graduated to not remembering its face or name) had shown me in another dimension. To my surprise, I won both games, which was incredibly shocking since my grandma took the life force from anybody she played games with. She made me cry numerous times while playing Uno as a kid. She was ruthless with the draw four cards! Good grief, I'm having tremors just thinking about it.

I distracted myself by talking to them about any other topic that wouldn't even graze the idea of me being gay. I didn't avoid it out of shame (I moved on significantly from that notion) but because I didn't know how to say it. The words were easy; the delivery was not.

By the third hour, it was apparent that they enjoyed spending time with me. In the same sense that I viewed my grandmother as the embodiment of a pure human, I think they viewed me as the epitome of what a grandson should be. Some could argue that it was misguided. I called them, not because I had to, but I wanted to hear about their days of kicking ass in bingo or the constant stream of doctor's appointments. I visited them when I was home because the little voice in my head that fucked up everything in my life insisted that seeing them was the one good thing I could do. I loved them dearly and was not ready to shatter their view of who I was.

I left the apartment sometime later, knowing I wouldn't see them again until the wedding and feeling icky that I'd have someone else do my dirty work.

"How'd it go?" my mom asked me immediately as I walked into the house. She was stalking and waiting for my arrival.

"I didn't tell them."

"Aw, Vin. Why?" she said with a mixture of annoyance and understanding.

"I . . . I don't . . ." I trailed off, not wanting to finish the obvious statement.

*How long are you going to keep this up? You have a boyfriend for fuck sake! Granted, you cheated on him real good. Better luck next time!*

In the moment, I felt bad that I didn't have the courage to tell my grandmother and the disappointment that oozed from my mom, but I didn't want to be Gay Vin. I wanted to be Intelligent Vin, or Witty Vin, or Caring Vin, or any other assortment of adjectives that didn't need to be capitalized. I didn't want the first thing people recognized about me was that I was gay. I didn't want people to tiptoe around the topic with the fear they would say something offensive or crude. I wanted to remain Vinny Boy or Vincent or just Vin who happened to be gay but not a single person minded it. This is the longest coming out story ever and I'm sorry for that.

"Should I tell her?" my mom asked, pulling me from my thoughts.

"Yeah, that's probably easier."

"Okay," she paused. "You know, once I tell her—"

"The whole Seven Kingdoms will find out." She stared with a look of confusion. "I know. I'm ready for it. It's long overdue. Just promise me one thing."

"What's that?"

"Don't paint me as some victim. My story isn't a struggle—it's just who I am. I don't need pity from anyone. I'm the same kid that mowed everyone's grass in the neighborhood and played football with their sons. They can save their sympathy for people who need it."

She nodded. I trusted my mom would never do that, but I felt better mentioning it.

"I love you so much," she said and stepped closer to give me a hug.

*Liar. Cheater.*

It echoed in my head. I wouldn't be forgiven. It wouldn't be forgotten.

"I love you too," I said, leaning into the hug.

"Let's go to the party next door. I know everyone will be happy to see you."

We moved to the kitchen where we each grabbed a plate of food. We gently nudged the dogs out of the way. They were eager to get a bite or two of what we had. We left through the front door and took the short walk across the street. I hesitated for a moment as we rounded the corner into the backyard. The tent shot up into the sky and expanded across the grass. I reminded myself one more time that I was a

*Liar.*

*Cheater.*

And with a fake smile, I continued into the crowd, ready to pretend that everything was fine.

Everything was *always* fine.

# eighteen

## CLUBS

At this point, you may be wondering several things:

1.) Why are you writing this?
2.) Why is this structured like a novel if there's no intention for anyone to read it?
3.) Why have you been so honest?
4.) Who is the *you* that YOU keep referring to?

Okay, so maybe you haven't been wondering about any of those things, but I'll give you the answers to them anyways to promote transparency. (I understand this gesture seems silly considering that I just made up the questions an unknown reader may or—likely—will not have. It is delusional. Grab a ticket for a one-way ride to Stupidville with a quick stop in ThisJokeIsNotActuallyFunnytown!)

Let's start at the top.

It began as therapy. I own a MacBook and it hadn't seen much action since college except my forays into the world of porn. I wanted to utilize a resource I had, and with a fondness of writing, I figured the easiest story to write would be my own. I finished the first one and felt invigorated. I accomplished a task that many people are never able to finish. I told myself the first one would be the hardest to write, which it was. After it was "done," (I put that in quotations because the beast has not been edited or read by another person to tear it to shreds) I took a month off and then dove into the second one. I'm not saying this is better than the first, but it has been easier to write for whatever reason.

This leads to the next question. In order for this to feel like it's worth the effort, I was determined to structure this like a book with dialogue and chapters and proper formatting. Let me just say that writing dialogue is such an ass sore. Capturing half remembered conversations and different personalities is something I was not prepared for. It's the logic of *fake it 'til you sound somewhat plausible.* With absolutely zero experience of writing anything worth more than a B+, I didn't have high hopes I'd ever write one "book" let alone two! And consider how meta it is that I'm mentioning the writing of the first book while working on the second. Who the fuck does that?!? It shows my inexperience and complete disregard for adhering to the rules. But now it just sounds like I'm bragging.

In regard to question three, who said I was being honest? Right, I did since I posed the question. Whether you believe it or not, this has been the most truthful I've ever been in my entire life. We all slip in lies into our daily lives as easily as pouring creamer into coffee, but I assure you that running through this exercise would do me no good if I lied. You'll have to trust me there. The perks of this never leaving my laptop is that I can sleep peacefully at night knowing that nobody's grubby eyeballs will skim the pages, looking to critique and bitch about the contents of my "book." Or maybe, I'm just enough of an asshole to lie about not lying.

Last question! When you think about it, who is anyone? Aren't we all just blobs of matter floating on a pebble that has miraculously found itself on a rotating path within an ocean so large our minds couldn't possibly fathom the infinite nature of it? Okay, let me backtrack and cut out the philosophical bullshit. So, I lied. Slightly. I want someone to read this when it's done. Sure, the plot is tied together with a half-broken shoe lace, the grammer is worse than should be expected for someone who has access to spellcheck, and the self-deprecation didn't go away even though I promised it would, BUT I think someone—*you*—will be able to look past that. *You* will want to hear my story. *You* will want to know why I'm not around anymore.

I'm going out on a wobbly limb and guessing you have thought of one final question.

5.) Does any of this matter?

Listen here, you tiny turd: none of this matters. It's just another story you'll forget about in a day. But that's okay. I never claimed this ramble was anything more than a cathartic attempt to feel like I'm not a complete waste.

I almost forgot. I'm holding onto one more killer secret. I'm very proud of it and can't wait to fill you in, but to ratchet up the drama, I'm going to keep mum on it until the end. Ya know, I'm trying to keep you invested somehow.

To wrap up: I enjoy these excursions that pop up occasionally and completely break any momentum I have in my writing. Usually, you have to pay for them, but I'm giving them away for free.

Don't say I never did anything nice for *you*.

## nineteen

## RIBS

The sun tried its best to break through the blinds in my bedroom. Between the angle I had them tilted and the position of the apartment in general, the light had zero luck. The room continued in its shroud of darkness.

I woke up slowly. There was no rush. It was Saturday morning.

There was a stirring underneath the covers. Izzie was waking from her slumber and attempting to worm her way out from the cocoon she built up. With the motion on either side of him, Evan opened his eyes and stared over at me.

"Good morning," he groaned. It sounded like it hurt to utter the words.

"Oh my god! Who are you? Why are you in my bed?" I asked in a panic.

"It's too early for that," he said, unamused.

I turned over to face the door, away from the light that wasn't entering the room and away from Evan.

We had one of those talks the night before. One of the talks that was becoming increasingly common. I'd assume my position on one end of the couch and he would be on the other. We'd both be hugging our legs close to our chests, which someone with a brighter mind would take as us being defensive towards each other. The conversations always started out innocent. He'd ask about my day to which I'd give a short reply and then I'd ask him about his day. It was becoming more apparent he was not enjoying his job. He slyly threw in hints of him looking elsewhere but confirmed that switching jobs again would not look good on his resumé. With the pleasantries out of the way, we would dip into the sensitive topics. I struggle to remember how we maneuvered into them, but without fail, we always did.

By the end, silence was the kid that sat between two feuding parents or, in our case, between an upset couple.

"Vin," he said, poking my back. "Are you mad?"

I rolled back over to face him. He was always cold in my apartment, so the covers were pulled up tight against his face. He looked worn. Not just from the night before, but from life in general. Who wasn't?

"About last night?" I guessed. "I'm not mad. I'm just growing tired of having those types of conversations with you. We seemingly skipped over the honeymoon phase and went to the phase where we just nitpick one another." I paused before chiming in with one last thought that came out as a whisper. "How did we get here?"

Back to the couch. We dove into the topic of how Evan wasn't sure if I loved him. He felt he was constantly begging for my attention and affection. He claimed I wasn't emotionally available. My first instinct was to put on my northeast hat and immediately get defensive and angry, but I choked back the emotion. It was a statement that didn't make sense to me because I was a complete fucking mess. My emotions were fluctuating every second, but they hit the force field and evaporated, never making it out beyond my brain. I tried to explain that I loved him, but . . . I stumbled with the words. I am still fumbling with them now. I loved him, but I didn't know how to show it. Physical touch felt forced to me even though the primal side of me craved sex. Words of affection were hollow and came out as if someone had prepped a speech I was reading for the first time. The audience would be watching—the same, unsatisfied one as always—and would cringe as I butchered getting the words across. I just didn't know how to act normal around him, to not be afraid. Did that mean he wasn't a good fit for me? It would assume so. We had very few commonalities and strikingly different demeanors, and, yet, those wasn't deal breakers for me. We just needed to push past this point of not understanding one another.

The conversation eventually fizzled out with no real resolution and with him undoubtedly feeling as if his boyfriend didn't actually love him. He shuffled off to bed. I stayed out in the living room, playing Xbox for a while because I knew if I laid down next to him in that dark room, every unholy thought I ever had would consume me and drag me back to the barren room with the repainted walls.

How did we get here? *Asshole, are you really that stupid?*

"Do you hate yourself?" he asked, ripping me back to reality.

"Uhh . . . what . . . why do you say that?" I stopped briefly. "Actually, it's a valid question so I'll answer it." I turned away from Evan, staring up at the ceiling. "I don't think I hate myself, but I certainly don't *like* the person I am."

"What's the difference?" he cut in.

"Maybe there isn't one. Sorry, this wasn't a question I was prepared to answer from the press corps today. I might be depressed. There has never been a day where I didn't want to get out of bed or struggled to pull myself together for work, but there have been numerous occasions where I've sat in this apartment and mentally reviewed a long list of things I need to improve on. I'd wear myself down with the over encumbered thoughts that would put me into a spiral. I'd begin to resent myself and my lack of progress. I'm not an expert, but I'm guessing depression can manifest itself in a variety of ways. I have never felt good enough. I hate how I resort to sarcasm or can't accept compliments from people. I hate that I still don't feel comfortable around you to be myself or show you how much I care. I have absolutely zero self-worth. I don't know how all this happened. I'm sure I could talk to someone and they would help me identify the root cause or at least give me ways to adapt and deal. But it feels cheap. Shouldn't I be strong enough to handle it? I live on my own, have a great job, and an awesome boyfriend, but it isn't enough. My brain keeps sabotaging me, insisting everything I do just isn't quite up to par. I'm driving myself insane. So, to answer your question: Yeah, I hate myself. I hate everything I can't control and for the things I can control, I'm never satisfied."

*Liar. Cheater.*

I flipped back the covers and moved over to the window.

"Maybe it is simple. Maybe I need to change my perspective," I said while I tilted up the blinds to finally let the light in.

Evan watched me intently, gearing up for a response. Instead, he sat up in bed and continued his stare.

"What?" I said with a chuckle.

"I'm sorry."

"For what? Any issues I have are my burdens. I'm not a miserable person. I love to laugh. I love to be around people that rip me from my existential crises that I seem to face more often than ever before. I love how I can travel on any random weekend. I love my family and how they continue to support me living a thousand miles away. I love when I get to sit on my couch and veg out with video games to forget about the absurdities with work. I love that I get to read and escape from my reality. I have a lot to love in my life. I love you, more than you'd ever realize."

This was another vivid reminder that love is such a useless word. I put Evan on the same pedestal as video games. Yikes.

Izzie fully emerged from under the covers and looked back and forth between Evan and me.

"I think she is ready for a bathroom break," I suggested.

She hopped off the bed, which must have been like jumping off a cliff without a parachute, trotted across the room, and out the door.

Evan slowly moved out of bed and came over to give me a hug. He continued to keep me close for a long time. The worn face from earlier was replaced by something more alert, more worried.

"We need to stop those conversations. They are depressing," he finally said, referring to what we talked about the night before.

"I completely agree, and they definitely will. Something for us to work on."

In hindsight, it never changed, but is that surprising to *you*?

# twenty

## LONG ROAD TO **RUIN**

"The acceptance criteria for this user story aren't fleshed out enough. How is the customer supposed to know the functionality being delivered? What about QMO? How will they be able to test? You gotta remember that the ACs need to follow the INVEST model. I'm sure you learned that methodology at some point. We are very reliant on getting this functionality delivered without any defects. As an analyst within the pod, you are the . . ."

I stopped listening. Or rather, I didn't care to listen anymore. I was sitting across from my boss during our one-on-one. It was a meeting that was supposed to occur once a week, instead, I found myself on a cadence of only once a month.

I stared past him, out the windows, and toward the runway of Love Field. I was so close to freedom. I could be over at the airport in fifteen minutes and on a flight within an hour if I planned appropriately.

But nah.

I was stuck under the dim glow of the fluorescent bulbs that seemed to age everyone. I was stuck with the same bullshit series of tasks and the same bullshit meetings and the same bullshit of trying to prove my intelligence and competence. I was stuck at a job I continued to feel disdain for within a company I loved. I was stuck in an endless loop of an aggressive drive home each night to cleanse myself from the angst of the day. The frustrations from work followed me from the parking garage of my complex, through the hallway, and into the apartment as if I was holding onto a leash. I couldn't shake the feeling that I was over the job. I told myself I could quit. That would show 'em! I had enough money to keep myself afloat for a few months. I was sure to find something else before the money pit ran out.

The spiral. It chased me in every facet of my life.

I was getting ahead of myself. I was predicting the future. I snapped back to reality and found myself sitting across the table from Athena.

*How did I get here? I was just in another meeting. While you are here, how about another reminder? Liar. Cheater.*

Time floated like a feather in the wind. It would settle but it was hard to determine where or when.

"What's up? What's happening?" Athena asked, looking over at me intently. She picked at her spaghetti squash. It was the third day in a row I'd seen her with that lunch, if my memory was correct.

"The usual. What about you?"

"The usual. Well, actually, I am going to . . ."

I stopped listening. I always enjoyed my talks with Athena, but between the everlasting frustrations of work and the mudslide I was experiencing with Evan, I was removed. She motioned her arms, indicating something big. I watched her, but at the same time, I was staring through her at the person walking by behind.

Anders.

In the two months since the Lorde concert, our friendship deteriorated even further.

I had a party back in April. Naturally, Evan was there along with a series of background actors. Anders showed up in grand fashion with three other friends. I met all of them at previous times, but we still encountered the awkward "introductions" where you didn't want to embarrass the person and tell them that you've already met. One of Anders' friends, Eli, was weirdly drawn to Evan. At the end of the party, Eli told Evan that if he and I ever broke up they should hang out. They swapped Instagram accounts and called it a day. Evan casually mentioned it to me the next day and it made me want to dive out of the car and head-on into the grille of an eighteen-wheeler. I was angry at Anders for bringing over a creep, but I was also still so insecure in the relationship that I imagined Evan snickering in a corner and beginning the conversations with Eli would lead down a romantic path. Obviously, those delusions didn't go away before EDC and Grindr guy came into the picture and we know the result of that weekend.

That situation helped solidify how little I needed Anders as a friend or acquaintance. My time in Dallas was tarnished with fuck-up after fuck-up, but one thing I was improving at was dropping the dead weight (with one notable exception that always took up space in my mind). I didn't have a quota with friends. Anders served his purpose as fodder and the pioneer of mediocre conversations at work, and I was finally okay with him fading into obscurity.

I watched him walk by the table with acknowledging either of us. That was fine by me. He was never an important part of this narrative anyways.

". . . They have been enjoying it so far, so I'm looking forward to visiting them in Denver," I caught the tail end of what Athena said.

"Denver is a cool city! I would go back again. Probably not during the wintertime though," I said.

"So," she said before inhaling another forkful of squash, "how are things going with Evan? You know I had to ask."

"No problem. Just know you better give me an update on Stavros. Are we still referring to him as Stavros or can I shout Jag for the whole building to here?" I asked, looking around to see who was nearby if I did decide to follow through.

"Jag is an acceptable name to use, but with discretion."

"Fair enough." I continued to pick at the salad in front of me but found it about as interesting as sitting at the DMV.

"Well . . ."

"Right. Yeah. Things have been interesting. We keep having these really depressing conversations when we hang out. It dampers the mood and I'm not sure how to avoid them."

"What causes them to start?"

I shrugged. I didn't have a better answer than that.

"I see. Not much help I can be there. I like Evan though, so figure it out," she said, jabbing the fork in my direction.

"Yes ma'am. I would never let you down. I'd tell you more about the inner workings of my relationship, but I doubt you want your ears to bleed today."

"Hmmm. I can schedule you in on Wednesday for an hour if you'd like to do it then."

"That would be fantastic. Thank you for fitting me into your busy schedule. I am honored."

"You're doing great. Keep up the good work," Athena said. She packed up her empty container and moved from the table.

"Wait," I said, remembering our deal, "you didn't tell me about you and Jag."

"Maybe some other time," she said with a smile and walked back toward our seating area.

Motherf'er. She did that to me all the time. I needed to learn to not give up the goods until the other party was sitting at the negotiation table too.

"Hey!" someone called out.

I turned around and saw Anders. *For fuck sake.*

"Have you been ignoring me?" he asked with a wide grin.

"I don't think I could even if I wanted. You have a way of showing up."

"Let's hangout sometime soon! I haven't seen you in forever. I need to hear about Evan and, uh, anything else you may have going on," Anders said with practically no care.

"You know me. I evaporate into nothing when I step outside this building. I barely exist."

"Anyways," his smile flinching for a nanosecond, "we will meet up next weekend. I'm sure you'll be in town, yeah?"

"Oh absolutely."

"Great!" he said with one final fake smile and sauntered off to go torment some other poor soul.

To close the loop on this: I was going to write a chapter chronicling the gathering we had, but it was painful enough to experience in reality, so I'd rather not relive it through prose.

✦

The major downside of keeping my phone on Do Not Disturb was, naturally, I missed every single call I received. It must have been really annoying for the people calling me because the first time you did, it would go directly to voicemail.

I left work that afternoon, grabbed my phone, and saw a missed call with a voicemail from my grandma. That's unusual.

I listened to it and the gist was an ask to call her back.

After leaving the campus, I returned her call, setting it to speaker phone. If I was going to be distracted while driving, I didn't want to make it as obvious.

She picked up on the third ring.

"Hi Ann," said the familiar voice.

"Hi Grandma. It's Vinny. I got your voicemail."

"Oh! Vinny! The caller ID always comes up with your mom's name, so I just assume it's her," she announced with a laugh.

It was how we started off every conversation for the past five years. I didn't mind. I enjoyed the innocence behind it and her voice always perked up when she realized it was me, which melted my dead heart.

"No worries. So, what's up? Is everything alright?"

"Yeah, yeah. Everything is fine. We just hadn't talked in a while, so I wanted to see how you were doing." In actuality, I was home less than two weeks ago and saw her, so there was something nefarious going on.

"I'm good. Same old stuff. Just driving home from work now."

"Your mom always calls me on the way home from work too. It must help to pass the time, huh?"

"Yes, it does. Much better than being completely focused on the traffic in front of me."

Several beats of silence.

"Uh huh. Well, I spoke to your mom this past weekend and she told me."

Ahhhh. I should have known. The dam was let loose. The zoo animals released from their cages. The STD was being spread around the colony. The metaphor was being milked until its nipple was sore.

She continued. "I just wanted to call and tell you that Walter and I love you very much. This doesn't change a single thing about the way we see you. We just want you to be happy. You are still our grandson," the words took longer to come out by the end. She was crying.

Everyone seemed to want me happy, but do you think anyone knows how unhappy I am? I have tried to make it as obvious as I can to you.

The comments were expected, but a wave of relief passed through me. Another barrier crossed without incident. I was continually worried about how people would respond and absolutely none of them had been adverse about it—with the exception of my father. And even in that scenario, it was the shock and unexpected nature of it that threw him off guard. Of course, people can say one thing but believe another. Whoever that was the case with, I was none the wiser.

"Thanks Grandma. I appreciate you telling me that. It means a lot. I stressed to Mom that I didn't want her telling people and making it seem like I was any different from the person they knew."

"Okay. Well, I'll let you get back to driving. Are you coming home for your birthday?"

"No. I will be heading up to Cape Cod again after my birthday, so I won't be able to."

"Aww. Okay. So, I won't see you until the wedding then?"

"I don't think so."

"Oh. Okay. Well, I will call you in a few weeks on your birthday. I always need to remind myself I can call you sometimes! I just never want to bother you."

"It is never a bother to talk with you."

"Okay Vinny. Talk to you soon," a blip of hesitation. "Love you."

"Love you too."

I ended the call and continued to sit at the red light, enjoying the reprieve from the stop and go traffic. Our exchange was simple, but there wasn't a need for it to be more than that.

Every time I talked to her, it was like she gave me all the XP available and automatically maxed out my character level. I felt lighter and happier and satisfied.

The feeling never lasted, but it was nice to cling onto it for even the briefest of moments. It helped me believe that one day I'd understand what that permanently felt like.

## twenty-one

## THE PIECES DON'T FIT ANYMORE

Seeing a familiar face after a long time was an odd phenomenon. You knew who they were and what they looked like—unless something brutally drastic happened—but so much time would have passed. You thought about how their life continued on without you and you were relegated to a special guest role within their story. There might be subtle changes you weren't aware of or traumas they endured without your knowledge.

I walked into the Cedar Springs Tap House knowing I would find Benji sitting at one of the tables. He confirmed with me five minutes earlier, as I began my trek over from the apartment, that he was in fact sitting at one of the tables. My mind had a hard time wrapping itself around the concept. Shouldn't he be in London?

Most of the time that answer would be yes, but after nearly a year, he was visiting Dallas to catch up with friends and family.

We stayed in contact through weekly text messages telling each other to have a good week—go figure. Sometimes the conversation would expand beyond the initial pleasantries and we would dig in deeper into how the other person was doing. It was nothing revelatory. Most times it felt like I was chatting with a pen pal, not someone I spent a year and a half with.

And to think I was so butthurt over who Evan went to EDC with and I was over here grabbing dinner with an ex. My goodness, Vincent Besser is an annoying individual.

Anyways, upon walking into the tap house, I scanned the room. It was of modest size with a modest crowd.

I spotted the lanky figure immediately, shacked up at a table jutting out from the wall. His back was hunched over, staring at the menu in front of him.

"Hey Benji," I said as I reached him. He turned around, stood up, and gave me a hug.

"Hey hey," he responded. He looked no different from the last time I saw him.

We took our seats.

I wasn't sure what to expect. In some respects, it felt odd to see him sitting across from me because of how final it seemed when he left the year before. Transplanting yourself to another country really gave someone the excuse to not follow up with any people they left behind. I wouldn't have blamed him if he did that to me, but Benji just wasn't that type of person.

I had no idea what to talk about with him, so I started out simple.

"How's it going?"

"Every day is just a joy," he said, pursing his lips. His sarcasm was more expert than mine in many cases.

"You must like it though if you are still out there, right?"

"Um, yeah, I guess. I'm really just trying to find a job that will actually pay me some money before I start going to school full time."

"Solid plan. And what do you want to go back to school for?"

"Well, I'm not sure yet." Typical Benji answer.

"Okay . . . you should probably figure that out before you start applying places."

"You right. I have just been trying to lock down a group of friends. Grindr is a wasteland and you already know hook ups aren't my thing. I'm stuck in this weird half-relationship with a guy right now. He doesn't want to stay together because of the age difference but I don't see a problem with it. Every time we hang out, we end up doing stuff, so the whole thing makes no sense."

I was trying to keep up with what he was saying, but he moves at lightening pace and drifts from topic to topic without warning.

"I want to hear more about it, but can we change the topic for one second?"

"Mhmm."

"I'm sorry for how it all went down last year. I didn't treat you the way you deserved, and I know you'd never admit to it bothering you, but it should have—"

"—don't be dumb. That shit was hurtful as fuck. I'm just not petty and didn't let it ruin our friendship or whatever it was by the end. But continue," he said, twirling his finger to indicate that I should, in fact, continue.

"Okay. Yeah. I understand. I . . . I lost my train of thought now. Uhhh," I thought for a moment. "I do value you being in my life and I know distance makes any friendship tough, but I hope we always stay in touch."

The waiter finally came over and broke up my shambling apology. We both ordered beers. I had never known Benji to be a fan of beer, but London must have straightened him out.

"Wow. You really went right for it when you sat down. I'm impressed, and I do appreciate it," Benji said after the waiter left. "You know I'm a nosy ho and will be bothering you all the time," he finished with a smirk.

"You always follow through with that threat. I'm terrible at reaching out to people, so I'm glad you take the initiative."

"Why don't you?"

"Why don't I reach out to people? Because I've convinced myself that all the people around me don't actually enjoy me but have found a way to tolerate my presence. I always feel this uneasiness when I text someone or suggest making plans. I guess I'm afraid of rejection. But, honestly, who knows. I have given up trying to understand why I respond to things the way I do."

"Morbid as usual."

"I'd say I'm working on that as well, but that would be a lie," I said.

He snapped his fingers in front of my face.

"You gotta get over this. No depressing Vin in front of me. You can save that for your quiet time," he said, frowning over at me.

"You got it," I closed my eyes for a moment and then reopened them. "Problem solved. Crisis averted. The bunny was put back in the hat. I'm not depressing anymore."

"Praise the Lord."

The remainder of our dinner was a myriad of random stories and general rehashing of the past year. None of it was exciting and there wasn't a salacious ending where anything happened following the meal.

Obviously, if I am only meant to be a special guest star in his life then the same could be said for him in relation to my life story. I say that to justify his cameo appearance in this written record. I'd say he was a fan favorite, but that would imply anyone has read this thing or that I had the ability to write compelling characters!

The conversation I had with him gave me the courage to reach out to the other person I'd been thinking about.

Dylan.

I didn't owe him an apology. We both treated each other poorly and I wasn't salty about any of it. I felt compelled to meet up with him because I was concerned. There was a nagging feeling that he needed help. I had no explanation for the feeling except that it was a near constant thought that blipped through my mind.

I texted him and demanded to get dinner, in the nicest possible way. We talked on occasion and usually the conversation lasted only a few exchanges before he stopped responding.

It was along the lines of how Lee and I were interacting these days. He certainly fell out of sight even though the promise of us being friends was something he agreed to, whether he realized that at the time or not. It was a theme that people scattered once I got into the relationship. Maybe it was a good excuse for them to finally leave.

I was tired of getting the cold shoulder and didn't understand what had changed. Things leveled out in the month or so after we "broke up," so I was confused when Dylan disappeared out of my life.

He agreed to dinner (after a span of eight hours without responding) and picked me up one night after work.

I walked outside the complex and around the corner. There was one car idling at the curb. It was the rustic BMW I had seen a few times last year. The front bumper looked as if a horde of zombies had shambled into it. It was dented in various places, but still functional.

I took two leaps over the shit infested grass, landing on the edge of the curb. I hadn't been that nimble since I outran the cops back in ninth grade (a different story for another time).

Once in the car, the overhead light quickly faded before I had a chance to glimpse at the driver. A mental image populated my mind and I assumed Dylan still fit it.

"Hello," he said in a swanky voice with a twinge of nervousness to it.

"Howdy Dylan. Can I get a hug?"

"Sure," he said, unsure of the entire situation he found himself in.

The hug was awkward over the center console.

I eased back into the seat. "Any recommendations on where we should go?"

"I figured you would have picked the place."

"That was a silly assumption. Okay. Let's see . . . what about that restaurant we went to? Some soufflé joint where we had to wait forever for the food."

"Rise?"

"I would, but I am in the car."

"No, you—" he paused, realizing I was only kidding. Or was I?

"Yes. Rise. That would seem like a fitting name for a restaurant that makes soufflés," I said.

We were still idling at the curb. I briefly wondered if he forgot how to drive and if I would need to take over.

"We can't go there," he said, shaking his head. "That is only someplace I would go on a date. It is too fancy. Aren't you seeing a boy?"

"Let's get two things out of the way: this is certainly not a date and I am not dating a boy. Evan is a twenty-four-year-old male. Christ, you make me sound like a pedophile when you say 'boy' like that."

"Okay. Then why am I here?"

"Because I thought we were friends and usually friends hang out, but I may be wrong. I haven't consulted the handbook in a while."

"Oh."

"Dylan, which restaurant would you like to go to?"

"Breadwinners. It is in the same shopping center."

"Wonderful."

He finally pulled away from the curb and went toward our destination.

The ride was gloomy. An unsettled air coursed around Dylan. He was never in a happy place when I saw him in the Ago, but he seemed worse.

The conversation was minimal as he focused on going thirty over the speed limit on every road while I gripped my legs and fought the urge to tell him to stop driving like an asshole. He had precious cargo in the passenger seat!

We whipped into the parking lot. He spotted two empty slots.

"Is that a handicap spot? I have a mirror thingy if it is."

I squinted past the headlights and up to the blue sign. Even with new my glasses on, I still had trouble seeing at night.

"Looks like a handicap spot. Wait—how do you have one of those?" I asked, pointing to the card as he hung it from the mirror.

"My stepdad left it for me."

"Oh."

Dylan lost his stepdad a year ago. He was the best parent Dylan had. His mom was bipolar and a cataclysmic wave of shifting emotion. His dad seemed like a snob, which may have explained where Dylan received some of his uppity traits from. The loss of his stepdad was incredibly hard based on how he eluded to it. They would spend hours working on the car or having a drink together after dinner. I think it gave Dylan a sense of family and the idea that he could belong somewhere. As with most good things in life, it was taken away from him prematurely. His stepdad slowly deteriorated into nothing and Dylan watched the entire thing. Cancer was an absolute motherfucker and showed no mercy on even the strongest people.

But my mind wandered to how his stepdad must have felt. The imminent doom was approaching and there was nothing he could do to stop it. What did he feel in the last days he had? Knowing myself, I'd have regrets about all the things I never did and the people I never met. How would I have handled such adversity? It was hard to fathom without finding myself in the situation, but life was bizarre, and it was entirely possible I would one day.

I didn't pry into it any further. Instead, I pulled the door handle twice, once to unlock it and the second time to open it. German engineering at its finest.

We walked to the front door of Breadwinners and stepped inside.

It was crowded but we managed to get a table right away.

After sitting down, I asked Dylan the question that I was seemingly asking every living soul recently.

"How's everything going?" I glanced up from the menu, finally taking in the person right across from me.

His clothes were baggy and hung loosely off of him. The sweatshirt and running pants were probably the bare minimum attire he could have worn to the restaurant. His hair was disheveled with the dark brown color pushing out the bleach blonde at the ends. It was long and started to come down over his ears, making him look even younger than he already was. His eyes were focused on another table and sunken in. I doubted he was getting much sleep. I wasn't sure if he heard my question. He just looked . . . lost.

"Dylan, did you hear me?"

"No," he said, looking back at me.

"How's everything going?" I repeated.

"I moved out of the apartment you used to come to. I needed the change. I have this bitch of a downstairs neighbor that keeps leaving me notes whenever I play my music. You remember that subwoofer from the old apartment? Sometimes I like to crank it up and she has to complain about it. What a bitch. I have so much work I need to get done and the music helps me focus—"

"That's not really what I was asking you. I mean, I'm glad you got a new apartment, but let me ask it another way. How are you?" I said, stressing the question.

"He moved back in." The he being his ex-fiancé.

"What? Why?"

"Because I love him."

"But he cheated on you? You deserve better than that."

"I think he is doing heroin," he said absentmindedly. "Again, I think. I was suspicious before but never caught him doing it firsthand."

Somewhat stunned, I said, "Dylan, you need to get out of there. You can't put yourself through that again."

"I will tell his family. They need to stop being oblivious to what he is doing to himself."

"Dude. For fuck sake. Are you listening to anything I'm saying?"

"Quite frankly, I'm not."

I was at a loss for a response. The waitress came over and we ordered our food and drinks. Dylan stayed with water. I went with a beer since the conversation was quickly derailing.

"Why wouldn't you be listening?" I asked.

"Because you don't know shit. All you do is badger me with texts and making it seem like I'm some orphan that needs a home. I don't need your sympathy. I just want to be left alone. All the stuff I'm going through right now, I will get through it without you."

"Then why did you agree to meet up?"

"So I could tell you this in person. Maybe you would finally get the hint that way."

I was holding back the frustration trying its best to boil over.

"Dylan, I keep *badgering* you because I care. You may think it is misplaced or that I only reach out to you to make myself feel better or some other lame logic, but I promise you I know how everyone could use a little help in life. I just wasn't sure if you have anyone who is doing that for you."

"I do, so I don't need another ex of mine to act like they know what's best for me."

"I'm sorry you are still upset about what happened between us."

"I'm not upset—"

"You sound like you are."

"Please don't interrupt me . . . I'm not upset. I just don't understand why you keep trying to talk to me when you have a boyfriend. It's weird."

"The only interest I have in you is being your friend. I'm not sure of any other way to say it. You must not be used to this or something. Unfortunately for me, I have a long history of staying in contact with former flings."

"So we were just a fling?"

"For fuck sake . . ."

"Answer me."

"No, Dylan. We were not a fling. I really liked you. We just weren't meant for each other. Terrible timing for sure. I'd prefer if I didn't have to rehash the specifics."

I was getting another headache. I grabbed at my forehead in a feeble attempt to rub the pain away.

"Are you okay?" he asked.

"Yeah. Just a headache." I continued the massage my head. "We can leave if you want. I don't need either of us to sit here if the other person is going to be miserable."

"Are you miserable right now?"

"No. Just tired."

"Same. Anyways, we already ordered the food."

As if given a stage direction following Dylan' comment, the waitress came over with our meals.

I slowly picked at the food, an increasing level of discomfort and uninterest took away most of my appetite. Dylan, on the other hand, inhaled his. I offered up mine and he gladly accepted.

"Tell me about the boy," he said. It seemed like all the French fries he had went to his head and he completely forgot about the rest of our conversation.

I told him as much about Evan as I could remember. It was never easy to give the life story of someone when you were put on the spot. You told it in fractured sentences that never added up to anything more than a tiny part of what you knew. I managed to relay the information to Dylan about how Evan and I met, what Evan does for work, his dog, and his interest in . . . I blanked. I realized in that moment how I knew nothing about what Evan liked, mainly because none of them intersected with mine. I blamed the headache for the lapse of memory, but I knew it was bigger than that.

"Seems like a good match," Dylan said after I finished giving him the details.

"Yeah, he is," I said, barely believing in the statement.

"Do you mind if you grab the check? Dillion hasn't paid me yet even though I have been working my ass off on several clients on top of all the schoolwork I'm falling behind on." He pushed the bill in my direction. It met some resistance against the stickiness of the table.

"I don't think I have a choice at this point." I pulled out my phone and grabbed for the credit card in the pocket attached to the back.

I threw the card down onto the bill. Plastic beats paper.

✦

After Dylan dropped me off at my apartment, I realized I needed to figure out why I kept reaching out to exes of mine. It was unhealthy to not let them go. If they wanted my friendship, they could seek it out.

Recently, my life felt like it was devolving into a series of unpredictable conversations. I'd fall asleep and wake up in the middle of a heavy conversation with Evan in tears on one side of the couch and me not knowing how we got there on the other. Or I'd wake up and be sitting across from Benji or Dylan and wonder what brought me there in the first place. I didn't enjoy the repetition.

I got nothing of substance out of the dinner with Dylan. I felt no better about our friendship and certainly didn't believe he was in a stable place.

The most pathetic part was that I'd forget about him. Not forever but for a few weeks. Enough time would pass until I'd suddenly remember him and feel an intense wave of guilt that I hadn't reached out. So I would and then I'd find myself in the same tiring situation.

I never learned. Blame it on stubbornness or human nature.

# twenty-two

## GUIDING LIGHT

I got a tattoo.

It was something that had been on my mind for a long time. The idea of adding a permanent piece of art to my body was thrilling. I understood the hesitation others had and why some chose not to, but I saw it as an opportunity to add some creativity to the flesh suit I'd be walking around in for . . . however long I kept walking in it.

The one thing that made me nervous was how the tattoo would be perceived. I worked in a corporate setting, and, quite frankly, people were uptight about piercings, tattoos, hair color, or anything else that made a person stand out from the crowd of middle aged, soon-to-be-gobbling-up-Social-Security type people. Even at [REDACTED], it was rare to see someone who was unique.

I wouldn't have had concern if the tattoo wasn't in a visible location, but the tattoo was in a visible location. I got it on my right forearm. I was a lefty for almost everything I did, but it felt more natural to get the tattoo on that side. I wanted it in a place where I could always see it, always view it as a reminder.

I did my homework and scouted out various tattoo parlors in the Dallas area, but I needed additional help, so I consulted the only expert I knew to assist me with the details.

"Well, well, well . . . this is a surprise!" the voice said. He eyed me up and down from across the screen. "You look about the same, Vinny Boy."

"Hi, Red. Should we get the pleasantries out of the way? How are you? How's the fiancé doing? What's going on with the band? Where are you living these days?" I bombarded him with *the* questions.

To his credit, he answered all of them. (By the way, I apologize for not keeping you up to speed about Red. We talked on occasion, but given my preoccupation elsewhere, I didn't think our trivial chats enhanced the livelihood of this thing. So yeah, he got engaged to this guy from Ireland that he met during one of his excursions to Europe.) At a high level, he was doing well. The band was staffed with completely new members from when I saw them. They were still going on tours and performing gigs down at Key West when they had the time. Red's time on *American Idol* didn't lead him to newfound stardom, but he did make it to the Top 50 which I saw as a massive accomplishment even though he played it off as if it wasn't. He was living in Nashville and he begged me to go see him. The idea of being in that city again made my skin crawl, but the memory of what was there continued to diminish into the abyss. Oh, him and his fiancé broke up, so that sucked to hear. I wouldn't say I was shocked, but let's just keep that between you and me.

Following a lengthy side conversation into the array of details regarding the breakup, I slowly nudged the call back to its original intention.

"Red, I have no doubts you will find someone who is right for you. I know you say you're going to stay single for a while, but you have the amazing ability to attract people to you, so you'll find someone sooner than you expect. But, speaking of being single, can I get your help with something?"

"Oh my god! Did you two break up?" he asked with severe concern.

"Evan and I are fine. I just wanted to see if you were paying attention since you like to talk, but rarely have the aptitude to listen," I said with a grin.

He threw his head back and laughed. "Bitch—"

"See. There you go again with the talking."

"Oh, fuck right off to Evan's house or whatever the fuck he lives in. You got me fired up now. Always taking shit from you. . ." he trailed off. Nothing he said was serious, so I moved past the comments.

"Anyways, I need your advice on getting a tattoo."

His face lit up. He went to speak but stopped himself.

I continued. "I have been looking around Dallas for a place to go, but I could use your help in pinpointing *what* I should be looking for. Are there red flags I should watch out for? Is it okay to not like someone's design? How badly is it going to hurt? Ya know, things like that."

"Oh my god! My little Vinny Boy is finally letting his balls drop! About damn time. I'm happy to help but tell me what you are getting."

I told him and voiced the concern I had. No, not the one about it being visible. The other concern I haven't shared with you yet.

"Your body, your ink. You get whatever you want, as long as it means something to you. You already know that though, so stop asking me for validation. It makes you look silly," he said with a slight chuckle. "Okay, here's what you need to do . . ."

I took notes. That is not an exaggeration. I actually took notes as if I was back in tenth grade math.

After he finished with his tips and tricks, we chatted for a while longer, mainly about nonsense and the nonsensical things surrounding the nonsense.

---

Weeks later, after consulting the list of tattoo shops, keeping Red's advice in mind, and going to several consultations, I was sitting in the chair. My right forearm was exposed, shaved, and wiped clean.

The tattoo artist, Bianca, looked over at me. "You seem nervous. What's wrong?"

I glanced over at Evan and back at her. "I just want this to be unique. I know a lot of people get this sort of tattoo, so I need it to stand out."

"Honey, it is going to look great. Just remember that you are doing this for yourself."

I laid my head back and heard the rumble of the machine.

Why did I care if a million other people had a similar tattoo or not? We were all a bunch of cliché animals that the end of it all. We all ate and shit and cried and slept and cheated. Nothing about anyone was unique. This was always evident in how we communicate with each other. Nobody talks in the flowery language you read in John Green's books or quotes Robert Frost or The Bible like every character seemingly did on *House of Cards* or any other pretentious show. Consider the average conversation you have with someone. It is a series of yesses and noes, or umms and mhmms. The bare minimum is used to convey the largest message.

With the tattoo, it gave me a chance to be different, but it was foolish to believe I was. The reason I write is for you to see that maybe—with the slimmest possibility—I am slightly different from the rest. I don't write with big words or try to change your mind on complex topics with paragraphs of useless metaphors (I might be guilty of that actually). I know I lack subtlety in my writing and that I don't allow you to think for yourself instead of always giving you the answer, but I don't want to leave doubt. How did we get here? *Why* did we get here? I've lost the thread and the rationale for this rant. It is another example of my brain ripping me in too many directions. Let's regroup.

The tattoo didn't take long, and as Red said, it didn't hurt too bad. I watched as it took shape.

Bianca wiped the tattoo several more times. "Want to take a look? I could tell you were purposely avoiding it the whole time."

"Yeah. I'm sorry. I just wanted to see the end result."

"It's okay, darling," she said, moving away her hand so I could see the full tattoo.

Evan stepped closer, staring down at it with me.

It was simple, as intended. A compass with the four cardinal directions stretching out on my forearm. A small, dashed circle encased the center of the two intersecting lines. I elected not to have the arrows marked with the actual direction. I figured I'd remember what they were without that. Instead, I had a small airplane where the south line ended to indicate the reason why I had moved down to that part of the country. For the east line, I settled on a symbol of a house. For obvious reasons, Pennsylvania would always be my home, wherever I was. As for the north and west lines, there was nothing there yet beyond the arrow. Maybe my story would take me there, but not quite yet.

I knew every time I looked down at the tattoo, it would help me to focus, to re-center me. Wasn't that what a compass was for? To tell you where to head when you were lost? I had felt lost too many times since moving down to Dallas and a tattoo wasn't going to help me resolve the issue, but it was comforting to know that it could be a start.

Was it heavy-handed? Sure. But I kept reminding myself of one thing: I didn't do this for anyone except myself.

I told Bianca how much I liked it and thanked her profusely.

After getting it wrapped and given instructions for how to take care of it, Evan and I stepped out of the tattoo shop to be greeted by the midday sun.

I thought about letting the compass tell us the way home, but that would have been silly.

## twenty-three

### (UN)LOST

Friday night.
I was alone on the couch, decompressing from the week of work. Evan was doing the same and we decided that meeting up on Saturday would be better.

It was unusually silent in my apartment. I was too lazy to get my phone and start any music. The cars whizzed by outside, moving faster than I would have thought considering a stop sign was a short way down the road. The occasional roar of a passing plane always kept me thinking about work. After a long stretch of dullness, my upstairs neighbor waddled across the floor, each step more pronounced than the last. She yelled. Some poor soul was on the other end of the phone and had to get their ears abused by her high-pitched cawing. I was able to tune it out with ease and returned to staring at the ceiling to think about . . .

Nothing.

People claim it is impossible to think about nothing because the act of thinking about nothing is actually thinking about something. Who are those people? I want to meet them.

Whatever.

My brain was free of the noise, the worry, the doubt, the anxiety, the million other intangible things that controlled me from the broadcast room.

Do you know what the worst of the intangibles is?

The pain. The pain of all the stupid, inane, senseless things you've ever done and knowing with severe clarity that you will do it again.

That was at another time though. Currently, I was free from it, running slightly faster than it could catch me.

I eventually got tired of nothing and made the effort to roll off the couch and snag my phone from the kitchen counter. I scrolled through Reddit, entering into the echo chamber of narrow thoughts and reposts of content I saw on the site a week ago. One of the most popular websites in the world and yet it was entirely pointless. Discussion within the threads were cringy and commandeered by bots trying to sway public opinion with differing opinions being downvoted into oblivion. But I still used it every day, so I guess I was the foolish one.

Bored of that, I moved over to Facebook. Now that's a fun website! I got to peek into people's fake happiness. I would get a glimpse at hundreds of my closest friends and what marvelous things were happening in their lives. Vicky got a new car. Wonderful! Dean finally got that job he had been gunning for after putting up a multitude of posts complaining about the company and their interview process. Congrats! Michelle posted twenty-eight photos of her newborn kid, but no one had the balls to tell her that the baby wouldn't be on the cover of any Gerber products. Awww! Gregorio told the world how bad of a mood he was in, but he then refused to answer any comments asking what was wrong. Silly guy! Gwen posted a controversial article from a third-rate blog of some anti-vax lunatic who claimed that vaccines caused autism, argued with anyone who disagreed, and bitched at them to NEVER comment on one of her statuses again. Classic! Uncle Lou posted an article from Fox News about how our illustrious President was the sexiest thing since the flaming hot Cheeto was created. Old people are so cute when they spread fake news! Littered between the massive piles of shit posts were the mounds of ads from sites I visited five minutes earlier. Crazy!

It was a pit of stupidity. Facebook, Twitter, Instagram, Snapchat, YouTube, or whatever the new thing would be in the next year. It didn't make a difference. People loved the rush of getting a retweet or a like or another subscriber. It was that drip of morphine you continually pined for. We crave the attention and affection of those who are meaningless to us. After creating that post or video, they sit back from their laptop or phone and reenter the misery of the world with the rest of us. The thoughts and prayers didn't stop the violence or disasters. The cute videos of puppies didn't help to cure the crippling feeling of loneliness that is slowly sinking its way into everyone.

Am I bitter? You probably wouldn't believe me if I said otherwise, and I can't fault you for that. I just get tired of the façade that people put up to impress others who are doing the same exact thing.

I tossed the phone aside, returning to just me and the nothi—

And it hit me.

I needed to get out of the house. I knew if I didn't, I would spiral.

I got off the couch, changed into something more respectable, and left the apartment in a rush. The air outside was muggy, the full weight of summer was no longer an idle threat from mother nature.

I had a ten-minute walk ahead of me to clear myself from the spiral. It sat on the periphery with a wide grin. Sometimes there was no warning when it would happen. I could have laid there and let it consume me, but I would have done something regrettable. I would have thought about the lying and the cheating and the *fucking* headaches that wouldn't go away. I would have downloaded Grindr and found the—

Liar. Cheater.

Enough.

I refocused on the walk. I continued down Congress. I'd eventually have to make a left and come up to Cedar Springs, but I enjoyed the few minutes of quiet. In a city as large as Dallas, you could still find pockets where you heard the crickets and strange creaks two houses away. I looked up. Even in the quietest places of Dallas you still couldn't see the stars. The light pollution was severe, as you'd expect for a city with over a million people. My mind began to drift again, but to something more positive. I was standing out on a ramp leading from the garage to the backyard. The dogs were out roaming the area, trying to sniff out an unoccupied spot. The weather is warm, but not with the sogginess of a Dallas day. The fireflies appear and vanish in a wink, scattering across the yard. One of the dogs takes interest and I can hear the snapping of jaws moving around. I finally look up. The number of stars seem infinite; it pales in comparison to what I saw on trips that brought me to more secluded lands, but my mind brought me back here. Why? There was no answer because none was needed. I continue to stare upward, wondering what it takes to get to one of those shiny, dead lights, to be free from the plagues and worries of Earth. How lonely it would be though. Traveling through space, knowing you'd left it all behind but maybe you didn't actually leave it—you ran from it. Desperation drives people to do irrational things. Could I see myself leaving Earth to escape my problems? No, that would be ridiculous, but I did wonder if there was a planet where life was easier and the weight of my brain and all the shit that forced itself into it could be lessened. That was assuming my problems were location based and not me based.

A nose nudges me. I look down, back toward the grass and the dirt and my entire existence. I lock eyes with a dog, a much younger version of what he currently is. He's ready to go back inside and so am I.

I step through the garage door, shutting it behind me and returning to my present self in Dallas.

The sounds of Cedar Springs grew rapidly as I covered the last block. The Strip would be crawling with people of various sizes and shapes and colors. It was the least judgmental area of Dallas I knew filled with the most judgy people you could imagine. Did it make any sense? Nah, but you learned to roll with it.

I went inside JRs—the same place Evan and I had gone at the tail end of our first date. I pushed past the clusters of roaming bodies on the first floor and took the back stairs up to the second.

Two people were sitting on the stained couch at the top of the steps. Their bodies so intertwined that it was hard to tell where one person ended and the other began. I heard a chuckle from behind as I forged ahead to the bar.

They had the windows open, so there was no escaping the heat. Fine. I'll accept my fate. I wore a dark shirt to hide any of the sweat stains that would appear.

*Why are you here?*

It was a question I was avoiding. Instead, I contemplated what I wanted to drink.

"I'll take a Jack and coke," I yelled across the bar. The bartender nodded and went to work.

I indicated that he could close the tab with a quick motion of my hand slitting my throat. He understood the gesture and printed me out a receipt.

"Thank you honey," he said with a smile as he dropped the receipt and moved along to the next customer.

I snatched my drink from the bar and walked outside to the railing, placing my drink on the ledge. The Strip was a three block stretch of gay bars. On that particular night, nothing of note was happening so the usual density of population was present. I was like a drunk person on a balcony in New Orleans with the view I had, except I wouldn't be showing my boobs for beads. I had a great sightline everything below and beyond.

It was early, but people swayed unsteadily on the sidewalk. Their yells permeated up and pierced through the music that echoed behind in the bar. Many were in groups, arms slung around each other with laughs radiating out into the night. A few wandered on their own, looking indecisively about where they should go next.

I wish I had a group of friends to go out with.

Evan was only good to go out about once a month. He was an old soul trapped in a twink body. Most times I didn't mind it because spending time with him was more important than spending money and being surrounded by greasy strangers. Sometimes though, the urge ripped through me to get out, to venture down to The Strip and be tangled up in people I could relate to. Our stories weren't the same—everyone's was slightly different—but we shared enough similarities that I felt at home. I felt like I could be myself. I could talk in a greater exaggeration with more hand motions that could knock out anyone in a three-foot radius. I could dance with my ass grinding into their pelvis, knowing they were enjoying it just as much as I was. I could leave behind the Vincent that was a Son and a Corporate Employee and a Brother and all the other things that didn't quite oppress me but also didn't give me the satisfaction I needed out of life.

Being an active participant while at The Strip wasn't always necessary, so I stood there and did what I did best: observed.

People were fascinating when you watched them in a casual manner. I certainly don't condone being creepy about it, but I do think you can learn a lot about someone from afar.

For example, a guy walked across the street, toward JR's. Nothing abundantly special about him at first glance, but he was worth dissecting more. His jeans were ripped in various places and he wore boots that looked like they belonged in the seventies. The button down was undone from the chest up. He walked with another friend but carried all the confidence. It was hard to make out his facial features but everything looked symmetrical. He had one earring in, which was a feather that draped down onto his shoulder. It was extra. It was what you'd expect from someone who was out on The Strip.

What did I learn in his time crossing the street before he moved out of frame? He was into fashion. That was apparent. Nobody dresses that nicely out to the gay bars unless they are looking for dick or they enjoy the act of dressing up itself. Something told me he wasn't looking for a hook up because most of the people who would approach him weren't his type. He'd enjoy the casual conversation with strangers but was always searching for a way out of it. His eyes would drift over to someone else. He didn't have the confidence to go up to them because the fear of rejection held him back. It didn't matter how many times friends told him he was a rock star, he couldn't correct the fear. So, he would stand there listening to the guy who'd offer to buy him a drink and suggest they go out on the dance floor. He'd do it because what was the alternative? His friend had wandered off to the bathroom and had yet to reappear. For someone that held so much confidence, he certainly had no clue what to do with it. The night would end up the same as many others: wasted time. He'd collapse onto the bed of his tiny apartment and think about when he'd find someone worth it. The thought would carry with him until the alcohol took over and lulled him to sleep.

I certainly didn't know a single thing about that guy, but it was nice to make stuff up though. It helped my brain not to focus on myself for a period of time.

I let my imagination wander on several other people that passed by, the thoughts getting more elaborate.

I continued this until I was left with just the melted ice in my drink. The line at the bar wasn't worth the wait, so I nixed getting another round.

Once outside, I went across the street and headed for Round-Up. It would be crowded. I'd manage.

The bouncer stared at my ID longer than expected before handing it back and letting me pass. It quickly turned into sensory overload. The noise from the karaoke bar to the right, the multitude of pool games happening to the left, the flashing lights from the dance floor straight ahead. I moved toward the lights and walked into the wave of people. I broke up groups as I wormed through the middle with the destination being any one of the bars.

I waited for the bartender to circle around the bar. I learned over the years that you needed to have patience when waiting for a drink, but you also needed to show some urgency. The best way to do that was to have your credit card out and visible. It meant you knew what you wanted, and you needed his bitch-ass to walk over and make you that damn drink.

It worked, and the beefy bartender sauntered over, giving me nothing more than a head nod.

I recited the same order from earlier. He nodded again. He grabbed a cup, dumped all the ice that ever existed, poured a dribble of Jack, and lathered up the rest with coke.

My man.

I slit my throat again and he slapped down a receipt. The price was egregious for the lack of alcohol but making a scene at a crowded bar was about as classy as going to Walmart and sticking all the oranges from the produce department down your pants.

I stepped away from the bar, my spot being occupied by the next eager idiot. I meandered for a moment and spotted a snippet of free wall space.

I leaned against it and continued to observe.

Did you expect this to be a story where someone came up to talk to me? Buhl, this isn't some Hollywood bullshit.

I can tell you with complete certainty I didn't speak to anyone that night. Of course, I could be lying.

I left the bar after it became clear they recycled the same playlist each week. I hadn't been there in a month and still heard the same Taylor Swift song at nearly the same time. Oddly enough, the crowd surged when the song started as if they didn't know it was going to happen.

I fought the urge for pizza and continued down Cedar Springs. Like any good tour guide, you never take the same route back.

I retreated away from the noise and lights and people. The clarity I felt for a few hours began to slip. God, I hated everything about my mental state. It was always out to perform chaos at the expense of just one person.

It was odd not to tell Evan I spent the night out at the bars. He could have checked my location on Snapchat, but he didn't suffer from the paranoia I did.

For once though, I was happy to fall asleep with a clear conscious minus the mantra that became all too permanent in the creases of my mind.

*Liar, cheater. Liar, cheater.*

Nothing would ever come of it though. I'd carry the secret to my grave.

*But Vin! What if someone does end up reading this and then they do find out your secret?* you may be wondering.

Shut it and let me continue to live in a delusional state.

Anyhow, I'll be dead before anyone finds out about my secret(s), but you need to have more patience before we get to that.

## twenty-four

### AND KNOW THE PLACE FOR THE FIRST TIME

Traffic jams tend to start when one person drives as fast as unnecessary and has to slam on the brakes. The person behind them does the same thing. So it goes for a quarter mile, half mile, two miles until you are left with a phantom traffic jam. All caused because of the stupidity of one person, and then replicated by the masses.

At fourteen stories up, I watched this unfold on the intersecting highways that weave through downtown. For a Saturday night, traffic was at its lightest and, yet, people still had a way of causing meaningless delays.

If that isn't a great metaphor for my life, then call me Ringo Starr and hand me a guitar.

Wait, what? Never mind. Moving on.

I pressed my nose against the glass of one of the windows in Evan's apartment. The flashes of light from Reunion Tower lit up his space every few seconds. I moved my attention away from the traffic forming below and toward the high rise that sat across the street from Evan's. Much of it was dark, either from drawn curtains or the absence of a tenant. In a few though, the strobe of a television cascaded enough that I could briefly see into the life of a total stranger. None were doing anything of interest or renown.

I stepped away from the glass, leaving a sizeable smudge to match the previous ones I had implanted on the other windows.

Evan was busy cleaning the apartment. St. Vincent seeped from the Alexa device that sat atop his dresser/TV stand. Evan was still riding the high from the concert a few weeks ago and continued to play her songs about pills, different cities, and mass erections.

I asked earlier if he needed assistance cleaning, but he insisted he could handle it on his own. He finished fiddling with the laundry and was now occupied by the impressively large stack of dishes scattered in and around the sink.

I plopped onto the couch and flipped open my laptop. I minimized away the Word document of the nearly completed "book," and opened up a fresh Safari browser window.

Sometimes I liked to do Google searches on random things to escape the Now. Usually the need to escape the Now was more prevalent, but in this case, I would be bored until Evan was done with his quest to return the Kingdom of Dirty Dishes to a subservient state.

I started with a simple topic, one that was nearby. House of Blues. I knew that the location positioned almost directly beneath him was not the only one, so I felt the need to gather more details. The Google search led me to the Wikipedia page. I read briefly and clicked on a link that brought me to another page. I skimmed that page until I got bored and found another topic.

Three clicks later, I read about a pie eating contest in Alabama where three people ended up dead due to the fruit being poisoned by a jealous ex-lover. How cliché. At least try to be more inventive than that.

In a series of further clicks I no longer recall, I ended up at a Wikipedia entry for something called Graham's number. If you're familiar, you may be wondering how I went from House of Blues to pie to other nonsense to math. I'm wondering right with you, but the answer would be uninspired and not important.

Not satisfied with the Wikipedia entry on Graham's number, I typed it into Google and stumbled upon a blog written by an incredibly sassy person who had an affinity for numbers. It was a fascinating read that spanned across two posts.

After a finished reading through enough of it to gain the power of knowledge, I turned around to fill Evan in on the news, but he beat me to the uptake.

"Why do I constantly do this to myself?" he asked me.

I didn't have an answer, so I posed another question, hoping he would have one. "Do what?"

"Let the dishes pile up."

"Oh," I said, pausing briefly to reposition myself so I wouldn't break my neck trying to talk to him. "I assumed you were about to have an existential crisis with me. Thank goodness. I had you penciled in for that on Tuesday."

"Not funny."

"I'm beginning to think *you actually think* that about most things I say."

He brushed aside the comment. "What do you want to do tonight?"

"You know what I want," I said, leaning to turn on the PlayStation.

"I'm not mentally prepared for that."

"We have one left. We—you mostly—need to finish it. It is worth it. I promise," I said, flashing a smile.

"Fine, but I get to be little spoon."

"Gross. I agree to your terms though."

I hit the power button on the remote and it eventually flashed the logo and then the home screen for the PlayStation. I quickly navigated to the HBO GO app and selected it. The load time was dreadfully slow, but it gave time for Evan to get himself situated on the couch.

"Are you ready for this?" I asked.

"I'll be happy when it's over. This show is a real downer."

"That's why I love it!"

We stretched out along the length of the couch. His limbs extending a bit beyond mine. I snuck my right arm under his head and placed my left on his hip. (Do you care about such meaningless detail?)

The app knew what we wanted and presented us with our prize when it finally loaded.

*The Leftovers.*

Let me hit ya with a brief synopsis for those that are uninitiated: The show is based on a book, which seems to be like a majority of quality television and movies these days. The catalyst for the show is that 3 percent of the world's population just fucks right off. Poof. Gone. They disappear, and no one knows what the frick happened. Cut to three years later. The viewer follows the town of Mapleton, New York as they move on with life. Some people lost everyone, others didn't lose anyone, but each of them have been dramatically shaped by the event and the lack of a logical explanation for it.

The characters are flawed and depressing and realistic. It obviously spoke to me on an emotional level.

Season one can be a chore to get through, but you'll be rewarded with an incredible two seasons after that, which, coincidently, expand beyond anything that happens in the book.

"I promise to be quiet," I stressed.

"I'm sure you will be."

I was so jazzed about the show that I usually talked through it, which led to some annoyance on Evan's part.

I hit play. In hindsight, I'd like to think that was the exact moment the text came through on my phone, but I never made the effort to sync up the timelines.

The screen flashed the familiar HBO logo and soon we were on our way.

Time passed, as if I need to keep telling you that.

An hour later, the credits rolled. Silence continued between us. Izzie gave a sleepy stare from the other of the couch and then went back to her nap.

"What did you think?" I asked.

"It was good," he said flatly.

"That's it?!? Well, what about the ending? Did you think she was telling the truth?"

"About what she saw? Yeah, I think she was. There wasn't any reason for her to lie."

"My thoughts exactly. It's why I love the ending. They didn't show a single second of 'the other side' or whatever you'd want to call it, but she created this vivid picture of what it was like. That imagery she spoke of was powerful and it could have been a total lie. It feels disingenuous though, so I'll always believe she told the truth. If she did lie though . . . all those years she spent hiding away . . ." I trailed off. The thought made me shutter. How easily we could leave people behind.

"I think you enjoyed the show way more than me. I didn't feel any emotional connection," Evan said.

"Why?"

"I don't know. Just because."

"Well, I'm sorry to have wasted your time," I said, making it clear that I was offended about him not liking a show I had no hand in producing.

People get weird about things they perceive as art. Sometimes people don't want you to discover that indie band or underground artist because they love the notion they are one of the select few who enjoys them.

Sometimes people like to knock acclaimed movies or books or shows because its edgy and nothing deserves to sit on too high of a pedestal.

In my case, I was bitter because I knew *The Leftovers* was top notch, so Evan being oblivious to that was annoying.

My thoughts were bordering on pretentious and petty, so I pushed them aside.

He responded after an exaggerated sigh. "You didn't waste my time. I don't have to like everything you do. The opposite is true as well. I'm very aware that going to the St. Vincent concert was a chore for you, but I'm appreciative you went. I hope you are appreciative I watched this show."

Damn his logic!

"Yeah, you're right. It's just a show after all . . ." I said, not feeling the need to elaborate further.

"I'm going to grab a drink," he announced to the audience that sat outside his windows, precariously perched on nothing but air.

We untangled from each other and he went rustling through the cabinets for a glass.

"So," I said. "Have you ever heard of Graham's number? I was reading about it before we watched the show."

"I have only heard of Graham's cracker."

I laughed more than I should have. "That was dumb. We will work on your jokes another day. Anyways—"

"Hold on," he said, finishing up the concoction he brewed. "Okay. Continue," he stated once he was back on the couch.

"Yeah, so. Do you want the full story or just the highlights?"

"It's just a number. How complicated could it be?" he asked, taking a sip of the drink and wincing at the taste.

"I'm not an expert by any means, since I've just learned about it, but Graham's number—for a period of time—was the largest known number ever. Of course, once he created it, people felt the need to create something bigger. Ya know, size matters to mathematicians and other smart folk."

"Wait, created a number? How's that possible?"

"Created probably isn't the right word. He discovered the number to prove some theory. I . . . I don't think that's exactly how it went, but that's not the important part. The summation is that the number he found is large. So large that our dumb brains can't comprehend the enormity of it."

Evan nodded, urging me to continue.

"Mind you, this number isn't infinite. It has an end point. Based on what I read, you can calculate what the last digits of the number are, but to write them all out would be impossible. The number of digits within Graham's number is bigger than the total number of atoms . . . in the entire universe! The whole fucking universe! We don't even know how big the universe is, or at least I don't have a clue."

"It's probably pretty big," he weighed in.

"Imagine how tiny an atom is. Now imagine how big we think Earth is or the sun or the galaxy. Now explode that out to be trillions upon trillions upon billions upon words that don't even exist times bigger. This number is larger than that. Insane, right?"

"Totally."

I leaned in closer. I was fully playing up the theatrics at this point. "The last thing I read before you rudely interrupted me earlier was this guy asking what it would be like. Strip away the idea that human bodies decay to nothingness after a blip of time—in the grand scheme of all things—and think about what it would be like to live for that long. You know that you won't live forever, but you sure as hell won't feel like it is any less than that.

"But that's boring to me. Immortality is a tale that has been woven for centuries. People search for it and kill for it and ludicrous stories are created centering around it. Baloney. No one wants to live forever or to live for Graham's number amount of time. What I think is scarier is considering that we are just a dot whose value is completely meaningless within that number. We are nothing. Absolutely useless to the history of time. Our problems and triumphs will be swallowed by the universe because—surprisingly—the universe does not revolve around Earth or any of its inhabitants.

"Think about *The Leftovers*. The world we glimpsed into lost 3 percent of the population, but what about the 97 percent that never made it to the other side and stayed in the reality we saw? Wherever the 3 percent went, they lost nearly everyone. The people they knew or loved or even hated—dots, all of them—became entirely meaningless the moment they vanished. I feel like I'm on the verge of some revelatory thinking, but that may require me to actua—"

In that moment, I absentmindedly grabbed my phone to check the time. It was an impulse I fought throughout the day and tended to lose out on. The screen lit up with a new text; the contents were hidden behind the passcode, but that wasn't important—the sender of the text was.

Faceless Nameless.

"Are you okay?" Evan asked. He might have noticed the shift in my expression.

"No. Not really. I wasn't really expecting that," I said mostly to myself.

"What?"

"Faceless Nameless texted me."

Obviously, I referred to him by name at the time, but no need to break the streak of degrading him by not calling him by his actual name.

"Oh. Wow. What did he say?"

"Don't know. Don't really care to read it now," I said. I tossed my phone onto the coffee table that used to be mine, but now was in Evan's possession. It skidded across and came to a stop a few inches from the edge.

"I'm sorry. I know seeing anything from him isn't easy. Do you want to finish what you were saying about Graham's number? I think you were about to break ground on something no one has ever considered before!"

"I wasn't. The gist is this: I ramble too much about nonsense. I'm a dot. You're a dot. That text is a dot. Whatever shit we have going on is stupid and complaining about things doesn't make them more important."

"Okay."

"I'm probably going to go to bed. Are you tired?"

"Not really."

"Me too."

"Then why . . ."

"Just going to try to run away from the assault I'm about to face by counting from one to Graham's number. Maybe I'll get halfway before I die."

"I'm here to help if you need anything."

"Thanks. I appreciate that."

"Vin?"

"Yeah?" I was off the couch and halfway to the bed. I turned around to face him, feeling that what he was about to say would be crucial to hear.

"I love you. More than you'll ever know. You make me really happy and I know sometimes we have tough conversations but it's just part of us growing."

"I love you too." The response was almost involuntary. How could I not repeat the words? I did still mean it, right?

I should have reached out to him and confessed how I needed him. I needed his help to run away from everything that sucked in my life. The pain, the endless stream of guilt and shitty thoughts, the constant recycling of idiotic notions that bounced along my brain, and all the other dots that were building up.

But I was too much of a coward to say anything.

part three

## GONE NOW

# twenty-five

## BLACK BUTTERFLIES AND DÉJÀ VU

The act of turning twenty-five was no different than turning twenty-four. Part of being a productive member of society meant I now worked on my birthday which was still severe whiplash from my childhood. Having a summer birthday meant I was free from celebrating it in the confines of a classroom and getting to spend a majority of them at the beach was an added bonus.

Even if it was the Jersey Shore.

The day was largely the same. The pointless meetings, bullshit emails, and empty conversations with people to pass the time were a staple of my servitude at [REDACTED]. Even on my birthday they weren't nice enough to spare me from the mundane.

I wouldn't say the text messages, Facebook posts, and other well wishes poured in; it was more like a trickle from that faucet the plumber had been out three times to fix but was never able to seal properly. Most of the messages were from folks where we had signed a contract long ago in some distant realm that required each of us to wish the other a happy birthday and then proceed to avoid and ignore one another for the rest of the year.

I shouldn't have cared that I never heard from certain people. While the day is important to me, it is just another one for a majority of the population. We all like to feel validated and comforted by the idea that others think about us when we are not around, so that simple message on a birthday goes a long way. I burned enough bridges and neglected to maintain others, which led to diminishing returns each year.

Okay, enough about birthday wishes. I'm just trying to analyze something that isn't worth the effort.

Surprisingly, I didn't have any plans for after work. It was a Wednesday, so Evan would be working late. We agreed that going out to dinner the next night would be easier. I had every intention of going home and pulling stuff together for the Cape Cod trip in a few days. That plan shifted when Daniel swung by my desk in the early afternoon and demanded we go out and grab dinner. I agreed and he scampered off to think of a place we hadn't been to yet.

The workday passed without much happening and I soon found myself in my car heading to the restaurant. It was outside of the city, which meant we were going to hit rush hour traffic. While everyone else may have been, I wasn't in a rush.

I talked to my mom for the duration of the drive, catching her up on the uninteresting things happening in my life.

At the restaurant, we got a table quickly even though the place was reaching critical mass. The waiter came over and gave an overblown speech on the history of the restaurant and the farm-to-table ingredients they used. I shook my head at nearly every other word to make it seem like I gave a shit about the ramble.

Once he was done, we ordered drinks and settled in.

Yada, yada, yada.

I'd much I'd love to give you the recap of our small talk, let's skip all that and dive into the highlight of the evening.

There was a point in my life where I had this grand vision that I would never come out. I would live my life like Rapunzel, locked away in a tower with the hopes I'd never have to divulge my secrets. With the passage of time and the development of basic wisdom, I discovered that was an impossible and idiotic line of thinking. There would have been no logical way for me to hide my sexuality for my entire life, but damn, I was impressed I lasted as long as I did.

And then, when it became clear I wouldn't be able to fool people forever, I anticipated that coming out would be executed like a telemarketing operation. I'd hire fifty people from a third world country, pay them a dollar for their services, and have them call all the people I'd ever known simultaneously to clue them into my big, gay secret. Some would be shocked, some would be confused, but the majority would wonder why I'd go to such great lengths for something so trivial. (In reality, everyone was shocked. I was like the straightest gay guy ever apparently. The only people who knew without a doubt (allegedly) were my friends from high school that used to call me a faggot every chance they got. They must have been using the name to address me and not as a slur.)

What my own imagination failed to realize was how coming out wasn't a one-time event but a continual journey that took significant time. I'd tell one person, a few months would pass, then some more would find out. You've read about a lot of them in the previous book, unless you skipped that and just happened to pick this up for a nickel from the hobo in the back alley.

Daniel was the next person in that journey. I was a weary traveler by that point. I had slayed the dragon and saved the kingdom half a dozen times and just wanted that part of my life to be done with, but I owed it to him.

"Tell me more about this book!" he urged at some point after our food arrived.

For someone who had no intention of letting other people read the book, I sure told a lot of people that I was writing. On some Freudian level, I wanted to be recognized for the work—even if it was bound to be a dumpster fire.

"There's not much to tell you. I think I'm almost done but knowing that would imply I have any clue about what I'm doing to begin with."

"Then why are you writing whatever you happen to be writing?"

My answer was largely the same as when I told Lee all those months ago. "I am trying to unburden myself."

He sat for a moment and chewed on a piece of his steak. "Okay," he said. "I think I understand. This book is nonfiction?"

"Correct."

"Then why are you being dodgy about the contents?"

My heart raced. Telling people would always be a chore for me, regardless of who it was. Coming out would never be easy, regardless of the circumstance. If you find yourself in the orbit of this situation, be patient and kind. What's the point of being a dot if you're just going to be an insufferable asshole anyways? Like you've heard me say before, everyone has a story, so take time to hear some. You may learn more than you deserve.

"Because that requires me to say I'm gay which is a large premise of the book."

"I see. That's unexpected, but okay! Makes no difference to me!"

"I'm glad to hear that." I picked at the remnants of the mac n' cheese that lay scattered in the bowl.

"I'm sorry," I continued. "As with most people, I wanted to tell you earlier, but this irrational fear controlled me, and I was always worried you'd be disgusted."

"To be honest, there was a time when I would have been. I was a much different person back in college, but I credit Danielle with helping me change. We saw how it has been for her brother and the impact on their family, so I think I've gained a deeper understanding."

The waiter reappeared. "Can I get y'all another round of drinks?"

"Yes please," Daniel said.

He cleared away the empty plates and glasses, freeing the table of the clutter.

"Also, I need to apologize for being somewhat distant these past four months. I have been seeing someone, which has severely cut into our weekend hangouts and after work expeditions into Halo," I said.

"Ah, it all makes more sense now. No need to apologize though. I'm happy you've found someone! You should know that Danielle has been asking about this book ever since you first mentioned it. She is super eager to read it."

"Why would she want to?"

"Because she cares about you, and—quite frankly—she might be a bit jealous since she has always wanted to write a book too."

"I imagine when she does someday it will be light-years ahead of mine."

"Tell me about him. What is he like?"

I wanted to say this:

> His name is Evan. Evan Ethan Eaton. Pretty cool, right? It sort of rolls off the tongue in a way most names don't. I like to imagine his parents knew how cool the name sounded when he was born and envisioned him as a movie star or some slanted celebrity, but I doubt that was the case. Anyways, I'm getting off track. We have only known each other for four months so I imagine my answer would and will be different at other times, but now, in this moment, I see him as a piece of art. Sounds dumb but bear with me. He is the artwork everyone walks by because they want to see the Mona Lisa or the statue of David or some other main attraction. One day, you go to visit this museum and take a wrong turn, separating you from the crowd that is marching forward toward the prize. You contemplate rejoining the group, but something compels you to continue on. You navigate down the long, straight hallway. Everything seems so sterile, so perfect until you reach the end

and see it. At first glance, the artwork looks normal—just another abstract concept. The shapes are oblong and scattered in a frantic manner as if the artist became unsure of how to finish. And then you notice the gash that starts in the right corner and extends across the painting in a wide arc. The canvas is frayed along the edge of the gash and creates a subtle discoloring that somehow matches the aesthetic of the painting. It's damaged. Not irreparable, but enough so that people no longer understand the meaning or appeal behind it. You are drawn to it though. You sit there for what may have been hours, but you don't care. You eventually cross over the barrier and touch it, running your hand along the gash. It's not so bad. You don't understand why you are fortunate enough to be the one standing in front of the artwork, but you're glad. You end up leaving the museum, never finding your way to what the masses have gathered to see because you're satisfied with what you found and know you wouldn't be impressed by anything else. Over time, you start pulling people from the masses to show them what you found. They are happy at your discovery, but still gravitate back to rejoin the crowds, leaving you alone again to admire what's waiting at the end of that forgotten hall. So yeah, am I comparing him to damaged goods? Maybe, but the point is I don't see it that way. I see it as him being unique and helping to rip me from the expectation of what I thought I needed—or wanted—out of a relationship. My perception of him is different than anyone else. If I used the same analogy on myself, I'd be a piece of artwork the kid from your high school art class cobbled together after huffing glue and markers for twenty minutes. With that mindset, I got lucky and sometimes I need to remind myself how fortunate I am. I just need to know if it will last.

Instead, I said this:

"His name is Evan. He is pretty cool. We have been trying to figure each other out, which hasn't been easy but I'm excited to see where it goes."

Our brains tend to work better in retrospect and contrary to what the movies tell us, we don't always have the quick wit or elegant response readily waiting.

Daniel nodded. "The four of us should meet up sometime."

"That sounds like a great idea."

The drinks arrived, prompting another cheers to being open with each other. Everyone kept some secrets though, so I'm sure Daniel still had a few he hadn't shared yet.

"Can I ask you something?" I posed.

"Yup."

"Did you and Danielle ever have times where you felt like you were bogged down in emotionally draining conversations? Like all the time."

"Of course," he said, shaking his head in agreement. "We had a spot we would go to: the Café Brazil on the opposite side of campus. We'd be in there until the early hours of the morning going back and forth on topics we knew nothing about but spoke in a manner that suggested we were experts. We learned a lot about each other, and it helped us to grow."

"It's happening to us as well, but I'm not seeing the happy path you are eluding to."

"It takes time."

"How much time before it just feels like failure?"

"I can't tell you that. You'll know when it feels like it's too much."

I took another sip of my drink, unsure of a response.

Daniel asked: "Do you love him?"

"Without a doubt, but that doesn't mean it is a relationship worth continuing. We are just extreme opposites. I'm amazed the mantra of *opposites attract* carries any merit because it certainly doesn't help us. I want to play Xbox and he wants to buy a fish tank. He wants wine and I'd rather chug a beer. He is content with spending the weekend at home and I am always itching to go to the bars. I'm starting to feel like I'm holding him back from something greater. It's almost as if I'm the thing before the thing, like the next relationship he goes into will be the one that carries on for the rest of his life. The thought makes me sad and frustrated."

"I don't know what to say that will help."

"It's okay. I'm not expecting you to solve my problems or asking you to. It is nice to talk to someone about it though."

"I'm always here for you," he said with a smile.

"Here's to turning twenty-five—may I live to see a hundred," I said, lifting up the glass. He did the same. They clinked and echoed across the emptied-out room.

We couldn't resist dessert and sat at the table for a while longer as we chowed down. I was stuffed by the end when the waiter came over and dropped off the check. Daniel quickly snatched it. "Don't even bother," he said.

"Thanks. This is a better birthday than I was expecting."

I had a long ride home that night. The air was stale and dripping with heat, but I rolled the windows down anyways. The wind pierced my ears. I turned up the volume to hear the music ("Ribs" by Lorde). I pressed my foot down on the gas; it took a second, but the car responded and began its steady acceleration. Fifty-five, sixty-five, eighty, eighty-five. The lights on the road ticked by overhead. I sped past the few cars that were out on the highway. The skyline of Dallas came into view with its assortment of colors extending high above into the blackness.

I was okay. And there was a chance that one day I would be good. I'd never ask for anything more. I didn't need to be amazing or fantastic or whatever other adjective I could muster up. Being good was *good enough* for me.

But I wasn't the only person to consider anymore. Was I still good enough for him?

# twenty-six

## BEST OF YOU

I had a second helping of birthday dinner the following night with Evan. To the surprise of no one, we went to Bowen House as a remembrance of our first date. I didn't mind since I assumed I wouldn't be paying for the overpriced cocktails and fruit fly sized appetizers.

I'd like to clue you into some sort of drama that occurred that night, but there was none. The night felt like how all of them should have been. The time slipped by gracefully and didn't feel like a chore. I guess it should never feel like a chore to spend time with the person you love but given the struggles we had been having, I was always afraid that our encounters would spoil before the expiration date.

After the second round of drinks, he pulled out a small box and slid it across the table.

"Happy birthday. It isn't much . . ." he trailed off. His face contorted to show embarrassment.

"You know there was no expectation of a gift in the first place."

"Yeah."

I opened the card attached to the top. It was simple in design with an even simpler message written inside:

> I wanted to say that you have the key to my heart, realized that was silly, and settled on this instead.
>
> Love,
> Evan

I looked up and smiled at him. He stared back, the light from the fake candle bouncing off his face the same way it did so long ago. He wasn't wearing glasses, so his stare was more of a squint. Evan's usually clean jawline was covered with a few days' worth of stubble as the stress of work caught up to him.

I loved him so much.

It would hit me at random moments how much my heart ached to be with him. Soon after, the weight of everything I have done would crash into me like an eighteen-wheeler barreling down the highway.

*Liar, cheater. You know how this works.*

"Fuck off," I mumbled. I rubbed my head to prevent the inevitable.

"You okay?"

"Yeah!" reassuring myself more so than him.

I tore into the wrapping paper and set it aside. I pulled against the two sides of the box to rip off the tape that blocked my path.

Inside, sitting in a manger of tissue paper, was a key.

I held it up and laughed.

"Please tell me that this unlocks a safe that contains several chunks of gold, the list of people in the Illuminati, and the directions to leaving this galaxy."

"Not quite, but it will grant you access to my apartment."

"Even better! This is sweet. Thanks Evan." I reached my hand out to grab a hold of his, a rare sign of public affection from me.

"I love you," he said.

"I love you too."

Evan's birthday was a shade under two weeks after mine. Do you know what I got him? A spiralizer for his vegetables. He went out of his way to get me something with meaning and value that costed him practically nothing and I got him a *fucking spiralizer*. I am such a worthless dot.

When we left the restaurant, we contemplated going somewhere else. We decided against it and, instead, he came back to my apartment and stayed the night.

If only every day went as smoothly as that.

## twenty-seven

## 400 LUX

I would like to take another brief interlude if you don't mind.
I'm becoming quite fond of these side chats we keep stumbling into. It has gotten to the point where I am actively thinking about topics we could talk about.

I've been thinking a lot about what kind of book I'd write if I wasn't so tied up in this shit. There is a grand vision I have of creating something entirely devoid of clichés. I want to write a horror novel where people don't make stupid choices or trip over objects that exist in another dimension. I want to write a young adult novel where the main character isn't chosen to save the entire universe from destruction even though they didn't know how to wipe their ass a day ago. I want to write a sci-fi novel where none of the characters are a deadbeat, alcoholic cop who stumbles into a large mystery that will alter life as we know it! I'd love to write a book where the villain doesn't grandstand enough for the hero to escape or the character we thought was dead show up at the last possible moment with some dumbass quip about how they cheated death and is always saving the hero's ass.

We are better than that!

It's impossible to avoid though. People are drawn to the easy and relatable. Sure, none of us are space pioneers or teenagers with the mission of saving the planet, but people have been indoctrinated with that sort of fiction for countless years that it's a hard pattern to break.

I believe though that people have the propensity to be challenged and experience something new. Evan has done that for me, if you are looking for a way for me to tie this back to the main point of this book.

I'm smart enough to know what I have written is not revolutionary; a single story never tends to change the mold of what already exists. But I do think that there are parts of this that are new to you. Maybe you have never read something where the main character is gay. Maybe you have never read something where the main character makes a nauseating number of mistakes and isn't supposed to be the hero. Maybe you have never read something where the writer breaks the fourth wall so many—likely too many—times. Maybe you don't actually care about anything I will try to convince you of. That's fine by me.

Reading is the most personal form of entertainment in my opinion. We go to theaters to watch movies. We go to venues to listen to our favorite artists. We go to forums and the water cooler to discuss the holy shit moments from last night's episode of *that* show. Most times though, we are alone when we read. We are in a quiet room, bundled under a blanket, and trying to escape the noise of the world around us. We are able to bury ourselves deep into the life of someone who doesn't even exist by reading a continuous flow of words on page after page after page.

Incredible!

That sounds so boring, but, yet, it manages to be better than Thanksgiving dinner.

I want someone to be entrenched by what I wrote and the story I have shared. I'm selfish, so fucking selfish.

I hope I get to write all those stories I have dreams of, but I don't think I'll get the chance to. Life has this problem of always getting in the way. Pretty cliché, right?

Two other things I wanted to mention before we dive into the Cape Cod trip.

Firstly, are you the slightest bit curious what Faceless Nameless texted me a few chapters back? If you were, I hate to disappoint you, but his text was nothing worthwhile. It was a ramble about a scenario he found himself in with [REDACTED] and wanted to know what the standard protocol was. So yeah, he essentially asked me a work question. I was annoyed because I'm not customer service and he texted me on a Saturday night. Bitch, I work Monday–Friday. The weekend is for drinking and sticking my hand in my pants for long periods of time, not questions related to work.

Because I am a loser and still repressing the misplaced love I have for him, I responded. It was a dutiful response that thoroughly answered his question. Do you know the text I got after that?

Nothing.

So fuck him. Fuck his entire existence. Fuck his idea that he can waltz in and out of someone's life without a care. Fuck me for ever meeting him, caring about him, or any of the other dumb shit I did related to him.

Fuck you Allen. You will get no more screen time from this point forward because I have given you more time than you ever deserved.

On a lighter note, the second thing to mention was that I wanted to spell out a word you have likely never seen on paper before.

You ready?

I don't think you are, but let's do it anyways.

C-O-C-K-A-M-A-M-I-E.

What a word! Ask your grandma about it some time since no one has uttered it in fifty-three years.

I don't know if we will sync up like this again before the end of the book. Given the trajectory of where things will start heading, it may not fit the narrative too well for me to be interjecting.

I'll probably do it anyways because I intend to be intrusive and a major inconvenience to you until the bitter end.

But if I don't, see you in the epilogue!

# twenty-eight

## WAKE ME

Sequels are rarely better than the original. They tend to be a retread of what was previously done with minor variations.

The same could be said for my return to Provincetown.

I boarded a plane in DAL and flew up to BOS without incident. My head bobbed against the window with each bump of the flight, which didn't help me sleep much. I'd heard horror stories of people who contracted infections from leaning up against the windows, but that never stopped me from living with no regard to my health.

I lingered around Logan International Airport. The terminal with all of the [REDACTED] flights was sectioned off to a portion that required several escalators and taking a long stroll underground. My ferry over to the island was still a few hours away, so there was no rush to get to the dock.

Watching people at the airport was an odd juxtaposition. You were in a public setting, but many times it felt like you were intruding on private situations. People sat stretched out across several seats, their legs splayed on luggage, and stuffing their faces with a quick meal before moving onto the next flight. Others would carry out conversations on the phone that moved into uncomfortable territory for those who sat nearby. Nobody wanted to hear about the boil on your back or how Tilda cheated on her third husband with the governor of Utah. You'd see folks having a mental breakdown when a flight was delayed, or if they were running late. People were open about their feelings at the airport because most had a destination in mind and an important reason to be going there.

Needless to say, Logan was no different.

After finding a spot at a gate where a flight had just departed, I put my headphones back on and quietly observed my surroundings.

People watching was an art and being subtle was an extremely important aspect. Stare too long and someone will stop what they were doing, but to not stare at all would be doing that person a disservice by not paying attention to the odd thing they were partaking in.

For example, there was a middle-aged man with no distinctive features who was two rows away from me. He was occupied with his phone and held it close to his face, almost to the point where his nose was touching the screen. The man was so absorbed that he didn't notice how every thirty seconds his hand drifted up to his face. He would extend a finger and insert it deep into his nose, probe for a second, and absentmindedly stare at it. Unimpressed with the results, he would flick it off in the direction of the poor lady sitting behind him. I watched him repeat this process several times until his rational side kicked in. He quickly removed the finger lodged in his nostril and glanced around to see if anyone was looking. I had been but looked away sharply before we made eye contact.

Another person, sitting closer to me, was munching on some fast food and left half a sandwich on the floor. They gathered up their stuff and walked away without a care for the mess they left behind.

Someone else was up at the ticket counter bitching at one of the agents about how their boarding position wasn't automatically upgraded even though they were an Obsidian-Gold Tier Third Cousin Twice Removed Newly Baptized rewards member. The agent wasn't impressed and pressed a button that catapulted the passenger through the air where they landed with a loud thud against the wall near the bathroom.

"Reminder to all passengers," the agent said over the intercom, "we will no longer upgrade Obsidian-Gold Tier Third Cousin Twice Removed Newly Baptized rewards members. We will only upgrade those who are Bronze-Iron Tier Partridge in a Pear Tree with Four Cacti rewards members to first class. Thank you for your understanding! Also, the flight to El Dorado has been delayed eighteen hours so you fuckers better start walking." The intercom crackled as she disconnected. Several looks of confusion passed between people sitting by me. A few others began packing up their belongings with a dejected look.

For the record, the airline whose flight was delayed rhymed with Smelta. You know what they say: the one who Smelta, Delta.

I looked down at my watch and was shocked to see the time wasn't midnight. That was a pleasant change. Instead, it told me to get my ass to the ferry.

I obeyed the command and made my way through the underground labyrinth. Once outside, I called an Uber and was quickly scooped up. No pleasantries were exchanged between us as he was focused on maneuvering around the growing crowd forming on various streets throughout the city.

Another day, another protest. Someone had to fight for the future.

He kicked me out of the car on a side street and I walked the last two blocks to the pier. I located the fast ferry that would be taking me over to Provincetown.

I shouldn't have dawdled at the airport because the line to get on the ferry extended for a quarter mile in an orderly fashion. Each person I passed was more attractive than the one before. Perfectly tanned with short shorts and tank tops that worked hard to show that bulging boobies was the new normal apparently. I recalled that Xander told me I would be coming up at the start of Twink Week.

Fuck.

He always complained how Twink Week was a conglomeration of all the New York City models who lived their lives at the gym just for this specific week. The hotels and houses would be packed with orgies of unprotected sex and rampant drug use. They would leave shitty tips at the restaurants where they would have four mimosas before 9 a.m. Dick Dock would be packed at sunset when anonymity ruled the beaches.

I took my place at the back of the line. I was dressed in jeans and a T-shirt. I looked like a nun compared to everyone else around me. The wind would occasionally pick up and push my shirt against my bulging stomach. I put my arms in front of me to cover up the imperfection.

I shouldn't have cared. I had a boyfriend and didn't need approval from anyone in that line or in Provincetown, but to act like I wouldn't have wanted attention would be like saying the Great Depression was pretty great and an enjoyable time for all involved.

So I did care. Sue me. I didn't plan the trip again to take another stab at finding an inconsequential hook up I'd instantly regret. I went to escape the tedium of Dallas and because I missed the beach. I was always trying to escape.

*Liar, cheater.*

My brain didn't talk much anymore except to remind me of the words I was starting to forget.

I was lost in thought when the line began to move. We all shuffled toward the ramp where the echoing sound of luggage being dragged across the metal slats could be heard.

By the time I made it onboard, the luggage compartments at the front of the ferry were overflowing. One of the workers was pointing us toward the main cabin. I walked in and saw all the luggage was being stuffed there. Stacks were leaning haphazardly toward the twinks who were lounging in the seats. If one of the bags fell, they would have been flattened beyond recognition.

I tossed my rolling bag into the pile. I'd sort it out later when we docked in Provincetown. I spotted a seat in the middle of a row and excused my way through. I sat down, knew no one would bother to engage in conversation with me, and put my headphones back on. I cranked up the music to avoid hearing the constant announcements over the intercom and the chatter of conversation from every direction.

I looked around the ferry. People were packed in tighter than the luggage. They were standing in aisles, sitting on laps, and trying to take up as little space as possible to save room for friends. It was bizarre to be surrounded by so many people and not care for any of them. I imagined that many were successful in their careers and life endeavors and likely nice people, but they all just looked like a bunch of twats. You could attribute it to jealousy on my part.

I passed the time by listening to the same expanding playlist I had been building on Spotify since college. There was no limit to how many times I could listen to "When You Were Young" by *The Killers*. It was timeless.

An hour and a half later, we slowly pulled up to the dock on the edge of town. We began the unloading process without much fanfare. I managed to dig my bag from the pile and proceeded to wait in line. It took another fifteen minutes to make it off the ferry. Everyone scattered like cockroaches toward the main thoroughfare of town.

I followed the same path I took a year earlier. Xander was working at the restaurant and told me to meet him there.

One of the pleasant things about a small beach town is that most of it stays the same. I passed by the familiar trinket shops and divots in the street. I saw the same houses with the same sun-bleached residents smoking cigarettes on the patio. I waved over at them. Just kidding, I'm not a fucking weirdo who actually engages with strangers.

The walk grew quieter the further away I got from the epicenter. I passed by Xander's house. While it would have been easier to drop off my stuff before heading to the restaurant, that would have required common sense on my part. Instead, I continued my walk down the hill.

I made it to the restaurant a short time later. I could hear the sounds of conversations and plates clanking together through the open windows. It seemed moderately packed for an early afternoon.

The breeze from the water rustled my hair in various directions. I needed to do something with the mess I had.

Through the door I saw a sticklike creature stalking behind the bar.

Xander.

I crossed into the restaurant, past the hostess, and straight to him. There was only one other patron sitting on one of the stools. He looked vaguely familiar. I took a seat three spots away from him.

Xander looked up from the drink he was making.

"Wha—whoa!—You made it!" he yelled. He walked around the bar and gave me a hug.

He looked the same as last year, so no sense in describing him again.

"Can I take your bags?" he asked.

"You can, but there is plenty of room here," I said, pointing to the space between me and the next seat.

The other guy at the bar looked over with a crooked smile. He quickly turned back to the television and wiped his mouth with a napkin.

"How have you been? Actually . . . do you want a drink? That's the more important question," Xander said.

"A drink would be great. Maybe a Long Island? We have plenty of time to catch up later, so I don't want to bug you too much now if you are busy."

He gestured to the bar and entire restaurant. "Does it look crowded?"

"I mean . . . no," I said after looking around.

"Exactly. Let me make your drink and grab you a food menu."

Xander scurried off to complete the tasks at hand; I turned my attention to the television propped in the corner.

"Welcome to the 5 o'clock news at 3 o'clock. I'm Generic Blonde Anchor and this is Gross Old Man. Our top story tonight: the President did what? After a series of bizarre Myspace posts, critics and alligators alike are calling for an explanation to the confusion that has spread across the country. Messages seen here—from AOL chatrooms—show the growing concern with the President's posts. User MyFatBonerLeansLeft wrote 'We need a Prez who will stand up 2 thos bullies out on Venus. There's a reason it rhymes with Penis! It's because they are a bunch o' puszies!' Well said. He sounds right leaning to me. Ha! Ha! Gross Old man, any thoughts? No, okay. Please continue to smile creepily into the camera you disgusting fuck. He sexually assaulted me more times than Chris Brown beat up women, but no one seems to mind. We all know that the only reason anyone watches this drivel is because of my tits and that half the population has the brain capacity of roadkill. You hear that, you dumb cretins! I can say whatever the fuck I want, and you'll still watch because you are fucking stupid.

"Anyways . . .

"Let's focus our attention to another story. Earlier today, there was a mass shooting in which twelve thousand people were killed. We will not miss any of them. We will be sure to keep you updated on the one taking place tomorrow. Rumor has it that at least fifty thousand are expected to die in what many are already calling an 'unprecedented act of violence only eclipsed by the mass shootings that took place on January 4, January 18, February 1, February 8-15, March 3, March 5, March 21, April 12, April 27, May 1–29, June 27, and June 28 of this year.'

"Back to our main story. We have just received breaking news that the President has just sent a carrier pigeon to every citizen to inform them that he expects each to contribute to the force field being built around the country to protect the citizens from any mosquitoes entering in through the air. Trying times indeed! We hope you will contribute the money you don't have to this noble cause because I certainly don't intend to even though I have enough fuck you money to fuck everyone in all of North America! Twice!

"We will be right back with more!"

The screen cut away right as the Generic Blonde Anchor's wig slid off, exposing the wires attached to her head.

Xander came back with the food menu. "Now for the drink!" He scurried off to the other end of the bar.

"Hey," I called over to the guy at the bar. "Do you mind changing the channel?" I motioned to the remote laying in front of him. The television droned on with a commercial about Toilet Water, America's favorite lite beer.

It then transitioned to a commercial about a new drug on the market called Pill. Flashes of happy, lifeless people propelled across the screen to show the miraculous wonders of Pill. Side effects included death, hypertension, limb loss, stubbed toes, death, fever, headaches, chills, death, cold sores, dry scalp, itchy palms, sweaty knees, death, anal discharge, eye pus, boogers, cancer, brain lesions, long-term memory loss, and death. The voiceover went at blazing speed, but I think I caught them all. The upbeat commercial ended with a funeral and this fun jingle: *We makes lots of money because you spend yours at will / Thanks so much for being a slave to our Pill!*

"Sure," he finally said, wiping his mouth once again. The bowl in front of him looked like it had clam chowder in it.

He hit the remote and flicked to the next channel. "Our top story tonight: the President said what?"

"Can you find another one?" I asked.

"Sure," he said. The drool began to pour from his mouth. "Sorry," he chuckled. "The news always gets me going. I tend to vomit, but I still enjoy it. Sometimes the bullshit can be too much, ya know? You wonder how people could forget to use their own brain."

I nodded in disbelief and recalled how I knew the man. He was the same one from the bar a year earlier that was puking. People never changed.

He clicked the remote once more. ". . . I'm Generic Blonder Anchor . . ."

Then again. ". . . March 21, April 12, April 27 . . ."

Again. ". . . fuck everyone in all of North America . . ."

Again. ". . . fuck everyone in all of North America . . ."

Again. ". . . fuck everyone in all of North America . . ."

"ENOUGH!" I shouted and slammed my fists against the bar. People from the beach a couple hundred feet away stared back at me through the window, likely wondering what the disturbance was about. Pigeons were swooping down toward them.

I took a breath and composed myself. "Um, could you find a channel that doesn't have the news on it?" I suggested.

"No can do, pal. It's the only channels we get out here. All news, all the time! We are so informed. Isn't it great?" he asked, dry heaving into the bowl that clearly didn't have clam chowder in it.

He continued to flip through each channel to show me he wasn't lying. The same news story dominated the headline with the same exact wording and tone and robotic anchors.

I turned away from the man and the television, unable to decipher what had just happened.

Xander set down the drink in front of me.

"Took you long enough. Actually, can you give me your keys? I'm not feeling so well, and I want to take my stuff to your house."

Brief confusion passed through Xander's face, but he dug into his pocket and handed over the keys. "I still have a few hours left here. Meet you at the house later?"

"Yeah. Sure. I'll be there."

He turned his attention away from me. "Goddammit Ross! How many times have I told you not to put on the 5 o'clock news?"

"But—but it's not even 5 o'clock . . ."

The sound drifted away as I shuffled to the door.

I was met with intense sunlight and squinted until my eyes adjusted.

I went back the direction I came, thinking how no one would ever believe that happened. Sometimes reality is stranger than the lies I come up with.

## twenty-nine

## PANTOMIME

I dragged my bag up the steps to the house and had to take a second to catch my breath.

I fumbled for the keys and eventually unlocked the door.

It swung inward to reveal the dated kitchen. Dishes were stacked in various places and two bags of chips lay opened on the kitchen table. I crossed into the living room, which is where I would be staying again.

Nothing had changed. That was becoming the overarching theme of my life.

The couch was still the ugly green color. The floor dipped in several places to simulate a lazy rollercoaster. The air was stale and sticky from the lack of central AC.

I dropped my things near the futon and went to the bathroom to take a shower. I knew Xander wouldn't mind. I pulled off my shirt and caught a glimpse of myself in the mirror. I'd lost a few pounds in anticipation of the trip, but I still had a gut that protruded out. My chest was bare because no one liked a hairy chest, contrary to what Evan said. I stepped closer to the mirror. The bags under my eyes never seemed to disappear anymore and the sagging of my left eyelid continued to get worse. I was quickly crossing into Forest Whitaker territory. My hair was a jumbled mess.

I stepped into the shower and stayed in there for a long time. I continued to move the valve until the water was scalding. It hurt, but I grew accustomed to the slight throb that settled in after a minute or two. Pain didn't bother me as much anymore.

Afterward, I returned to the futon and finished writing the last chapter of the book. I had an epiphany in the shower and was granted the gift of sight.

Xander trudged into the house several hours later. The sun had just ducked behind the nearby houses, turning the room darker by the minute.

"Howdy partner," I said as he stepped into the living room.

He threw himself down onto the couch. "What's up?"

"Just finishing up something." At that point, the writing was completed. Sure, I needed to edit the unliving shit out of that monstrosity and figure out how to format it in a digestible way, but it was DONE! I never knew how lonely it would feel to finish the writing and not have anyone to tell about the accomplishment. Writing was a solitary job, especially when you're an amateur. *At least you're here.*

I closed the laptop and stared over at him. "How was the rest of your indentured servitude?"

"Made good money. It really picked up after you left. Are you feeling better?"

"Yeah." *I never felt unwell to begin with. I just needed to escape from the oddities that were there.*

"Perfect. Let me shower and then we can grab dinner."

Xander got off the couch and disappeared around the corner. I heard his footsteps on the stairs and down the hallway to his room. Several minutes later he reemerged and went into the bathroom.

An hour later, we were settled into a seat at a restaurant on the west side of town. It was past the main intersection where the ferry dropped me off and away from the horde of people mingled in the area.

"What's your recommendation?" I asked as I flipped through the menu.

"I've only been here a couple times. I don't get out much."

"Even when Colby comes to visit?" Colby was Xander's boyfriend.

"I work the same amount when he's here. The only quality time we get is when I go down to Boston."

"Are you still thinking of moving in together after the summer?"

(Let me pause for a second. You may be wondering how we moved past the debacle of last summer when I was a raging dick. It may seem like there were no repercussions from my actions. You would be correct in that assumption because, contrary to popular belief, not everyone holds unreasonably long grudges. In Xander's case, I apologized, and we went a long while without speaking (likely due to him being busy), but the next time we did everything was fine. It's this thing called maturity and healthy relationships tend to be built on the concept. Obviously, my behavior was poor, but it was acknowledged and moved past. I just wanted to clue you in as to why you would not be hearing any dramatic conclusion to that thread.)

He laughed from across the table. "I am still planning on moving to Boston but definitely not moving in with him. His apartment is a total mess and his roommates keep multiplying. I'm looking for something quieter."

"Do you see that as a warning sign for the relationship?" I was grasping at straws in a futile attempt to keep the conversation going.

"Nope." Well, that answer's that.

Not wanting to press the issue further, I steered our chat to hear about the details of his move to Boston—which part he wanted to live in, what sort of job he wanted to get, and whether he would be taking trips back to Provincetown. I won't bog you down with the details of just another conversation.

You come to realize after twenty-five years of questionable existence that not much exciting happens. You wake up, drive yourself into the same dull job surrounded by the same predictable people, and come back home to complete the same routine before you head to bed. The days are filled with meaningless conversations that do nothing to advance the plot of your life. You live for the days when something outside the norm happens and gives you an ounce of hope that life can actually be different.

We exited the restaurant an hour later. Xander entertained the idea of taking me to a bar, but quickly remembered he had an early call the next morning for work and nixed the plan before it ever took flight.

On our casual stroll back home, we spotted two men walking in front of us. While that was not an uncommon sight in Provincetown, the fact that people were stopping and staring was. The sea of people seemed to part as they neared, which opened up the path for us to continue walking behind.

"Do you get a lot of famous people that come up here?" I asked.

"Didn't I tell you about the time I smoked a cigarette with Emma Roberts?"

"I don't recall."

"Yeah, I was bartending at a party for that guy," he pointed to the stranger on the left in front of us, "and went to grab a cigarette. Out walks Emma

Roberts and we chilled outside for a bit. She was nice. Also, do you really not know who is walking in front of us?" he said with a distinct lack of care.

"I am not the best with the back of people's heads. Not one of my talents. I prefer the front most times."

"It's Ryan Murphy," he said flatly as if they were best friends.

"No way! Do you think he would be offended if I walked up and told him I could write a better season of *American Horror Story* than he has in the last five years?"

He looked over at me. "Don't you dare."

"Or what? Do you honestly think I would do that?"

"It wouldn't be the dumbest thing you've ever done so I wouldn't put it past you."

We continued walking as I contemplated what he could be referring to. My mind flashed to an instant during my trip to visit him in Kansas City. I did something so embarrassing, so stupid, so idiotic that I don't even want to recap it for you, which is saying a lot since I told you about that nasty threesome I had. I've had some low points, but that was the grand poohbah of them all.

Ryan Murphy and his pal picked up their pace. A pile of papers swung in his right hand as he waved around his left in a way that suggested he was trying to put a killing curse on his buddy.

"Sadly, I know exactly what you are referring to," I said with slight shame.

"It's okay. No one expects much out of you," Xander said.

I picked up my pace and moved past Xander. "Don't yo—" he called out before giving up the rest.

I closed the gap between me and Mr. Murphy.

"Excuse me, are you Ryan Murphy?"

"Fuck off," he said with a flick of his hand. He thought I was a fan. How foolish.

"Gladly, but I wanted to tell you I could write a better season of *American Horror Story* than you ever have. I'm not sure you understand the basic concept of plot and making anything seem believable. Musical numbers and covers of forgotten pop songs are never the answer to making your characters entertaining."

"Fuck off."

I was beginning to think they were the only words he knew.

"Just thought you should know—"

"Fuck off."

"Are those the only words—"

"Eat my dick."

"Great! We're making progress. Top notch dialogue we are having here. Be sure to include this in episode five when everything will inevitably just crumble into itself."

"Eat his dick too," he suggested, pointing to his silent companion.

"Tempting, but no thanks. I have enough diseases already and that man looks as if someone dipped him in honey mustard and threw him in the oven for thirty minutes at 350 degrees."

He stopped walking.

A crowd began to form around us like you'd see at a fight during recess. People were addicted to the drama that didn't include them.

"Do you know who I am!?" Mr. Murphy declared with a distinct lack of authority. He finally turned around to face me. He was about my height with a face sliced and injected more times than a Thanksgiving turkey.

"Obviously . . ." I said. I wasn't sure if it was a trick question.

"I have more money and power than you could ever dream of! I could fuck that guy over there," the pointed at a skinny dude with a face like a lemur, "and it would be the only accomplishment of his entire life." It was dark out, but I could see the lemur blushing. He likely wasn't used to the attention. I had read one time about how shy lemurs can be.

"You sound upset. Can I mention one last thing?"

"Fuck off."

"Back to that I see—"

At this point, Xander grabbed my arm and pulled me aside. Murphy and friend continued on, giving out their "Fuck off's" as if they were buy one get all of them for free.

"What the *fuck* is wrong with you?" Xander hissed. Not literally, but more in a metaphorical sense because he was upset. If he had actually hissed, I probably wouldn't have understood what he said considering I am not a Parseltongue.

"I just wanted to prove that I can constantly do dumb things. It's my life's work," I said cheerfully.

"I can't stand your existence. It's nauseating."

The rocks scattering under my dragging feet brought me back to reality.
"You still here?"

"I was just daydreaming. Sometimes my imagination goes off the deep end. The weird part is that I have a hard time remembering what's real or not." I feel like I had read somewhere about the shyness of lemurs.

"Fascinating."

Once we were back at the house, Xander went to bed. I pulled out my laptop and sat in concentration trying to think of titles for my chapters with my never-ending Spotify playlist being the source of inspiration.

✦

I returned to the spot that practically set my whole life in motion a year earlier.

The walk was the same. I took the direct path down the crowded street that soon fizzled out to nothing more than a few stragglers that occasionally passed by. My feet ached by the end of the trek. The flip flops provided less support than the dad that left for milk and never came back.

The beach wasn't as packed as last time since it seemed like everyone was over at the nearby hotel pool. The hotel was *the* place to have raging orgies. I heard some people refer to it as 23inMe Hotel, as in they were hoping to get a good variety of DNA samples inside of them by the end of their stay.

I sat on the beach for a bit. The pathetic waves calmly crashed onto the shore. Umbrellas were set up in various spots to shield the inhabitants from the sun.

*Fuck. I didn't put sunscreen on again!*

I kept my shirt on to avoid any new damage. The tan line from the year prior had finally diminished to be faintly noticeable.

I wanted there to be some great awakening or level of enlightenment but lightening hardly ever strikes twice.

Conceding that the charm of the place wasn't as grand as the year before, I pulled together my belongings and left for the jetty.

The man-made jetty stretched for a mile and connected to the fishhook that curled back around to the south of the island. Last year, I only walked halfway. I intended to go all the way this time and explore what was on the other side.

The traffic was light as I hopped from one massive slab of rock to the next. I realized the flip flops were just a hindrance so off they came.

The few people I did pass by barely looked in my direction. They were focused on the task at hand. One slip would result in a nasty fall into the jagged rocks on either side. It wasn't a dangerous walk by any means if you were paying attention.

It took me the better part of an hour to reach the end of the jetty. It faded out into sand and scraggly bushes. The sand was hot under my feet, so back on the flip flops went. Each step sent a wave of sand that sprayed out behind me in every direction.

I followed the people who were ahead of me over the small hill. At the top, the island opened up into a moderate strip of more sand and shrubs.

I crested over tiny mounds of sand and heard the sound of heavier waves lapping against the shore. I saw the beach. More dots were stretched out along the expanse of space. Many were alone; a few were clustered together with friends or family.

I staked my claim and fell back against the towel that laid on top of the sand. I stared up at the sky. It was devoid of any clouds, no shade from the sun that day.

It didn't take long to realize the walk wasn't worth the time. It was just another normal beach.

*Would you just shut the fuck up and enjoy something? You got a problem with everything. Take a fucking break for once.*

Why did the beach have to be anything special? Couldn't it just be a beach? Couldn't it just be a way to pass the time while Xander was at work? Why did I feel the constant need to always be doing something?

They were questions I didn't have answers for.

In an effort to distract myself, I pulled out my phone and noticed a new email had come through. Surprisingly good service for being somewhat far away from town.

It was from Evan. The subject line read **just so you know**.

Ominous.

There was nothing inside the body of the email except for an attachment. My mind raced. It would definitely be a set of photos chronicling my infidelity. He decided to hire a private investigator because I was acting stranger than normal lately. It would have been an insane thing for him to do, but my brain clung to the idea like a child to their favorite toy.

I opened up the attachment.

If I had been paying attention instead of jumping to irrational conclusions, I would have noticed it was a Word document he sent, not pictures.

It was a page long, single spaced with breaks in between each paragraph. It looked something like this:

> I never had a home growing up.
>
> With each divorce or job change, my mom and I would be off to somewhere new. By my count, I lived in nine different states by the time I went to college. I learned to not get attached since things seemed to fall away easily. I rarely had a group of friends I was proud of. I never even bothered to learn the names of the streets around me or where the nearest movie theater was.
>
> I continued this trend after college. Sure, it was great to be settled in one location for nearly five years, but with that came the heartbreak of my relationship with Kieran. To watch something that felt so certain crumble away was deeply unsettling. In the aftermath of that, sometimes I'd wake up in the middle of the night with nightmares about what was. Other times I'd wake up alone and wonder about what was to come. I have always been encumbered with worry and doubt and all those other emotions we like to pretend don't impact us but keep us in a constant state of fear.
>
> You know I left South Carolina to move to Michigan for my first job out of grad school. The feeling of breaking out on my own and away from that old life was indescribable. But it didn't last. The job became tedious and the thought of moving up within the company seemed like a false hope.
>
> So I did the only thing I knew and found myself in Dallas. I told myself this was it, this would be where I would figure it out. I'd have a great job and makes lots of money and buy a house I could fix up to call my own.
> Instead I got something better. I found you.
>
> I know you hate when I get sappy, but I don't think you understand. You were never part of the equation. I was quickly becoming content with living my life and figuring out the whole romantic piece in my 30s. Love could wait since it had scorned me just enough times to make me scared.

```
And to be honest, you terrify me. I still don't know
on some days whether you love me or just passing the
time.

I'm worried I am on the cusp of another change. One
that would take me away from Dallas. Away from you.
It's the only thing I know. Because right now, I don't
know if this relationship will carry far into the
future. I want it to work though.

I desperately want to find my home.

-Evan
```

I was speechless, not that there was anyone around I would run up and discuss the letter with, but I was left without clear comprehension of what was going on. I knew he was unsure about us sometimes, but to hear it stated without buffers was tough.

I tried to read it again, but my eyes kept darting around the screen, and I had trouble ingesting any of the information.

I sat up, still holding the phone in my hand, and stared out into the ocean. It was nowhere near as blue as the sky. It was the East Coast after all.

To avoid a spiral, I took my headphones out, quickly connected the Bluetooth, and navigated to Spotify. I played the first song that came up. I stood up, shook off my towel, and started back to the jetty. I needed to keep moving to outrun any chance of an implosion, any chance of wondering more about where Evan would go.

✦

That night, Xander and I went out to one of his favorite bars on the west side of town. The basement would be packed with twinks looking for dick. We elected to stay upstairs.

He bought the first round and we settled onto a bench outside on the porch. He went into detail about his day and rattled off the names of multiple coworkers I had never met before. I nodded and listened and interrupted when it felt necessary.

I was still thinking about the email though. What a whiplash that was from the rest of the trip so far. I had texted Evan once I got back to the house and let him know I read it. His response was brief and just said we can talk about it more when I was back in Dallas. I had a million questions for him, but one kept circulating in my head. Why now? Why would he send that to me while

I was on vacation? (I'm sure you are thinking *But Vin, you just wrote out two questions!* As a friend of mine one said, fuck off.) Maybe he was going through the same thing I did when he was at EDC. Maybe he didn't know how to vocalize the words or afraid if he did I would get upset. Regardless of the answer, I felt like a failure. There would be a way to fix it though. There had to be.

My internal struggle was cut short when I noticed the trio sitting in the corner to our left.

There was an obese man sitting on a motorized scooter with hardly recognizable features due to the excess that sagged off him. The man in the fedora beside him was of similar size and wearing a pair of glasses that constantly slipped down the bridge of his nose. The third guy, wearing a skirt, wasn't as heavy but was still traveling full speed toward Type II Diabetes. He was on top of Scooter, making out with him passionately. Skirt's ass stuck out far enough for Glasses to have his hand far up it. They continued in this manner without a care.

"Xander," I said, quite unsure of myself. "Do you see that guy getting fisted over there?"

He turned lazily to his left. "Oh . . . yeah. That's Fred Fisty. He is a local around here who's been known to get used like a sock puppet."

"Are you fucking kidding me?" I asked in disbelief. "What is wrong with this place?"

"Don't kink shame," he scolded me.

"But . . . we, uh, we are out in public. There must be better places to do that."

A pleasurable noise radiated from my left. I didn't have to look over to understand that Fred was experiencing the full thrust of a fist being lodged in his ass. Above the sounds of the moans, I heard a distinct *pop* like when someone takes a lollipop out of their mouth.

Xander shrugged and took another sip of his drink. "You want another one?" he eventually said.

"Yes, but we need to go inside."

"Fine with me. I'll teach you to be more accepting. Don't worry," he said as he stood up.

The grunting and squishing sound faded as we reached the bar.

Xander ordered another round and insisted on paying. He always had a wad of cash with him after working and was quite generous with it. He slapped down a twenty and told the bartender to keep the change.

"I've come to realize that money never leaves this town. I spend it at the bar now and then Denny here will come down, grab a drink, and give it right back to me," he said.

I nodded in understanding. I concentrated on my drink, hoping that if I finished it fast enough, I'd forget about what happened.

When we left, I had a slight sway with each step. I looked up and saw how the stars burned brighter than the nothingness I was used to in Dallas.

# thirty

## EDGE OF DARKNESS

"Are you ever worried about being forgotten?"

Xander was rubbing sunscreen onto his legs. We were already at the beach. Any plebe knew you had to put on sunscreen at least fifteen minutes before exposure to the burning blob in the sky.

He looked over at me. "Your brain is constantly fucked up, isn't it?"

"Answer the question," I said, squinting over at him. My reflection was staring back at me through his sunglasses.

"You'll have to explain what you mean. Also, do you want some of this for the tattoo?" He shook the bottle near my face.

I snatched it and put a healthy amount on my forearm. I was guilty of not putting it on before going outside too.

"You better be careful with that," he continued. "It would be tragic if it faded."

"Tragic is a strong word but I understand the sentiment. Thanks." I handed the bottle back to him and he stuffed it back into his bag. "Anyways, what I mean is: Are you worried about how one day you'll be dead and there will potentially be no one here who will remember anything you did?"

"What—why? Never mind. I'll answer it, but I want you to note I think this question is stupid."

"Noted."

"I am not worried about being forgotten because I'd be dead. I doubt I'll be concerned about it, but that's a whole other topic entirely. And, I don't put too much care into making an impact. I'm just here to live and meet good people."

"Seems like a dull existence."

"Not everyone is meant to be in history books."

Without hesitation, I said, "I had a coworker that died. Back in January. To call it sudden would have been an understatement. He was there on a Tuesday and gone by Wednesday morning. I remember getting a call from my boss that night, which was extremely odd. I was drinking for some reason and very quickly tried to sober up when I saw the call. When I answered, his voice was real stoic as he relayed the news. I hung up from the call and sat in stunned silence. I asked the guy I was hanging with to leave. I didn't know my coworker well; I was new to the team and he was immensely shy. But he was so young. Like only a few years older than me. I hate to speculate but I think it was self-harm. People that young don't just die . . . Once you start down that path, you think about what you could have done differently to help them. Or even worse. What if it was something you did that drove them over the edge? That's a foolish thought . . . Anyways, I tell you this because after the tears and sadness washed away, he was forgotten. Now, six months later, no one talks about him anymore. It's like he never existed and was nothing more than a dot on a whiteboard that got erased with everything else. And that freaks me out. What would I leave behind if I died tomorrow? Who would talk about me six months after I was dead? What about a year? Fifty years? It would keep me awake at night if I was ever able to sleep to begin with."

Xander took a moment to digest it.

"I get it. I'm sorry for your loss. You need to understand you will likely be forgotten and that's okay. It won't happen right away but after enough time passes it certainly will. That doesn't lessen the things you did accomplish though."

"True. I can't help but think of the most outrageous things and fixate on them. Contemplating my life is not something I enjoy doing, especially when I'm on vacation."

"Why don't we talk about something not as depressing? How about politics?"

"Absolutely not."

"Religion?"

"No!"

"The War of 1812?"

"Xander . . ."

"The destruction of the Great Barrier Reef?"

"Try again."

"Let's talk about global warming and how people still don't believe in it."

"I'm depressed enough as is."

"You pick something then."

"Tell me about Dick Dock."

"Why? There's not really much to say about it."

"Then it'll be easy for you to tell me."

Okay—it's . . . it's just a dock under the bar that always has the afternoon parties. Remember that?"

I nodded.

"Once it gets dark out, the place gets flooded with strangers looking for sex. People will just scamper off into various places down there and start going at it."

"I want to go."

He gave me a concerned look.

"No," I continued. "Not like that at all. It's more of a morbid curiosity type of thing."

"Yeah, I get that. We can go, but it won't be what you expect. There is nothing glamorous about it. Anyways, what do you want to do for the rest of today?"

I told him.

We lounged on the beach for a while. Xander dragged me into the water several times. It was cold and only enjoyable once I got numb to the temperature. It reminded me of all those summer vacations to the beach where I loved to swim in the 55-degree water. I'd spend hours out there boogie boarding or sitting in the shallow water of low tide. I missed those days.

Eventually, we trudged back to the boat that would bring us back to town. The trip was a calm one after we made it past the rocks that were put in place to break up the big waves from reaching the coastline.

I sat with my head against the side railing, bobbing gently with each movement of the boat. Xander had his face buried in his bag.

The sun dried us out.

It was always odd to me how sitting out in the sun took away your will to live.

After we docked, we went in the direction of the grocery store to pick up a few supplies.

 ✦

"Are you sure you want *me* to do this?"

"Uh huh. You're gonna do great," I said.

"And what if I mess it up?"

"Buhl, it's not that big of a deal. You and I both know that whatever you do will be an improvement over how it is now."

"You're right," Xander said with a laugh.

The contents of the package spilled out across the table as he tore into it. He shook the package and a pamphlet of paper fell out. He looked at that first. Xander read for a while before he spoke. Once finished, he instructed me to take a seat at the table by slapping the chair several times.

"First, I need to take this bottle and do some shit with it. Then this bottle and do some shit with it. Then we wait. Then you wash your hair . . . and shit."

"You want me to shit after washing my hair?"

"If you need to, but I didn't see any mention of it in the guide," he said, consulting it one more time just to verify.

"Proceed then."

He did. There wasn't much to it. A ten-dollar hair color kit from the grocery store wasn't the most sophisticated thing in existence. After the two bottles were emptied and massaged onto my head, we waited twenty minutes for it to soak in. During this time, we discussed what I wanted to do for my last night in Provincetown. (Most of the week passed since I received the email from Evan. None of it was overly exciting.) I was indifferent to what we should do, so he took charge and determined we would grab dinner and drinks at a small place down the road from him.

Once the twenty minutes were up, I stuck my head into the shower and washed out the excess color. Water, tinted with black, circled around the drain before disappearing down it.

I grabbed a towel from the hook and dried my head, leaving behind numerous stains that I apologized for. Xander didn't mind.

"Oh. That looks great! I like it!" he said after I tossed the towel aside.

"I hope you're not just saying that because I have to go home and live with it."

"I'm not. I'm proud of my work," he said. "Take a look," pointing over to the mirror.

I did. It looked better and more natural than the dark blonde/orange color I dyed it a few months ago. The black matched well with my new tan. I always felt dread after making a change—the tattoo, my hair, trying a new face wash—because I was paranoid what others would say or think. Nothing new there, I suppose.

"Thanks Xander. I appreciate your commitment in helping me not look like a complete disaster."

"Oh fuck off. You know you're hot."

"Maybe I watch too much porn but I'm a solid two point three out of ten. In Dallas, you could knock off another point since they are so judgmental."

"You act like you don't have a boyfriend who probably doesn't care how you look at this point."

"Oddly enough, I forget sometimes that I do."

"We need to work on your confidence."

"No. I need to work on this," I lifted up my shirt and flashed my stomach. "I've been trying. Going on vacation is always tough but I'm sure I'll get back into it when I get home. Just another attempt to get myself better."

"You talk about getting better a lot."

"Not as much as I used to. You don't know the half of it. I've moved onto bigger and brighter things."

"Like what?"

"Fuck if I know," I said with a shrug. "Maybe I'll figure it out one day though."

✦

We found ourselves seated at the restaurant bar and, naturally, Xander knew every other person who walked in. He called them darling or honey and they'd have outlandish conversations that lasted no more than a minute and always ended with the promise they would catch up soon. It was exhausting to watch, so I imagine it was even more tedious for him. The constant pressure to always be on, to always be in networking mode or exude a friendly demeanor. In a place like Provincetown, you never knew who would sit down next to you and the potential influence and wealth they had so it was vital to always be flawless.

We were halfway through our second drink and devouring our food when a man plopped himself next to me. He was dressed in slacks and a button-down tucked in. He looked way nicer than either of us.

Xander noticed the new visitor. "Oh. Hi Fred!"

"Girl, how many times do I have to tell you not to call me Fred? I only go by that when I have the skirt on," he said with a whisper.

"What is your actual name then?" I asked.

"Edgar Poe."

"Don't tell me your midd—"

"It is."

"Get off it. Your name isn't actually Edgar Allen Poe."

"My parents saw an opportunity and took advantage of it . . . And what's your name?" he asked.

"I'm Vin."

"Visiting, I presume?"

"Correct. It's my last night."

"What a shame. A cute boy like you would be fun to play around with. It's a pleasure to meet you."

I shifted in my seat and glanced over at Xander. He was on his phone, completely checked out of the conversation. I think he was bitter that he knew who Fred—Edgar Allen Poe—was but he likely had no idea who Xander was. That can be the downside of living in a place like Provincetown—people don't actually care about you.

(Also, I am so immensely tired of running into the name ALLEN. I mentioned the place ALLENtown a couple of times. Then there is the suburb of Dallas called ALLEN. Don't get me started on ALLEN wrenches! All it took was one banana, a Milky Way bar, and a lubed-up ALLEN wrench to cause a terrible night. I definitely do not recommend. Anyways, the name is like a stalker that watches you from outside your window while you binge Netflix and stuff cheese doodles in your face hole. I've concluded that ALLEN is a terrible name and I've decided if I run across someone with that name again, I will just switch it up. I will call them NELLA or LENLA or LLANE or ELALN or some other variation. I still have an attachment issue when it comes to the original FACELESS NAMELESS. I can't stop thinking about him even though

I promised you chapters ago I was done. But keep in mind why I can't stop thinking about him: PEOPLE DON'T CHANGE. I won't say it anymore once you finally get it drilled into your skull. It's pathetic but let me stop on this topic to avoid falling too much down the hate hole.)

I disregarded Edgar's comment and asked, "Do you live in town?"

"During the summer, yes. For the rest of the year I'm just a frequent visitor. My parents own a few houses here and I stay at one of them—perks of being an only child."

"What do you do for a living?"

"Not much. When I do actually work, I sell water."

"You sell water?" I said slowly.

"Did I stutter? Yes. I sell water. And let me tell you," he leaned in closer, "it's the biggest fucking scam out there."

"How so?"

"Do you promise not to tell anyone?"

I looked around. "It's not like I know anyone here and to be frank I'll likely forget this conversation before my plane takes off tomorrow."

"You don't have to be a dick about it," he said with minor frustration. "Anyways," composing himself again, "all my company does is scoop up water from the river out behind our warehouse and run it through one purifier. We then bottle it up and charge you ten times what we should because we slap a label on there saying how it's sourced from freshwater springs and other bullshit information. We are essentially giving you rainwater mixed with some sewage and a little bit of harmful bacteria—not enough to seriously hurt anyone though."

"How could you possibly get away with that?"

"Because the government doesn't give a shit about you and people aren't smart enough to look into the products they buy, which makes my job of selling super easy."

"Why would you possibly want to be a part of that?"

"I love money."

"But not as much as getting fisted, huh?"

"Honey, you got me there, I love to get fisted. Have you ever tried it before?"

"Can't say I have."

"You're missing out." He grabbed his drink and took a long, sultry sip while staring over at me. It was the sort of look you'd see in a crappy movie where the female lead would lock eyes with the hot guy at the other end of the bar and then the next shot is them going at it.

In this reality, the look he gave me was disgusting and we would never be going at it.

"I'm not missing out on anything."

"Are you sure?" he asked seductively.

"Are you fucking kidding me? You understand I have no interest in you, right?"

"I mean . . ." he said, taken aback. "I'm just trying to talk. Relax."

"See, that's the convenient response people like you always give. You always try to throw it back on the other person and make them feel stupid. You are a gross, old twat that wanders around this town looking for your next victim. You seduce them with your money because you could never do it with your looks. Most times though, I'm sure you have to settle for the geriatrics like I saw you with the other night."

"Fuck you."

"You hear that, Xander," turning toward him, "Edgar here is just trying to fuck. How foolish of me to think someone would just want to have a conversation."

"That's enough Vin," Xander said sternly.

"Fine." I turned back to Edgar. "It was a pleasure talking to you and I mean that insincerely."

Edgar did not respond and just sat in his seat with his face pointed downward into his phone. The full drink in front of him quickly disappeared. He slapped down a twenty and scurried out the door.

"What is wrong with you?" Xander asked.

"I was just being honest with him."

"Do you always have to be such a fucking prick?"

"How is any of this my fault? I didn't want to come to get dinner and get hit on by a complete stranger."

"It's Provincetown. Everyone is gay, and everyone is like that. Get over it."

"That seems like a terrible generalization, but I'll take your word for it since I'm an awful person."

"Just stop. I didn't say you were a terrible person. Why do you always have to spin everything in a negative way? I am really trying to enjoy spending time with you, but you wear me down. Always so pessimistic. I find it hard to imagine you actually have a shred of happiness. I don't know how your boyfriend puts up with it. I would have broken up with you a long time ago—"

I slid out from the chair and headed for the door. I heard Xander ask where I was going and say something about how I was always running away from my problems.

I didn't turn back.

Outside, the breeze rushed off the water, making it a pleasant night. I walked west. About a block and a half away from the bar, I nearly ran into someone who was walking like a zombie and staring intently into a bright screen.

"I'm sorry. I wasn't paying attention." I was, but I only seemed to be apologetic in the wrong moments.

"It's okay," the voice said staring up. "Oh, it's you."

Edgar had a look of disdain tangled up in a deep frown.

"I didn't mean what I said back there. Honestly, I'm not used to getting attention from anyone. You were coming on a bit strong though."

"I know. After being in this town for so long, you sometimes forget not everyone is looking for a fling."

"Where were you heading?"

"Dick Dock," he said without hesitation.

"Why?"

"To get dick . . . why else would I go there?"

We started to walk. I guess it was more of me following him. I had no intention of heading back to the bar or the house, so I was satisfied to go anywhere else.

"It seems unsafe first of all and, secondly, you seem like you are getting tired of the hook ups."

"I am. No doubt there, but sometimes you need that quick fix. You know what I mean?"

"I do."

The sounds of a thriving town soon greeted us. Many people were seated in the restaurants or grabbing drinks at a bar, but plenty were still wandering around in the street.

"Where are you visiting from?" he eventually asked.

"Dallas."

"I haven't been down there in forever."

"You aren't missing much. For as big of a city as it is, it sure feels like there is never anything to do."

"You probably aren't looking hard enough. There are always ways to get involved or stay active."

I nodded. Maybe Xander was right. I always had a propensity to view the bad side.

"So," Edgar continued, "how long are you going to follow me for?"

"I hadn't thought that far ahead."

"What happened to your friend? He looked very familiar, so I know I have seen him around before. I'm not very good with names though. Hopefully he didn't take offense to me not remembering or seeming like I didn't know him."

"I'm sure he isn't upset about that." I took a brief pause. "He started to get onto me about what I said to you, so I left."

"Oh."

"Yeah. I have never been one to take constructive criticism well, so I can't say I'm very surprised with my reaction."

"Something to get better at."

There's that nasty word again.

"Add it to the growing list," I muttered.

We continued to walk and weave our way down the street. A straggly man was playing a saxophone on the stoop of a closed storefront. He swayed back and forth as he played the melody of a tune I didn't know. The occasional passerby stopped, mesmerized by the sound and dropped some money into the basket. Even in an idyllic place like Provincetown, not everyone was fortunate enough to coast on family money.

"Dick Dock is right up ahead. You're welcome to join me down there, but I'll probably head off to do my own thing since you have made it clear you aren't interested."

"What should I expect?"

"I wouldn't want to ruin the surprise. Follow me."

He made a hard left and walked down a path in-between the big patio bar and the tiny bed and breakfast next to it.

A guy was sitting on the railing and called out to each person that passed by. "Have fun down there!"

I felt my face go flush even though no one would be able to see it in the darkness.

We slowly made our way down the decline and turned the corner. In front were the wooden pillars that held up the patio bar. It was low tide so the lapping of the waves against the wood was subtle like the sound you'd make while stepping into a bath.

Edgar turned to me. "This is where we part ways." We shook hands, which felt like an odd way to depart but I think he was afraid of what would happen if he went in for a hug. "Good luck in there. Don't do anything I wouldn't!" His shape disappeared into the blackness that was up ahead.

I stood there and began to notice the sounds of pleasure that intermingled with each other. I could hear people getting fucked. I could hear people making out. I could hear clothes being removed and tossed into the sand with a quiet thud.

I moved toward the blackness, not entirely sure yet what I was doing there. A part of me recognized how this would be an easy opportunity to escape from the email I had read days earlier, to forget about the impending conversation I needed to have with Evan, and to leave behind all the negative emotions that had been following me around for so long.

Another part of me—a more rational side—decided this wasn't for me. I didn't want to stand at a pillar and wait for some stranger to walk up, grab at my jeans, and quickly find what was underneath. I didn't want to hook up with someone I couldn't see or didn't know anything about.

I'd done that enough times already.

I walked through the blackness and went for the light on the other side. The quiet, destructive explosions of one's sanity could be felt all around me. That place had to be rock bottom for some. Thankfully, my rock bottom was hundreds of miles away, and while I shared the event with you, I'd never explicitly tell you which one. The walk lasted no more than fifteen seconds before I was out from under the patio and making my way back up to the street in an attempt to rejoin society and cleanse myself from the secondhand shame.

Nobody down there wanted sympathy, but I felt bad for them regardless.

Of all the things I may have lied about, do *you* think that experience was one of them?

Seeing as I had no other plans or friends in town, I headed back to the house. Xander was waiting in the living room.

"I called a bunch of times. Where were you?"

"Walking around. I didn't realize you called. I really need to take my phone off Do Not Disturb," I said as a mental note I'd never follow up on.

"Well, I'm sorry for what I said earlier."

"I'm sure you are, but you shouldn't be. It's readily apparent I still have some maturing to do. I should be able to listen to a friend give me feedback. It's not a very good friendship if you aren't able to do that."

He took a moment. "It always amazes me how you seem to have the right answer after the fact. You know when to apologize or take the blame for something. Can I give you some advice?"

"Sure."

"Go talk to someone. You have way too much shit rattling around in your head. You are going to run yourself into the ground. I mean this when I say it: you are an amazing person. You probably get tired of hearing it and you probably don't actually believe that right now. It can change though. You can change. It's not something you have to figure out on your own either. There is no shame in getting help. If I had to guess, I'm not the first person who has suggested this to you."

I shook my head.

"I love you Vin. You'll get there. It's going to take time."

I hate to admit it, but tears were building up. I wouldn't cry—I barely did anymore—but it was the closest I had been since last year.

"Get where?" I managed to ask.

"That's up to you."

# thirty-one

## The Room with Two Chairs

"You still haven't answered my question," she said mildly.

"What was the question? I must have missed it," he confessed.

She flipped onto a new sheet within her notebook and scribbled down something illegible given the speed and ferocity she wrote. Her face was covered in makeup to ensure the flaws stayed hidden underneath. The skirt she was wearing came down past her knees to preserve any sense of modesty that was lost in a time before he was born. It was easy to notice the gut that bubbled over her waistline as a result of not hitting the gym enough after having a couple of kids. Her hair was pulled back into a tight ponytail that barely reached her shoulders—

Sorry, this session is supposed to be about him, not her.

"What did you do last night?" she asked him again, apparently.

"I . . . I, uh, I don't remember," he confessed. He looked down and turned my hands over and found the somewhat faded stamp. It said BIG TOP. He must have gone out to the bars, which would explain why he didn't remember anything.

She blinked twice, staring and waiting for him to think harder.

"How long have I been here?" he asked instead.

"You have twenty minutes left," she said without checking the clock behind her. The hands were spinning rapidly in a counterclockwise manner.

"That didn't answer my question," he said with a twinge of frustration.

"Vincent, this is simple and must bear repeating since you seem to constantly forget: I ask the questions and you provide the answers. Breaking this routine will do nothing but cause you to lose sight of your goal," she stressed sweetly.

"What goal is that?"

"Vincent! WHAT DID I JUST SAY?" she shouted and slammed the notebook down on the table in front of her. The pen bounced off the notebook and rolled under the chair.

"I—sorry. I will stop asking questions."

"Save your apologies for someone who will actually care to hear them. Now, why can't you remember anything from last night?" she inquired.

"Looking at the stamp on my hand—right here—I think I went out to the bars and probably had too much to drink."

"That's incorrect. You went out two nights ago. This will be the last time I ask: What did you do last night?" she leaned in close and stressed each word.

"I don't remember."

"Fine. I will tell you since you are clearly trying to waste my time. You understand I could be talking to anyone else right now, huh?"

He nodded.

"Good, so don't WASTE MY FUCKING TIME. WHEN I ASK YOU SOMETHING, YOU ANSWER IT!"

"Okay," he muttered.

"You were out, whoring around with some stranger while your boyfriend sat at home and wished you were there with him. How does that make you feel?"

"I don't feel anything."

"Vincent . . ." her anger rising again.

"I mean, I feel like there is a void inside of me. I don't remember doing it, but I completely believe I did given my track record."

"Describe the void."

"I don't have any remorse for what I did. I am able to block out my indiscretions quite easily. The void opens up each time I lie to someone or hurt them. It swallows up any emotion I should be feeling and returns . . . well, nothing."

She scribbled more into her notebook. He didn't recall her ever reaching down to search for the scattered pen.

"Tell me about the voices in your head," she said.

"When you say it like that, you make me seem crazy."

"You are crazy. Answer the question."

"They, uh—I always assumed everyone else had the same thoughts that ran through their head. The constant notion that what you are doing isn't good enough. The casual reminder of all the shitty things you've ever done to knock you down a few pegs and make you humbler. The voices tell me things I already know but tend to forget. They speak like a choir, but without any harmony. They yell over each other with none being able to completely capture my attention. I figured that without them I would actually go crazy."

She scribbled more into her notebook.

"Going back to the hook ups," I continued. "I always used to think the aftermath was the worst part. The exact moment after both of you finished your business and laid there while the wave of regret swept in and washed you out to sea. I've learned that it's the complete opposite. It is the waiting beforehand that's the worst part. From the moment they confirm they are on their way over until they first step into your apartment. You sit there and mindlessly put on your shoes, making sure each lace is tied tight, so you don't trip when you go to let them in! You fix your hair, so it actually looks presentable. You slowly grab your keys and put on your glasses. At any moment you could stop and refuse to go, but you are in too deep at that point. The thought of your body intertwined with another is enough to convince you to let them in. The thoughts—the ones that always follow you around—tell you to think about him, to remember the person you actually love, but it's too late. The vicious cycle is nearing its starting point again and you have no escape plan. So, you continue to sit there, knowing your hook up is speeding over to be with you while you keep pushing yourself further away from him. Somehow though, you forget about all of it once the hook up arrives and you begin your interaction."

"Did you read that in a Grindr profile? So deep. How profound," she mocked.

"Maybe I did," he said defiantly.

She scoffed.

"Do you love your boyfriend?"

"Yes."

She flipped onto a new page and wrote NO! down the length of the page. She wrote it again and then a third time and a fourth. She continued to write the word until the page was covered entirely in the black ink. It dripped off the page and began to create a stain on the carpet below.

"DON'T YOU FUCKING LIE TO ME!" she screamed. She stood up and threw her chair toward the window. The glass exploded outward and the chair quickly disappeared out of sight.

"I'm not lying," he whispered, tears streaked his face and fell onto his shirt.

"If you actually loved him, you would never have done what you did. You would never have the constant contemplation about doing what you actually did, you pathetic scum."

"This isn't real."

"Of course it isn't, you fucking idiot. You are becoming unhinged. I am trying to save you, but you are a lost cause."

She sat back down. He looked over and saw the window was still broken.

"I'm not a bad person," he urged.

"You are the worst kind of person. You whine and blabber about wanting to change, about wanting to get better, but you continue to stick your dick in filth and defile the only good thing that has ever happened to you in your waste of a life. Do you not recognize this? DO YOU?"

"I don't recognize it," he said, wondering if what he had was a good thing.

She picked up the chair again and threw it out the other window. It shattered in a similar manner to the first. She adjusted her glasses and glared over at him.

"Recognize it," she said quietly. "If I have to say it again, I will pick up that shard of glass and stab you in the fucking eye. That's what you want, right? You want to feel. I can help you feel. I can help you see. Yeah, let's do that," she said as she moved over to the windows.

As she bent down to grab the glass, he said, "Stop! I recognize it. Okay? Please. I need help."

A twisted smile curled onto her face.

"Oh Vincent. Aren't you the one who always said you didn't need a therapist? And yet, here we are," she laughed grotesquely and walked back to the chair.

"I don't ever recall telling you that."

"I know more about you than I'd ever care for, you fucking waste."

He moved past her comment and responded to her previous question. "Everyone needs some help. It has just taken me a while to realize that."

"Good, good." She scribbled more into her notebook. "You are still a fucking waste though."

"I know. I have always known."

"When did you first know, Vincent?"

"The first time I said something hurtful to someone unprovoked. I was back in middle school and I think I was in—

"Vincent, I don't fucking care to hear about your sob story."

"But—"

"But nothing. You have five minutes left to convince me you aren't insane and a total fucking waste of organic matter before I call in Axis and he takes you away to the crematorium."

"The crematorium?"

"NO FUCKING QUESTIONS, ASSHOLE."

"It goes without saying you are the worst therapist of all time." He stood up and moved to the door. The handle wouldn't budge. Shocking.

"You can't leave here until I say you can. It's quite simple, you fucking waste." She scribbled more into her notebook.

He disregarded her comment and walked over to the windows. His feet crunched under the glass as he felt the shards dig in. The air that was pouring into the room was stale and acrid as if death was waiting nearby.

"I could do it," he finally said. "I could jump out this window right now." He stepped up onto the ledge and peered out. A floating mass of mist blocked any view for what hid below.

"Oh, here we go again. Another one of your idle threats. I have a long list of instances where the idea of committing suicide has crossed through your weak, feeble mind. Go ahead. Do it! Romanticize it. I don't give a fucking fuck what you do. Here, take this if you need any further motivation," she said, throwing the notebook at me.

It bounced off his leg and dropped onto one of the piles of glass. He hesitated briefly but moved toward the notebook and picked it up.

The pages weren't filled with notes, but of graphic depictions of him dying. One was by a noose. Another was in a car accident. The pictures were endless.

Her smile extended beyond the limit of her cheeks and up toward her eyes. "What do you think? Pretty neat, huh? I have more ideas I want to capture."

"You were never here to help me," he said just loud enough for her to lean in toward him. He tossed the notebook out the window and it disappeared into the mist.

"Of course I am. Why do you think you're here?"

"It's hard to say considering none of this is real."

"THINK VINCENT. THINK! WHY ARE YOU HERE?"

"Because I—"

"BECAUSE WHAT?"

"Because I am guilty. I feel guilty for the things I've done. I feel guilty that I don't believe in my relationship even though he has done nothing wrong. I hate the feeling that everyone I surround myself with just doesn't understand anything about me. I hide behind the veil of sarcasm and poorly timed jokes because I hate myself. I hate how boring I am, and I crave the attention of others who don't even know I exist. I despise that I hold people to an impossible standard they will never come close to and how the voices in my head create fake conversations that then leave me disappointed when they don't follow the outline I made up for them. It doesn't even make sense to say it out loud. I feel guilty for wanting to die when nothing traumatic has ever happened in my life. I . . . I thought that—"

"TIME'S UP," she shouted. "It is evident that your minuscule brain doesn't have the propensity to complete even the most basic of tasks.

"AXIS! Oh, AXIS! Get in here, sweetie. We have another body for you to dispose of. Vincent, I'd like to thank you for participating in this experiment. I will now be ending the tape."

"What tape?"

"This concludes Experiment Two-Five-Five-Three-Six," she said calmly to no one in particular.

The door burst open and the man he assumed to be Axis stood menacingly in the frame as most henchmen tend to look. His face was on sideways.

"Axis, make this painful for Vincent. This motherfucker didn't bother to try."

The man covered the space of the room quicker than Vincent expected. His mouth opened and closed like a fish gasping out of water.

With no alternative, Vincent stepped to the window and said, "I'll take my chances outside."

His body fell with an easiness that was new to him. The shattered window vanished from view as he passed through the mist. There was nothing for a long period of time—or at least it felt like a long time. It was impossible to tell. He continued down with thoughts of nothing passing through him. He was at peace until—

He felt contact against a hard surface. His head smacked several times against it before lulling to the side and coming to a rest. He tried to move but couldn't.

He was broken.

He tried to call for help but the mist choked any attempt.

It was painless. His fractured body had bones sticking out the skin. He saw bits of his brain floating in blood as it continued to pool and amass around his face.

A wave of sleep drifted through me and he knew he was ready to move on. He was going to wake up and free himself from the confines of this twisted nightmare.

He closed my eyes, excited at the thought of returning home.

He opened them slowly and looked on in disbelief as he found himself back in the room with two chairs.

"Hello, Vincent. Let's try this again shall we?"

# thirty-two

## I'M SO TIRED . . .

I held off on the conversation with Evan for as long as possible.

I landed back in Dallas sometime in the afternoon. Nothing noteworthy happened on the ferry ride back or the endlessly long non-stop flight back to DAL. Before all that though, Xander and I stood on the pier near the ferry. We hugged each other, and he rested his hands on my shoulders.

"Don't be a stranger. I know that life gets hectic and the weeks tend to bleed together, but don't forget you have a friend out here," he said with a flash of a smile. "You're gonna get there. It's just going to take some time."

I shook my head. "Thanks for everything. Coming up here for the past two years has been a nice change of pace to what Dallas is. You need to come back down!"

"I will take you up on that once I get settled into Boston."

I never did see Xander again (at least up through the timeline of this book) and it's not because we drifted apart like so many of my other friendships, but because the time did bleed together, the weeks turned into months and before I knew it, I was distracted and sitting in an average Tex-Mex restaurant.

We aren't there yet though.

Evan knew what time my flight was landing since I texted him the information before I took off. He was almost as bad as my mom, in which they both demanded to know when I was boarded and as soon as the plane touched ground.

I fulfilled my duty and sent him a text to announce my safe passage and arrival in the Big D. His response was almost immediate. He was excited I was back and wanted to come over. I didn't think the meet up would be centered around the contents of the email, but rather, he just wanted to see his boyfriend again.

I told him I would need an hour to get home and attempt to get my life in order. In truth, the clothes sat in my luggage for two days before I strained myself to throw them in the hamper and then it took another three days from there to do the laundry. Finally, it took two more days to gather the strength and mental fortitude to pull the clothes from the dryer and fold them properly. Toward the end of that span, I was free balling it to work and wearing the same pair of socks for multiple days.

That hour passed by rapidly and Evan was outside waiting. There were three possible ways to enter my apartment complex. Below you will find unnecessary detail about each:

1. <u>The Balcony</u> – While this was my preferred choice for people to get into my apartment, most neglected to use this way since it was a perilous trek over shrubs and a six-foot high railing. To me, it was a rite of passage, but others did not see it as such. I provided a chair to soften the fall from the balcony, but the incentive proved not to be great enough.
2. <u>The Poop Wasteland</u> – The name was given due to the excessive amount of dog feces that lined the grass outside the door. Sometimes it reminded me of Easter Island. I wondered how the poop got there and arranged itself in such an orderly fashion. The smell of shit and piss stung the nostrils each time. If only the owners could collaborate on a way to remove the turd bombs, but alas, they did not have apposable thumbs or hands or bags or any other gadget that would make it possible. Maybe future generations can solve that problem.
3. <u>The Runway</u> – On the opposite side of the building was the final way to enter. A long concrete path led to a keypad and then another door that let you into the building. Whenever Evan (or anyone else) indicated they were on this side, I would hustle my way over there. If I beat them to the door, I'd make them act like they were walking down a runway and modeling the season's hottest line of clothes. Everyone always objected from doing it, which was a real shame because I enjoyed laughing at other people's discomfort.

I let Evan in from The Poop Wasteland. It was his usual choice.

We hugged and kissed like a couple who didn't have a dreadful conversation waiting in the shadows.

Once back in the apartment, he let Izzie loose and she zoomed around and rubbed her face on all the furniture.

He put his stuff down and turned to me. "I'm happy to see you! It feels like it has been forever."

"Only a week, but I think it's probably the longest we have been apart," I said flatly. Something was wrong with me. I didn't know what, but I felt anger and disgust boiling up toward him. I tried to shove it down with the rest of my emotions I kept behind several locked doors.

"So, how was it?" he asked.

"It was a really good time. Somewhat relaxing and on the plus side I didn't get an awful sunburn or out myself to any of my family members." I managed to summarize a week's vacation to almost nothing.

"That's great to hear."

"How was your week? I imagine the holiday helped to break it up."

"I can't stand it there anymore," he began. "We have such a high turnover rate that I can't possibly find replacements fast enough. The candidates I do show to management are never good enough and then they have the audacity to bitch at me about not filling in the vacant roles. On top of that, my manager is absent half the time and the other half is incapable of performing the most basic tasks. Everything is a fire with no way of ever putting it out. I'm tired of it. I shouldn't be—it hasn't even been a year yet—and I know the optics of switching my job yet again, but I have started to apply elsewhere. Just putting out feelers to see if there is any interest."

I stared over at him until I was certain he was done talking. He had a way of taking long pauses and then always accusing me of cutting him off.

I attempted to stay rational and continue to push down the disgust. "Are you looking in the Dallas area or . . .?"

"Both. Obviously, there are significantly more opportunities outside of the city though."

"Uh huh. Is that what prompted the email?"

"Yeah," he said, the word nearly getting caught in his throat.

"That was pretty out of character for you."

"You think so? It feels like the opposite for me. I don't ever feel comfortable talking to you. You always look so angry and you get upset without any notice. Writing to you seemed like the simplest way to get my thoughts across without worrying in the moment how you would react."

"I see."

"I love you an incredible amount, but I am worried you don't."

"Why would you think that?"

"Because Vin, you are distant when we hang out. It seems like I'm interrupting and that you'd rather be alone. You are hardly affectionate. You—I hate talking about this."

"You brought this up by sending that email. You had to know this conversation was going to happen."

"This conversation happens every fucking time we see each other! You have to know it. We are in such a debilitating state of melancholy and it is completely fucking with me. I stress about you constantly and the state of this relationship."

"I'm sorry," I said quietly. "We can work on things."

"We have to."

The rest of the conversation was promises from both of us on things we would improve on. I always found our communication to be honest—possibly too much so—but Evan seemed to differ. We would work on that. I would try to be more present when we were with each other and I would begin looking for someone to talk to, preferably one that didn't break windows or draw pictures of my untimely death.

Evan would attempt to not be so analytical about everything. He was wound up so tight. I wondered if he was capable of laughing or releasing the tension that always sat in his shoulders. He acknowledged this flaw and we talked through ways to change it.

It was overly diplomatic. It didn't change that on some level I was certain Evan had already given up on the relationship. You don't just start applying to other jobs without consulting the person you were with if you were actually in a serious relationship.

The nagging feeling that I resented him on the most basic level never receded; it crept back into the shadows and laid dormant until another time.

I had a party at my apartment that Saturday.

I wasn't very good at hosting, but I learned all you needed was free booze and decent music. People were content enough with that to not complain about much else.

Evan and I celebrated his birthday earlier in the day since he stressed he didn't want to make a big deal out of it. A somewhat fancy lunch was all he wanted. Fair enough.

With that out of the way, we drove around to gather supplies. I wasn't expecting an insane amount of people. Given it was toward the end of a holiday weekend, most folks would be out of town.

We walked out of Kroger with some munchies, a bottle of wine, ice, some fruit, and Kool-Aid.

We walked out of the liquor store with a cheap bottle of vodka that was sure to sting the nostrils on the way down.

We walked into my apartment and concocted the drink. It was nothing more than jungle juice fancied up with slices of fruit to bring out the flavors.

I cleaned up in a few choice places and began the wait.

Nearly an hour later, Daniel and Danielle were the first to show up. Daniel carried his favorite scotch in the crook of his arm like a newborn. Within two minutes of being in the apartment, the bottle was opened with a distinct *pop* being heard over the music.

"You know," I said to him, "I have the mixed drink over there."

"Maybe later," he said, dismissing all my hard work.

Athena and Jag arrived sometime after. By this point, almost everyone knew they were dating, even if they refused to acknowledge it.

Then other people I have never introduced to you showed up but, of course, you met them that night.

In total, there were around ten people in the apartment when we reached critical mass.

Pockets of conversations broke out across the living room. I walked over to Daniel and Danielle who were sitting on the couch, bent over my scrapbook.

"When did you do this?" she asked.

"Senior year of high school. It was for my psychology class."

"Nice turnout," Daniel said, motioning to the people in my apartment.

Danielle nodded in agreement.

"Yeah. I like when everybody that stayed in town has a chance to meet up. People are so keen on traveling and forget how chill a house party can be."

"Evan seems like a nice guy. I'm happy for you both," he said. Given my trip to Provincetown, Daniel and Danielle hadn't met Evan until that point. Surprisingly, it wasn't awkward when they did—just another person to introduce them to.

"Thanks," I said, taking a long chug of my drink. "He is an awesome person. We are just trying to find a balance right now. He told me the other day he is looking for jobs outside of Dallas, so that was rough to hear."

"Give him a reason to stay here," he said just loud enough to be heard over the music.

"He is so focused on his career and buying a house and being a fully functioning adult that I don't think I'm such of a draw for him right now."

"Bullshit," Daniel said.

"He has been staring at you all night. He loves you a lot. I can tell," Danielle said. I trusted her judgement more than Daniel's. She had a more mature vibe to her even though she was several years younger than him.

"I'm not sure I am cut out for a relationship right now. I just don't have as much figured out as I once thought. But"—another chug of the drink—"no sense in dwelling on that now. Do y'all need a refill?"

"No," they said in unison.

I stepped away and entered into the conversation several other friends from work were having. The end result of that was shots. Evan and I didn't empty the entire bottle of vodka into the pitcher, so the remainder sat idly in the freezer, waiting for its next victim.

The shot ratcheted up my level of intoxication to a dangerous degree.

They tried to rally me for another one, but I declined. I didn't intend to ruin the whole next day for myself.

I stumbled over to Athena and Jag.

Evan was preoccupied in another conversation. One of the things I respected about him was his ability to venture out onto his own in new situations. He didn't need to cling to me the whole time.

"How goes it?" I slurred.

"It goes," Athena said. "Thanks for putting this together."

"Of course. I never mind doing it."

Jag draped his arm over my shoulders to stop himself from swaying. "I love you, man."

"I can see he has had his fair share for the night," I said to Athena.

She nodded in agreement. A smile passed over her face. If she was annoyed by Jag's level of drunkenness, it didn't show.

Jag told Athena and I he loved us several more times until he wandered off to another part of the room, likely looking for an empty shot glass to refill.

"He is going to have a rough morning," I said.

"Surprisingly, he doesn't get hungover too much," she said casually.

For a brief moment, I was at a loss at what to talk about with Athena. It was the weekend and discussing work happenings didn't seem appropriate. Quite frankly, for the length of time I'd known her, I'm not sure I actually knew too many things about her personal life.

"Random question: Where does your family live?"

"Denver! Remember when I went there a few weeks ago? It was to visit them. My parents moved there recently from Alabama. I have two sisters that moved out there as well and another one that's down in New Orleans."

"That's right," I said, thinking too hard about if she had told me that information before. "How do they like Denver?"

"They love it so far. They haven't had to deal with a winter there, so we will have to see how that goes."

"I thought it was a cool city when I went there with my mom. I don't think I could ever live there though."

"Mhmm."

"How are things going with you and Jag?"

"They are fine."

"That's it?"

"How are things with you and Evan?"

"They are fine," I said with a grin.

"Fair enough."

It's amazing how sometimes we refuse to be honest with the people we are closest with.

I felt a tap on my shoulder and was presented with another shot glass. I slung it back without hesitation and recalled the next day about how that was my undoing.

## thirty-three

# TIMEBOMB

Remember when I said we wouldn't meet up again until the epilogue? That wasn't exactly true. In my defense, I did say there was a chance I wouldn't make it until then before cutting in. With that in mind . . .

Hello again! Time for us to have a little chitchat.

Have you ever had something unexplainable happen to you?

Mine happened while I was in college.

I was working for the summer with my parents at the lumber store. I was a glorified stock boy. Every day, there would be shipments of different materials that needed to be tallied for inventory and then placed out on the shelves. It wasn't a glamourous job, but my dad paid me well and everyone seemed to like me.

I would get these awful headaches. The ones that send a stab coursing from your head all the way down your body.

It happened on and off for weeks. I told my mom and it freaked her out enough that she demanded I go to the doctor.

I was a healthy twenty-year-old, so I didn't anticipate there would be anything wrong.

At my appointment, the doctor did his usual line of questioning and I answered everything satisfactory. He then took the stethoscope and asked me to take deep breaths, placing it on my back and then my chest.

His face strained slightly to listen as the cold end of the stethoscope was pressed up against my chest.

"Hmm. Your heartbeat seems slow and irregular," he said without much worry. "Let's do an EKG to confirm."

Sure enough, the EKG confirmed his initial thinking. He set up an appointment for the next week at the cardiologist a few minutes down the road. He said it was precautionary and how I shouldn't be too concerned.

I contemplated telling my parents that everything was fine after the visit. I didn't want them to worry. They had other things to be concerned with like how their jobs were quickly killing them.

The contemplation didn't last long though. I was bad at keeping secrets (sometimes). I broke the news to my mom, and she was thoroughly freaked out.

I'll shrink the story a bit. The next month comprised of several visits to the cardiologist and trips to the hospital to do extensive tests. Everything came back fine. I passed the stress test. My liver or kidneys appeared to be functioning normally, but I don't remember anymore why they tested that. My heart didn't have any noticeable abnormalities. The cardiologist quipped about how I was the youngest patient he ever had.

In the end, everyone agreed it may have been some sort of virus that was causing my heart to behave strangely. Even with the notion that I was perfectly healthy, I continued going to the cardiologist until I moved to Dallas. He would always urge me to cut back on the sodium and that losing several pounds would be beneficial.

For a while, I wished the answer wasn't as opaque as it was. I needed something concrete.

We all strive to seek out every answer to each question we have. It's human nature. I wanted to understand why the headaches started, but no one seemed concerned about those once my heart issues came into the spotlight.

As time passed, the headaches did fade away and for a long time I forgot they ever existed in the first place.

Until this point in the story.

The headaches returned. I had been having them in a hectic pattern for months. To me, there was nothing explainable about them.

I held off on going to the doctor until it became clear they weren't the only issues I was noticing. An odd, twitching sensation started happening in my thumb, steady for hours until it suddenly stopped for a small period of time. It wasn't painful, but something I hadn't experienced before.

In hindsight, I should be thankful for the headaches. Without those being an annoyance and somewhat prompting me to go to the doctor, I may not have found out as early as I did. Not that it would make a difference in the long run.

　　　　　　　　　✦

It wasn't a very good story, but one I thought was worth sharing. Sometimes it is the small, seemingly inconsequential moments that really come back to fuck us in the ass.

I promise this will be my last interruption until the end.

One final thing: After all this writing, I still don't understand how semi-colons work. Should I put one here; or here; How about two right here;;

A quick Google search would likely land me an answer, but I never enjoyed doing things the easy way.

Oh well. Something to get better at.

# thirty-four

## LIKE A RIVER **RUNS**

The Dallas-Fort Worth area is a smattering of urban and suburban environments constantly shaping and morphing to the growing population. A particular area in Arlington is home to both the Rangers and Cowboys. The city decided the allure of those two teams wasn't enough because they built an entertainment section called Texas Live.

Texas Live was going to be another smattering of buildings that would cater to the pre and post-game crowds from the sporting events. Attached to it would be a moderately sized outdoor venue that would occasionally have artists come through to perform.

I was always on the lookout for bands coming through Dallas—especially the ones I actually cared for.

I think you can see where this is heading.

Texas Live opened in the sweltering heat of August with a weekend full of shows. The first band on Thursday was trash and I had no interest.

The Friday night show was very, very, very, very interesting. It was completely unexpected.

Can you guess who it was?

If *you* are actually reading this, then you already know.

◈

The Rangers were away for a weekend series with the Yankees, so the area was practically deserted. The looming structure of the new baseball stadium was taking shape behind me as I parked in the lot next to Texas Live.

"Took you long enough!" Evan said as he stepped out of his parked car several spaces away from mine.

"The traffic was terrible. I finally understand your struggle."

I walked over to him and leaned against the car.

"Only a ten minute ride for me. It was so nice," he said smugly.

"How was your day?"

After a brief hug, he recapped it to me as we ventured across the parking lot. He was still dealing with a high number of resignations that were leaving the site in quite a pit. He droned on and mentioned names of people I didn't know or cared about. My mind wandered to meaningless topics that swept me away from the present. I nodded when needed and interjected once to affirm I was paying attention.

"Where do you want to eat?" I asked. I was just full of thought-provoking questions!

"The place right here that will have generic bar food at a grossly inflated price," he said, pointing to the restaurant we were walking up to.

Inside, it was quiet. Waiters meandered around with no purpose. All attention focused on us when we got to the hostess.

"How many?" she asked.

"Two," I said, unsure of myself.

She bent down toward the iPad and her fingers danced across the screen. She raised her head in a bout of confusion and peeked around the corner to examine the expanse of empty tables. Returning to the iPad, she mumbled something to herself and continued clicking away.

"Sorry about that," she said. "We are still working out the kinks. Follow me please."

She led the charge to a high-top table toward the back row of televisions.

"Enjoy!" she exclaimed after dropping the menus on the floor and turning heel back to her post.

Evan bent over and grabbed them. "That was bizarre."

"Honestly, I've been noticing an increasingly strange number of events happen over the past year. I don't get bothered by them anymore."

"How was your day?" he asked.

This is the state we were in. This is the state we have ALWAYS been in. Who am I trying to kid? We didn't know how to engage each other in conversation except for the pleasantries that pass between two strangers.

I told him about my day. I told him about the man that walked through the front door, laid down in the lobby, and did six sets of ab curls before getting up to leave. I told him about the lizard that was sitting in the cafeteria sipping on a coffee with eighteen shots of expresso in it while a woman next to the lizard griped about a secret society of lizards who were threatening to overtake the country. I told him about how I sat in a meeting where the topic was how the cure for cancer was found over two decades ago, but the government was hiding it because Earth was too damn crowded and some people just weren't meant to thrive and be alive. I told him I didn't mind since no one I knew had cancer. I told him about all of this or none of it. The truth is nowhere in the middle.

The waitress came over, introduced herself as Sertiaw, and asked us if we wanted beverages. Of course, we did.

"Your day sounded like it was good for a change," he said.

It felt like a subtle dig to my constant complaining, but I didn't pursue it any further.

"I'm just glad it's the weekend." There it was. The summation of my life.

"By the way," he grabbed my arm, "happy six month anniversary!"

It was an odd coincidence that the concert landed on our anniversary. I mentioned to Evan several times how we didn't have to go and could have gone out for a nice dinner instead, but he insisted we go to the concert. I think he was tired of hearing me talk about them and finally wanted to hear for himself if they were any good.

Six fucking months. Who would have thought I would be in a committed relationship for that long? I figured I would be out huffing crack or running a cock-fighting ring out of my complex's parking garage before I'd end up in that situation, especially after the events of the year prior.

I wasn't better. That's for damn sure, but I saw the clearing out in the distance. Sometimes though it became foggy and covered in an overgrowth of trees when Evan talked about looking for another job. In those moments, I was weak and returned to a destructive form of thinking that ripped me away from any sort of happiness.

I loved Evan and I focused on the difficult situations (were they really that difficult though?) rather than the countless times when we shared each other's company without any issues—

But what's the point of replaying those happy moments to you? They were just a smokescreen—

Anyways, I digress.

Dinner was mediocre, but we managed to have conversation that didn't cover the topics of work or our numerous complaints about life.

Back outside, the line to get into the venue snaked around the perimeter of a water fountain that was shooting out spurts of almond milk in spontaneous intervals. We took our place at the back and waited for the gates to open.

The line inched forward at a leisurely pace, but we eventually found ourselves at the front and passing through the metal detector.

I stepped through the entrance and was immediately taken back to when I saw Bleachers at House of Blues. The intimate nature of both venues meant it was impossible to get a bad spot; still though, I wanted to be closer than when Arturo forced me to hang back.

I wondered briefly what Arturo was up to in that moment. I figured he was a thousand miles away on another trek with Warp Tour. I found out later he was standing ten feet away from me for the duration of the show.

"Let's move to the front," I urged Evan and grabbed his hand.

People were loitering around and not packed into the space yet, so we easily moved within spitting distance of the stage.

"I'm going to get a beer. Do you want one?" he asked, leaning into my ear.

"Sure. I'll have what you're having."

He took a step back, oriented himself, and went off in the direction of the flashing sign that said BEER. It was easy to miss.

This gave me a brief moment to survey the crowd beginning to form around me. Unlike my previous experience with Bleachers where it felt like I was chaperoning a high school dance, the people at this concert seemed closer to my age. I stared off toward the stage where the curtain was drawn with the image of Bleachers latest album. Jack Antonoff stood proudly with his arm across his chest in a regal manner. The title of the album was *Gone Now* and sometimes I wondered if he was. His lyrics eluded to struggle and—of course—wanting to get better. Was he a happy person? I'd never get the chance to ask and yet I still contemplated how I could help him if he wasn't.

*Why don't you start with yourself firstYou don't want to be too far goneWhat's the fun—*

A hand caressed my back and a beer magically appeared in front of my face. Shiner Bock. Not great, but it was impossible to outrun.

"Thanks." I grabbed it from him and took a long sip.

"You said there was an opener, right?"

"Yeah. This band called Joywave."

"I'm assuming they will have at least a few good songs . . ." he said, trailing off.

"You know what happens when you are caught assuming."

"Huh?"

"You make an ass out of you and . . . ming. That didn't turn out like it should have," I muttered to myself.

We didn't have to wait long to find out. The lights dimmed as the sun was nearly set in the distance. I could feel the beads of sweat rolling down my back; it was an inescapable reality during a Texas summer. Joywave jolted out onto stage in a massive burst of energy that carried through their set. They didn't have too much space to work with, but the singer bounced around like he was coked up.

Sometime later, Joywave exited stage right and the lights dimmed again to hide the stagehands who were setting up for Bleachers. Music blared from the speakers and I occasionally placed a song.

I'm sure you'd love to hear exquisite detail about the concert, but I'll spare you from that, except for one portion.

And let me put a disclaimer that even though I have dabbled in the art of music, I am an unknowledgeable twit, so if I misspeak here, it is my fault.

About halfway through, Jack told the crowd about how much looser the band was when they were playing shows now. They were done with their official tour and in-between albums, so they were just enjoying the infrequent experiences. He then asked his keyboard player to play a B-flat note. A low, throbbing hum radiated from the stage and felt as if the note had taken up residence inside of me. It was haunting. It felt like the gimmick that every horror movie deployed before hitting you with a jump scare. He told the crowd that the note evoked sadness. He then asked the keyboard player to step up the note one octave (???) or scale (???) or SOMETHING. I'm really out of my depth here. A more pleasant sound spread throughout the venue. He said this note was hope. He talked about how closely we straddled the line between the two. He then moved into a stripped-down version of the song about his dead sister and how he had no other choice but to keep moving similar to how a river runs. Was it poetic? You bet your butt it was.

Honestly, I'm not doing justice to the way he described those notes. I waited too long to recapture this situation for you and I regret it. How he spoke was empowering and it really made me feel like he understood what it was like to be out of place, to be slightly derailed but not enough so that everyone questioned whether you were alright or not. He could fake being better just like I could. That's why a majority of people I interact with would be absolutely disgusted about the things I've told you. I have grown to be perceived as this pure, angelic person who can be sassy but also truly caring. Most don't know about the mental gymnastics I constantly put myself through or the myriad of hook ups that I partook in to satisfy a part of me I don't even understand anymore or the filthy mouth I have or the endless thoughts of death. Nobody knows I wanted to get better and failed and that my window for doing so is rapidly closing. People rarely take the time to get know others the way they should.

Afterwards, I sat in the parking lot as all the cars around me surged to the exit. I blasted "I Wanna Get Better" on repeat, thought about that B-flat note for the entire drive, and realized it kept ringing in my ear long after that night.

# thirty-five

## CHINA SHOP

Despite the personal drama creeping in the shadows between us, I still wanted Evan to meet my family. He came home with me over Labor Day weekend. My aunt got married down in the Caribbean and was having a reception in New Jersey to celebrate.

We snagged a rental car from the airport and headed north. As we passed through Easton, I said I would show him around town when it wasn't completely dark out, so I stopped myself from spoiling anything.

We pulled into the driveway and grabbed our bags from the back. Porch lights shined back at us from each house and it was enough to confirm that everything still looked exactly the same.

I went to the front door, turned the handle, and stepped inside . . .

> *Familiar sights and familiar sounds*
> *Became quite the sensory hog*
> *Until we were greeted,*
> *By a white, shiny dog;*
> *Bounding down the hall with glee*
> *Soon one dog turned into three.*
> *Toys were brought*
> *And tails wagged wildly*
> *Resistance was futile*
> *To put it mildly;*
> *They walked away covered in dog hair*
> *Without a single regret or care.*
> *Time stood still*
> *As the stranger approached the man*

*And all were surprised
When he extended a hand;
The son had finally decided
That any awkwardness had subsided.
A woman stood in the corner
With tears in her eyes
For reasons that you
Are likely to surmise;
The son would always be her little boy,
Forevermore her pride and joy.
The conversation would have continued
Until the polar caps thawed
But they eventually decided
To give it a pause;
They retreated to bed
Where they swapped some good h---
Packed into the car
On the very next day
The boy contemplated
What he would say;
"Hi, this is Evan
We met at a 7-11."
There was nothing to worry about
As the extended family knew
That the boy would be bringing
Someone new to the crew;
For being gay was not to be feared
His reputation would never be smeared.
The stranger walked around
And was greeted with hugs and smiles
As the love in that room
Went on for miles and miles;
The reign of The Stranger came to an end
For he was now known as The Boyfriend.*

*The celebration of marriage*
*Continued into the night*
*As they slowly began hoping*
*That the end was in sight;*
*The two had nothing else to do*
*But talk of the upcoming trip to Kalamazoo.*
*The night did end*
*As was most always the case*
*They packed back into the car*
*With cake and, oddly, a vase;*
*They went back west*
*And you likely know the rest.*
*The next day consisted*
*Of a tour through the town*
*So The Boyfriend could see*
*How it all went down;*
*All the memories came back*
*Especially ones from that cul-de-sac.*
*Life for the boy*
*Had never been hard*
*And yet he felt*
*Strangely scarred;*
*For the names he was called always stuck*
*Even if he claimed to not give a fuck.*
*Moving on from the past*
*Could be quite the chore*
*He longed for the day*
*Where he cared no more;*
*So that he finally can live his life*
*Without any of the needless strife.*
*Sometimes he wished*
*That he could do it all again*
*Starting over*
*At the age of ten;*

An unintended thought
For a redo is not what he sought.
He wanted to love himself
More than he ever had
To be the best friend,
Son, partner, and hopefully, dad;
In time, he would find his way
For that would truly be the day.
But he didn't know
That time was not his friend
And that he was quickly
Racing toward his end;
His mind returned to the task at hand
Saying how he had one more thing planned.
They traveled for a while to a place
That was largely unknown
Where the shrubs and trees
Were entirely overgrown;
To watch the last remnants of light
Disappear into another night.
He wanted to tell him
"Please don't go"
Instead they sat in silence
Listening to the stillness below;
To him, words never came easy
As expressing his feelings seemed quite cheesy.
There was not much more
To this part of the tale
For they did nothing more
Then hit the ole dusty trail;
Back at the house, they said goodbye
And you already know how the mother did cry.
He stared out the window
As the plane soared high

*Asking himself a single word*
*Why?*
*Not now he tried to plead*
*For he only wanted to be freed.*
*Why did you cheat?*
*Why did you lie?*
*Why are you so hellbent*
*On wanting to die?*
*For the answers he had none*
*He just wanted to be done.*
*Why did you cheat?*
*Why did you lie?*
*Why do you think*
*You deserve that guy?*
*For the answers he had none*
*So he continued to stare toward the sun.*
*Why did you cheat?*
*Why do you lie?*
*Why aren't you even*
*Going to try?*
*For this answer would not be fun*
*He knew he was not the one.*
*He ran from that truth*
*For far too long*
*Holding onto*
*That same sad song;*
*For this final thought would surely sting*
*Vincent was only the thing before the thing.*

# thirty-six

## TALK ME DOWN

I was first introduced to Troye Sivan the night Levi told me his name was actually Arturo and sent me into a tailspin for an awfully long time. *Blue Neighbourhood* was the album that played softly in the background. I promised—more like decided—I would go back and listen to it.

I eventually did and took a liking to his music. Fast forward to the more present time and Troye Sivan dropped his second album, *Bloom*. I also thought it was quality material, so naturally I snagged two tickets when he announced his tour.

I couldn't tell you exactly why I liked his music. It was the typical pop-like sound dominating the radio waves. His lyrics were honest and truthful about his experiences, but, in a sense, most musicians are like that if they have a hand in writing their own music. Maybe it doesn't exactly matter why I enjoy his music. I can tell you one thing for sure: he is attractive. Does that influence my liking of his music? No. The attraction isn't some teenage crush where I write his name in a notebook and put hearts around it or write graphic fan fiction about how he'd impregnate me; it is more about his personality and the passion behind his music. I understand the reality that we will never cross paths—no more so than I would with Jack Antonoff, Lorde, Foo Fighters, or any other band I adore—but what would happen if we did? I'd be a level of nothingness to him. Another face, another fan, another dot. It's a valuable lesson to keep in mind that you are never a large part in someone else's story (but you should still seek them out!). Of course, you are important to family and a select group of friends, but outside of that, you mean literally nothing to others. And that is totally okay. I have written about a healthy number of people, many that have only been mentioned sparingly, which is because they played a very specific part in this story.

Live a great story for those that matter to you and stop spending time worrying and thinking how you'd interact with people like Troye Sivan when it is something that will never happen.

Okay, but I probably like him because I seem to gravitate toward twinks. I'm an equal opportunity employer though.

You must be thinking this chapter is going to turn into some freak encounter I had with Troye Sivan at the concert. You are completely foolish if you think that happened. (If you are interested in reading about my fake, sexually charged encounter, please check out my Tumblr.)

Evan and I found parking in the garage a block away from the venue. The threat of rain hung in the air, as the wind picked up. We arrived early enough to grab food, which we intended to do after we—

My phone rang. I fished it out of my pocket and looked at the name.

"That's unexpected," I said, flashing the phone to Evan to see.

"Hmm. Are you going to answer it?"

"It would be rude not to."

I answered the call and Anders' voice said, "Hello. We are standing behind you."

I turned around quickly and saw a hand wave from behind a crowd crossing the street.

"I'm assuming you are going to the Troye Sivan concert."

"Yeah. Wait for us. We can all grab dinner together."

"Okay," I said, hanging up after.

Evan gave me a look after hearing the name Anders. Months ago, I had told him the numerous reasons why I wasn't a big fan of him and Evan seemed to agree. Through a few more random encounters with him, we both agreed going out of our way to include Anders in social events just wasn't worth the effort.

I shrugged. "He really put me on the spot. I couldn't say no."

Before Evan could answer, Anders and his friend walked up behind us.

"Hi," he said again in an overtly cheery manner. He hugged each of us as if we just came back from war. "So good to see you both! It's been too long! This is Josh. Josh, this is Vin and Evan. They are dating if you couldn't tell. Aren't they just adorable together?" He was the unfortunate embodiment of every stereotypical gay character from television and movies before Hollywood figured out being gay wasn't a compelling character trait. Nah, who am I kidding? They still love that shit.

We never heard an answer to that question. Instead, we shook hands with Josh and went to will call to grab our tickets.

The line was nonexistent, and we received them immediately. It was the only concert I'd ever been to where I couldn't use my phone to get into the venue. Having a physical ticket was always nice though. I still had ticket stubs from movies I went to years ago. They served as good motivators to try and understand why I had a propensity to see shitty movies in theaters.

With the tickets in hand, we sauntered over to Gloria's for dinner. Josh and Anders already had a reservation, so we bypassed the crowd waiting for tables.

We each ordered a margarita, which was wonderful until I realized they cost $9 each. It was a total fucking rip-off considering the Gloria's within walking distance of my apartment had $4 margs all the time. I'll tell you what: it is a real struggle to live in this world.

Evan and I were on one side while Anders and Josh occupied the other.

"So," I started off, "how do you two know each other?"

"We—"

"We have been friends for a few years now," Anders said, cutting off Josh.

"Oh nice. Just friends is not something you see too often within the Dallas gay community. Everybody always wants something more than friendship." I assumed Josh was gay only because I had never seen Anders talk about having any friends who weren't.

Anders quickly pivoted the conversation to be about work. Josh and Evan continued to chat on their own, which I was envious of. Anders spilled all the details about an upcoming org shift that would see most of the employees in my area have a manager change. He made me guess who I thought mine would be. I grew tired by my second guess and when I finally mentioned Daniel's name, a massive grin spread across his face as he took a sip of his marg. He said something along the lines of "You didn't hear it from me" or some other cliché crap you only heard in a movie from *that* one-dimensional gay character.

I forced myself into Josh and Evan's conversation to rid myself of hearing the drivel from Anders. Who the fuck wanted to talk about work on the weekend? I'll answer that for you: someone who understood they had information I did not. He reveled in the notion that he had power over people in the form of gossip and petty talk. It'll catch up to him one day. People like that always plateau because keeping up the charade is tiresome work. I shook off the thought with another swig of my drink. It was strong enough that a subtle lightness hovered around me.

The rest of dinner was uneventful. The real meat of the night came when we were waiting inside the venue before the concert started.

"Tell me more about yourself," I said to Josh.

"Yeah, well, I am going back to school to get my MBA. I work full time right now at a consulting company. I see it as a temporary thing until I graduate. I really want to move . . ."

He continued on for a while. I appreciated how a simple question yielded so much information from him, but all he did was provide the boring stuff that didn't say much about him. I nodded and smiled at the appropriate times and listened intently to what he said. He was a bit cocky and overly sure of himself, so my guess was that he'd end up in the banking industry once he settled down.

"How did you two meet?" I asked, pointing over to Anders, who was chatting with Evan. Bless his heart. He knew how to take one for the team.

"Tinder. A few months ago. I'm not sure why he lied about how long we've known each other. I don't see the difference and I doubt y'all would have cared to know that." He stopped, looked over at Anders briefly, and then continued. "We were going out on dates when we first met and hung out a decent amount. It all stopped suddenly. I never really understood why. Has anyone done that to you before?"

"Not that I recall." *Sure, go ahead and lie. Do what you always do.*

"Honestly, it sucked. Weeks went by before I convinced him to meet so we could talk through what happened. He told me he wasn't looking for a relationship and how we could just be friends, which is how I ended up here with him tonight. I look at him and wonder if he will ever be happy with someone. I think he truly wants someone important in his life but is unwilling to believe the right person has come across yet when he may have shown them the door already."

*Fuck me. Am I that similar to Anders? No. No, I can't be.*

I didn't get a chance to respond to Josh. The lights dimmed, and a surge of noise ramped up from the crowd. Evan came up from behind and placed his arms against my hips. He'd stay in that spot for most of the night as

Troye Sivan belted out song after song. He told the crowd several times about how nervous he was for his first show.

Here is the high-level recap:

- He played all the hits
- He danced around the stage with forgotten teenage rage
- Lots of frat boys were there, which just goes to show how Troye's appeal expands beyond the gays as well
- I walked away realizing what the title of the book would be

When the concert ended, we pushed to the exits with the rest of the group. I heard the rain before I saw it, even over the buzzing of the crowd. It was a torrential downpour and there was no cover from the exit of the venue to the entrance of the parking garage a block away.

We said our goodbyes to Josh and Anders since we knew we'd be heading in different directions.

It likely wasn't the most appropriate thing to say, but as Josh went in for a hug I said, "I have known people like Anders before. You can do better than him. Don't chase him because he will never do the same for you."

He stared back at me with faint recognition at what I told him. He took off into the night. I never saw him again after that, mainly because I didn't see much of Anders outside of work.

Evan and I made a run for it. We hopped over puddles and sidestepped the lucky bastards who had umbrellas and were in no hurry to get to their destination. By the time we made it into the shelter of the garage, my jeans were sagging off my ass due to the volume of water that was absorbed into them.

We trudged our way to the car and sat in it for several minutes until the other cars cleared out from around us. The windows immediately fogged up, so Evan cranked up the heat.

"Can you turn it down? I am dying over here," I said, halfway into the ride back to my apartment.

He turned the heat off and the only sound from the car was the methodic swipe of the windshield wipers.

"Why didn't you do anything tonight?" he asked, unbroken from his trance.

"What are you talking about?"

"I started to be anxious during the concert and you did nothing."

"When? I don't have any idea what you're talking about . . ."

"You never do. I pulled away from you during the concert and expected you to turn around and see if everything was okay. But you never did." He was starting to get upset.

"I didn't think it was a problem. I'm sorry."

"You always fucking say that! That you are sorry. How many times can you possibly say it? It is impossible for you to be that sorry all the time!" he yelled, gripping the steering wheel tightly.

"What the fuck is wrong with you? You expect me to know how *you* feel? I can barely understand anything about myself. You should have said something if you were feeling anxious. Simple as that."

He didn't respond for a full minute. Many times, we exaggerate the time between a response or how long it took to do something in order to improve a story but consider actually sitting next to someone in complete silence for a full minute. It's terrifying.

The windshield wipers continued their swift movement back and forth. Back and forth. Back and—

"Where is this going?" he asked flatly.

I should have done it then. I should have told him it was going nowhere. I would have come out on top and gotten the good side of things. Sure, it would have stung for a brief moment, but I'd finally feel free.

"This shouldn't be an argument. You can't be upset that I didn't know how you were feeling during the concert. I mean, being upset is your choice, but I don't think it's fair. I have stressed many times how important communication is with me. I don't do well with non-verbal stuff."

Another minute passed before he answered. Back and forth, but slower as the rain began to let up.

"You're right."

I felt extremely manipulative in that moment. I didn't want him to run from his feelings or wind up apologizing for them. I just needed him to understand what I was thinking. I was too much of a pussy to tell him that or much of anything for that matter.

"Are we okay?" I asked.

"Yeah."

"The Kalamazoo trip is next weekend. Do you still want me to go?"

"Of course."

"Sounds like a date then."
We didn't say anything else to each other for the remainder of the drive.
Back and forth.
Back and forth.
Back and forth.

## thirty-seven

## WHAT ARE YOU GOING TO DO WHEN YOU'RE NOT SAVING THE WORLD?

"Hello friend," she said, standing next to my desk.

"Hey Athena. What can I do for ya?"

"I think they forgot one of my boxes back in the old building. Are you up for an adventure?"

I looked around. "You are really blowing my cover."

She gave me an inquisitive look.

"I have been working hard to pretend I am doing important work here," I continued. "Now, you have come over and ruined that by beckoning me on this adventure . . . but I am totally in."

I got up from my desk and followed her out of our area and into the hallway. We passed by the culture center littered with people heating up their lunch and occupying the nearby tables.

"How was your weekend?" I asked.

"It was extremely relaxing. An embarrassing amount of Netflix. You had the concert, right?"

"Correct. We got to enjoy it with Anders," I said flatly.

"Oh fun," she said more enthusiastically than I was expecting.

"Totally."

We walked onto the bridge that connected all three buildings. Each wall was adorned with names of employees. I glanced briefly at my name when we reached it. Even when I leave [REDACTED] someday, my name would be a fixture on that wall.

Our team had recently vacated our space in headquarters and elected to move into the new building—and by elected, I mean we didn't really have a choice on the matter. The only tangible benefit I saw from the move was that I'd get to park in a six-floor garage to keep my car safe from the random spikes of heat we were still experiencing. Besides that, there was absolutely no positives to the building. There were even less windows than headquarters and only one set of stairs allowing you to get to the first floor without going directly outside and setting off an alarm. My brain tried to understand the illogical nature of the building construction, but I had more important issues to be concerned with.

"Can you believe we have known each other for over a year already?" I said, feeling an innate need to delve into the topic.

She looked over and smiled. "You've been a pretty awesome friend."

"How so?"

"You blindly follow me on all my adventures," she said cheerfully.

"All your adventures? This is the first one I recall having with you."

"Learn to take a complement!"

"Yeah . . . yeah. It is something I desperately need to work on. But, I am glad we are friends. It was a bit bumpy in the beginning and I think people still want to believe we are secretly dating, but I imagine they will get the hint eventually."

We passed into the headquarters building and bounded up a flight of steps. After rounding the corner, we walked into our old area. It was quiet except for the constant droning of the white noise from above. Another team would be moving into the empty space soon, but in the meantime, the remnants of the people who previously occupied the area was still evident. A few of the cubicle walls had random paper tacked to it; loose cables fluttered across the floor, an easy tripping hazard to anyone who wasn't paying attention; signs hung from the ceiling declaring the team name for each cluster of cubicles.

"It's sort of eerie," she said, echoing my same thought.

"I don't even remember where you sat. It looks entirely different without anyone over here."

She pointed toward the back and went that way. I followed behind, catching a glimpse of my old desk. I contemplated carving my initials under it, but that felt extremely petty. It's not like I had any emotional attachment.

"It's not here!" she declared.

"That doesn't make any sense. It's gotta be around here somewhere."

She vaulted up onto the nearby desk to get a better look of the surroundings. "It should be easy to spot. A giant, orange crate," she said to herself. "Nothing."

She hopped down and looked defeated.

"What was in that crate?"

"Nothing important . . ."

"I don't believe that."

"No, really. It was just my 'What Would Beyoncé Do?' plaque and . . ."

"And what?"

"The calendar."

"What calendar?"

"The day-at-a-time calendar you gave me for Christmas."

"WHAT?" I shouted. "WE HAVE TO FIND IT!"

"It did have some solid advice, so I'd be sad to lose it," she said quietly.

I had given Athena a YOU ARE A BADASS calendar that reconfirmed all the numerous ways she invoked being, well, a badass. In return, she gave me the calendar with a *New York Times* crossword puzzle on it each day. I've mentioned my abject failure in completing that unaided.

"Let's walk around this floor. We are bound to run into it."

No luck. We walked into other areas where teams were still sitting in. Some gave us weird looks as they did not take kindly to strangers. We scoured the hallways and checked the crevices where only a true kleptomaniac would hide their loot.

"What about the freight elevator?" she suggested.

"Good idea!"

We ripped open the door that the freight elevator hid behind, but no luck again. A moth smacked into the door, established its sense of direction, and flew toward one of the fluorescent lights that dominated the ceiling.

"Fucking heck," I said. "This is becoming annoying."

"We can stop. I'm sure it'll turn up at some point."

"Nah. We need to find this."

"Okay—if I were a bright orange crate, where would I be?" she asked.

"I would want to be with all my other friends. I'd be afraid on my own and it would be super lonely. Do you know where they were stacking up all the empty crates when people were finished with them?"

"Over by Belinda's desk, right?"

"Seems logical." Belinda was the admin for our team. "Let's check back over there."

Halfway across the bridge, heading back to our new building, I felt a sudden urge to ask Athena, so I did. "How are things with you and Jag?" She owed me an answer.

"You love asking me that question. You are more concerned about our relationship than anyone else," she said with a smile.

"I don't mean to pry. Y'all are just important to me," I said somewhat defensively.

"We are going to break up soon," she said, staring straight ahead.

"What? Why?"

"We are just opposites."

"But you two get along so well. I see it all the time." I recalled how often Jag seemed looser around her. He laughed more. The stress of his job melted away, even for just a short time.

"You're right. We do . . ."

"Athena?"

"His family would never accept him if he married someone who wasn't Indian," she muttered. "He hasn't even told them about me, so I am never expecting to meet them," she shrugged, trying hard to hold back her emotions.

I didn't know what to say. We continued walking. She eventually broke the silence.

"He is the same way I guess. He loves his family too much to do anything that they would disapprove of. I don't blame him for feeling that way, but I am selfish and can't help but feel he is throwing this away . . ." she trailed off.

"I'm sorry. It could work out."

"How could you know that?"

"I don't, but there's no harm in thinking it."

"I get tired of feeling, you know? Sometimes I wish all the stress would melt or go latch itself to someone else who could handle it."

"You seem to be handling everything well," I said.

She stopped and stared back at me. "I'm a good liar."

"Why would you? You can tell me—"

"The crates should be right over here," Athena said coldly.

They were. Several stacks of them were shoved up tight against the wall of the admin's cubicle.

It was the tenth crate I opened when I finally found the rest of Athena's stuff. A note was folded neatly on top of the pile of things.

"Found it! What's this?" I asked, holding up the note.

"Not here," she said quietly and motioned toward the empty huddle room a few feet away.

We walked inside and slid the door closed.

"It's a note from my grandma. She loved to write notes to us when we were growing up. She lived pretty close and still sent us each one at least twice a month. They slowed down a lot during college and I figured they would stop completely, but this is the one she sent me during my first week here. It seemed right to keep it on my desk."

"Is this the grandmother that just—"

"Yes," tears filling her eyes.

"I'm so sorry. I'm glad we found it then."

"Me too," she said quietly.

We sat in there and cried. She had barely mentioned anything about her grandma until that moment. People kept so much of themselves locked away, never to be seen by another soul.

"It's going to be okay," I said, giving her a hug.

"I'm not sure it will be, but it's a comforting thought and better than the alternative."

## thirty-eight

### GRAVES

"RIVER!" the voice shouted across the house. "DID YOU TAKE A SHIT IN MY BEDROOM?"

The manic scrambling of legs upon the hardwood floor were heard, as the dog ran for its life. Confused between the excitement of new guests and fear of punishment, River sniffed us briefly and fled to his hiding spot on the couch with his nose stuffed under a pillow. His tail wiggled uncontrollably until he heard the voice again. This time it was in the room.

"C'mon, dude. We have been over this. No accidents in the house."

The tail stopped wagging, but only for a moment.

*Thump. Thump. Thump.* It began again.

His way of apologizing.

"He takes these massive shits now. I guess we are officially out of the puppy stage," Delilah said with a smile she was trying hard to hold back.

"Thank you for the visual," Evan quipped.

We were standing adjacent to the couch and watched as River, the no-longer-a-puppy golden retriever, uncoiled himself. He quickly remembered new friends were in the house and bounded off the couch in search of his favorite red ball.

The whole ride from Chicago to Kalamazoo consisted of Evan suggesting he had a surprise for me. By his third time of bringing it up, I realized he couldn't surprise me with much else besides a dog, but that didn't take away from the excitement of meeting River.

"Apologies for the outburst. He had been doing well for weeks now. I didn't think he would have any issues."

Delilah had straight black hair that extended just past her shoulders with cheek bones that gave a dignified definition to her face. She had a fierce demeanor that was swept away the moment she started talking. To describe her anymore would give the impression she continues in this journey beyond the chapter.

Evan met her during the year he spent in Kalamazoo after finishing up grad school. They worked at the same company and continued to stay in touch after he left.

"Delilah, I love the color you have in here," Evan said, looking around. "Would you mind giving me the tour? I have been itching to get a house, so I may get a few ideas."

"Of course." She led him up the stairs.

It was true. Evan had mentioned several times he was really hoping to find a house. He lived in one with Kieran and missed the comfort that brought him. He hadn't mentioned us moving in together because I figured he wasn't necessarily looking at houses in just the Dallas area.

I stayed put with River, who found the red ball and sat patiently in front me.

I wrestled it from his mouth and rolled it across the floor. He chased after the ball with fierce passion.

"Do you think I should tell him? I'm afraid it will change things," I asked River as he brought back the ball.

I had received the news the day before. It seemed unbelievable enough that I had briefly forgotten about it when I woke up that morning, as if it was nothing more than a nasty dream. That wasn't the case though. I'd have a slew of doctor's appointments to go to, but I wanted to make it through ACL with the secret intact and not having to worry about it. I craved normalcy for as long as I'd be allowed. It would be my burden to tell others. I knew I should have felt something, but the void was there and swallowed the death sentence. The crime: being a tw—

River dropped the ball onto my foot and stared up at me.

"No answer?" I questioned. "Okay then—thanks for the help."

". . . expensive in Dallas. I have been shocked," I heard Evan say from the top of the steps.

"How is it?" I asked once they were back in the room.

"The house is beautiful! I remember that you were looking when I moved down to Dallas. How did you find this place?"

Delilah dove into the story. They started lobbing real estate terms that had no meaning to me, so I tuned out and began thinking about the news again.

*You got what you wished for*, I told myself. *You are lu—*

"Vin," Evan said, poking at my shoulder. "Any preference on what you want to do tonight?"

"I am good with hanging out here unless y'all are wanting to go out."

"The bars are somewhat far away." Delilah thought a moment and then continued. "How about this: we hang low tonight and then we plan on going out after the wedding tomorrow night. We can take him to the stock market bar," she said, speaking directly to Evan.

"Good idea! I used to love that place."

"The stock market bar?" I asked.

"Technically, it is called Kalamazoo Beer Exchange. It's a bar in which the prices of the beers change depending on how in demand they are. You can find some decent deals if you go at the right time," Evan explained. Delilah nodded in agreement.

"So, it's settled then." Delilah clapped her hands together and moved to the kitchen. "What are you two in the mood for?" she called back.

The next three hours consisted of us casually drinking and talking about a wide assortment of topics. It was great to hear the two of them catch up on the happenings of everyone Evan left behind in Kalamazoo and I was appreciative of the amount of questions Delilah asked me. She really seemed to care in getting to know me.

We stumbled into bed sometime later. As I stripped down to my boxers, Evan grabbed at them and muttered something about how I wouldn't be needing them. We started getting into it and before I knew it, I was fucking him. Without lube, which seemed like a miracle.

A sudden jolt of realization spread across his face.

"Uh oh," he said.

"What's wrong?"

"It feels like I'm going to shit."

"Okay, I can remove myself—that was an odd choice of words—what should I do?"

"We should probably stop."

I pulled my dick out from inside him. He leaned closer and grimaced. I knew what that meant.

Honestly, getting shit on your dick while fucking a butt was not an uncommon occurrence. It was certainly something I had encountered before so it didn't bother me, but Evan was embarrassed.

"Not a big deal. Let me just go clean it off."

I hopped off the bed and slowly opened the door. I wasn't sure where River slept at night, so I definitely wasn't interested in him making a lot of noise.

As I attempted to squeeze through the half open door, I smacked my dick on the molding. It made an impressive sound that certainly overplayed the size of my soldier.

"Oh fuck," I whispered, trying to hold back my laughter.

"Don't tell me th—" he started to say.

"Yeah," I said after closer inspection.

I could hear Evan stifling his laughter as I made a dash to the bathroom. I grabbed a wad of toilet paper and wiped off my dick. I tore off some more and returned to the room where I cleaned off the molding where a shit imprint of my dick was plastered to the wood.

I returned to bed after disposing of the evidence.

"That was wild," I said.

"Something for us to laugh about later," he said and turned over to try and get some sleep.

✦

The wedding party had done their entrances and sat in an orderly fashion across the giant white table that stretched the length of the room.

From the back corner where we sat, it was hard to make out the details of each person as the light was occasionally bouncing into my eyes.

"Please help me welcome—for the first time—" the emcee proudly announced, "the newly married couple, Mike and Leon!"

They appeared at the top of the steps with their hands held up triumphantly. Everyone stood up and applauded as they descended down and took their spots at the middle of the table.

The speeches began after that and lasted for quite a while. Without knowing anyone in the wedding party, there was significant emotional detachment from the speeches that were given, but I still enjoyed them, nonetheless.

Afterward, each table was summoned up for food. We waited patiently as the last table called, even though we were the closest. In the meantime, Evan was spending time catching up with his old co-workers that sat on either side of Delilah and me. They seemed genuinely interested in hearing how life had been since Kalamazoo and several tried to persuade him halfheartedly to move back.

I was happy to see him so comfortable. He fell into a natural rhythm with those people that I rarely witnessed in Dallas.

I realized how procedural weddings were and this one proved to be no different. Following dinner, many of the guests spread out across the dance floor or mingled near the bar. The group would be pulled together one last time for cake.

I'll spare you the intimate details of this wedding since we will deep dive into my sister's before the end of our time together.

"So, tell me about the cluster of gays over there," I told Evan at one point while we were out on the dance floor.

He looked over, furrowed his brow slightly, and leaned in close.

"I only know a few. None of them are overly exciting from the stories I heard . . . except for the throuple," he said nonchalantly.

"What did you say?"

"A throuple!" he yelled into my ear.

"What in the fuck is that?" I asked, pulling away and staring up at him.

"You, of all people, do not know what a throuple is?"

"That seems to be the case."

He leaned back and laughed. A full, deep laugh that had only happened on several other occasions in the time I'd known him.

"Okay—you see those three gays standing in a cluster over there by the table with the red candle burning at a 42-degree angle with the smoke rising at a rate of four inches per second—"

". . . Did you just stoke out?"

"Do you see them or not?"

He spun me around slightly for a better view. I nodded my head.

"They all fuck each other," he spat out.

"What's so special about that? It's somewhat typical in the gay world."

"Last I heard, they sleep in the same bed and do everything together."

"Oh my. That is interesting. A throuple, you said?"

"Yeah."

"What a great name. Do you think they would talk to me ab—"

"No. Do not talk to them about it.'

"But why—"

I felt a hand on my shoulder. Mike popped in-between us and spoke at length about how happy he was that Evan could make it to the wedding. He was even happier I was able to come with him. Happiness was the cool drug being sampled by everyone it seemed. Spoiler: the high wears off quick. He talked about how we seemed to be great together and he would love to come down to Dallas to visit. I tried to escape, but Leon showed up and started reiterating the same thing. Once he was done, Delilah walked over and practically repeated it all for a third time.

If only they knew Evan and I were like that poster of the kitten hanging onto a tree branch. We were so close to losing our grip. I was only the thing before the thing after all. Isn't that right?

If only they knew the only thing I wanted was to confront the throuple.

When the pod of compliments and general cheer broke apart, I headed to the bathroom. The line was long, so I had ample time to reflect on how good of a faker I was; how I was able to flash a smile when needed so that everyone thought I was okay; how I was able to lie and say how happy Evan and I were; how I was going to live a full and rewarding life.

What a crock of shit it all was.

Following my bathroom break, I found Evan back at the bar ordering another drink. As I leaned against it, waiting for him to get his, I glanced over onto the dance floor and saw the throuple engaged in a dance routine. They had their arms draped across each other and spun around in a circle. They were laughing as they tried to spin faster and faster. How adorable.

Were they happy? Not only were they gay, but they were in a non-traditional gay relationship. That was like the equivalent of starting a hand of Texas Hold 'em with a seven and two that are off-suit. Most people would consider folding, but they leaned into the hand, played it, and walked away with a pile of chips.

It was all an assumption though. I had no idea about the state of their relationship and the happiness each member had with it.

Just like no one had any idea about where Evan and I stood in our relationship.

Evan slid a drink over to me and I scooped it up. The throuple was leaving the dance floor and returning to the table with the red candle that was now burning at a 43.5-degree angle with the smoke that was rising at a slightly decreased rate of three point nine two inches per second.

"What's their names?"

"The throuple? No. No. Do not ask them about it," he said firmly.

"You said you knew a few of them. Come over and say hi. I will casually slip into conversation with one of them."

"Vin," he said in an aggravated tone.

"I cannot fucking stand when you call me by my name. It always sounds like I'm getting yelled at."

"Then don't do something stupid."

"Fuck you. I can talk with whoever."

He looked over at me, partially stunned by the outburst. He grabbed his glass of wine and went back to our table without saying a word.

I walked to the throuple and singled out the nerd. He had a skinny frame and wore glasses that screamed he got shoved into lockers by the jocks if that was actually a thing that happened in real life.

"You know Evan, right?" I asked. I couldn't think of a better opening line than that.

"Yeah. It's been a while, but we hung out when he lived in Kalamazoo," he said with hesitation.

"Oh nice. I'm his boyfriend. Vin. I thought I'd introduce myself to a few of his old friends. Nice to meet you!"

He warmed up slightly to this. "Hi. I'm Tommy. Nice to meet you too."

"So, what do you do?"

He told me in great length about all the boring stuff he did for his job. He really was a nerd. I rarely encountered them out in the wild.

"Sounds exciting," I eventually said once he stopped jabbering. I was so fucking tired of having people talk about work. It was such low hanging, rotten fruit. "Did you come here with anyone?"

"My boyfriends."

"Boyfriends?" I repeated slowly as if I didn't know exactly what he said.

"Yeah. I'm in a relationship with those two goofballs over there," he pointed to the two guys who stood on the opposite side of the table and engaged in conversation with Leon.

"How long has that been happening?"

"About three years now."

"Wow. How is it going?"

"It's great. We all had to move past the jealousy—sometimes you are just more interested in one more so than the other—but we realigned ourselves and things have been great since."

"Well, I'm happy to hear that."

"Thanks. What about you? How long have you and Evan been dating?"

*We broke up about ten minutes ago*, I considered saying. I would have to deal with the fallout of my rude outburst.

I told Tommy all the details he probably never wanted to hear. It turned into another conversation that was quickly going to derail into useless territory, so I cut it off and returned to our table. I was somewhat disappointed in the lack of juicy details of the throuple, but not everything was as exciting as it seemed from the outside. As long as they were happy or at least faked it convincingly enough for everyone else, then happily ever after to them.

*Not everyone is as miserable as you. Liar. Cheater.*

Evan was chipping away at a piece of cake. I don't know how he heard me over the music, but he turned around as I was ten feet away from the table and looked over at me. His face contorted in disgust and he turned back again to finish the dessert.

I sat down in the chair beside him.

"I'm sorry. That was a shitty thing to say," I confessed.

"It was," he said, peering at me from behind the glasses that slid slightly down the bridge of his nose.

"Do you want me to leave you alone for a bit?"

"Yes."

"Can you at least go out on the dance floor and be with your friends? I don't want this to ruin your entire night."

"A little too late for that, but I will. Just don't bother trying to apologize again. It's the same shit with you."

Evan and I barely spoke a word to each other for the rest of the night at the reception and the bar we went to after with Delilah. It was becoming a theme that we were ending most of our nights together that way. Whatever moments of levity we had felt like a distant dream.

The next day wasn't any better. The only reason I survived the drive back to Chicago was that he had the radio on and I was able to stare out the window and watch the boring scenery pass by at a blur.

I should have told him then. Not to gain sympathy, but because he needed to know. He needed to understand that I wasn't fine. I never was.

But like I always did, I made the wrong choice and sat there quietly all the way back to Dallas.

# thirty-nine

## SO LONG, **LONE**SOME

It had been a particularly long day at work. Some might call it grueling, while others would whisper under their breath and call it taxing or laborious. It was one of those days where the dam over at Shit River let loose and a mountain of brown, thick goo flowed into your life and didn't recede. I'd recap the actual events for you, but I'm afraid the number of acronyms I'd need to use would confuse you and make you think I was trying to feed you alphabet soup.

I walked as quickly to my car as I could without running. I deftly navigated all of the turns in the parking garage, avoiding the shambling corpses as they shuffled to their cars and the unaware drivers who attempted to back out of their parking spot without a care to see if any other vehicles were around.

The drive home was uneventful. I passed by the same lady I did most days. She weaved in and out between all the cars that were stopped at a traffic light near the hospital. She walked with a pronounced limp, had a mangled head of hair, proudly displayed half her teeth all yellow and decaying, and wore tattered clothes that sagged off her bones like most of what Dylan owned. I had seen videos where people sometimes faked being homeless and did it for a meager amount of extra money because they were bored, but I doubted that was the case with her. She hobbled past my car shaking a Styrofoam cup in my general direction. A massive wave of guilt swarmed inside of me to the point where I didn't even look at her. Out of my periphery, I saw her pause momentarily and stare into the window, hoping to illicit a glance from me. I didn't budge. My mind flashed back to the time when a lady in Philadelphia practiced the same tactic and when I gave her the cold shoulder, she told me to go suck a dick and spit on the window. I lost sympathy for any beggars that day and carried down the prejudice to Dallas.

I'm not a good person.

I pulled into the parking garage at my complex and kept driving. Normally, I would stop near the entrance and find a spot there since I lived on the first floor, but I climbed higher, past the second, third, and fourth floors. I finally stopped on the top level, only because I didn't have anywhere else to go.

One of my regrets was that I never drove up to the top of the parking garage at my old complex to see if there was a good view of the city. I wasn't entirely sure why the thought occurred to me in that moment and why I desperately needed to fulfill it.

The top floor was deserted. Perfect.

The walls around the perimeter were significantly higher than expected, but I guessed that it was to deter anyone from doing a swan dive off the ledge. I'd find a way if the urge was large enough.

I backed into a spot. It took me three attempts to get it right since I'm not fancy and my car lacked a rear-view camera. No matter though. There wasn't anyone around to laugh at my inability to park.

I stepped out of the car and carefully maneuvered my way up the hood and onto the roof. I sat cross legged on the top, behind the sunroof, as all the dirt and grime of the year since the car had been washed became smeared onto the asscheeks of my jeans.

I gazed upon the skyline laid out in front of me. The summer months were washing away into the brevity of fall, which meant that darkness reigned more and more each day. The sun had dipped out of sight and the lights from the numerous buildings downtown shined brightly back in my direction. It was no secret that I gave Dallas shit for its inhabitants, filthy roadways, and lack of general activities to partake in, but the skyline was nice. That's about the only positive thing you'll get me to say about it.

From the angle of where my complex sat, I was unable to see Reunion Tower or the Omni Hotel, which were always flashing in a multitude of colors. I saw the giant building, though, with green lights streaking down all four sides. Lord knows I had no idea what the name of the building was, but you'd know which one I was talking about if you looked at a picture.

The sound from pockets of cars crossing over the concrete slabs of the tollway floated around my head. The pacing of the noise was scattered due to the various speeds the cars were going. It turned melodic after a while, like a lullaby. I was alone. I stripped away the unpleasantness of the day. I didn't have to think about all the things I was unhappy about or not excelling at. Evan disappeared from thought. The fact that my car desperately needed an oil change floated away without a care. The awkwardness of a conversation I had with a coworker earlier in the day that left me feeling like an asshole became an afterthought; a worry for a different day. The million other nuisances—

*Ding!*

A distinct noise came from my right and broke me from my trance.

A body stepped out of the elevator doors once they were fully open. The shape moved slowly and without a purpose. A hiccup and a sniffle could be heard, somehow managing to come during a brief bout of silence from the tollway.

The shape stopped, looked up, and slightly startled said, "Oh. There usually isn't anyone up here."

It was apparent the shape was a woman. A good portion of her hair was tucked underneath a beanie, but some of it fell past her shoulders. Sharp, green eyes darted in my direction and seemed to linger past me like someone was drawing her attention. A slim, slightly long nose and prominent cheeks stood out from the rest.

"Sorry for crashing your hiding spot," I said with a pinch of guilt.

"I'm not hiding . . . I'm . . . I'm . . . saying goodbye."

"Saying goodbye to what?" I asked.

She moved closer to the car, but still kept her distance as if she was unsure whether I was a friend or foe. I didn't know myself sometimes, so I couldn't blame her.

The cars seemed to disappear. It was just us now and the intruding audience of silent onlookers.

"I'm leaving Dallas tomorrow," she struggled to say.

"Why?"

"My boyfriend got a good opportunity elsewhere. Isn't that usually how it works?" she asked as if I would have the answer.

"Where are you moving to?"

"Somewhere cold."

"What's your name?" I asked, trying to continue the conversation. I needed this interaction. Something told me I had to.

"Murphy, but most people call me Murph."

"Nice to meet you Murph. Funny story . . . I really wanted to name my dog Murph. After I saw *Interstellar*, I fell in love with the name. I ended up picking something else, but I still wonder if that would have suited her better."

"That wasn't a funny story . . . or even a good one," she said while her serious expression morphed into laughter. The hiccups broke up the laugh into small fragments. "Did you just compare me to a dog?"

"Well, no . . . at least I don't think so. I compared your name to my dog. In fairness, my dog is super badass."

"What's her name?" she asked. Murph folded her arms in front of her and took another step closer.

"Rigby."

"As in Elean—?"

I nodded.

"That's cute."

"Thanks," I said with a weary smile.

A few moments of silence passed between us. The audience could be heard shifting in their seats, munching on their popcorn, and leaning in closer to hear what happened next.

"Why are you following him out there if it's making you upset?" I asked.

"Because I love him. Because I trust we are going to work out far into the future. Because leaving the only place I know is the bravest thing I can do for myself."

"I left home once, which is how I ended up here. It's worth the risk."

"I know it will be."

"How do you know you love him?" I suggested to Murph.

She looked at me—more like through me. Her green eyes already told me what her answer would be. "You must not have ever been in love before."

"I . . . uh . . . I think I am."

"You aren't. What's your name, stranger?"

"I'm Vin."

"Vincent, if you are finding yourself in a situation where you can't give me—or yourself—a straight answer, without hesitation, to that question then you need to do some soul searching. I was high school sweethearts with my boyfriend. It hasn't been easy, and I am patiently waiting for him to put a ring on my finger, but I know I love him—fully, deeply, and without question."

*Liar. Cheater.*

"I see," I said, looking back toward the skyline. It was significantly darker now with the lights placed sporadically around the top floor being the only thing that kept me and Murph visible to each other.

"Got room for one more?" she asked but didn't bother to wait for my answer as she closed the gap, dipping in and out of the dark patches that separated us.

"If you put a dent in this pristine car, you are buying me a new one," I warned.

"Student loans are sucking me dry right now, so let's hope that doesn't happen."

She climbed up gracefully and slid in next to me. I didn't think there would be space, but her slender frame took up less than mine.

"So," Murph continued, "tell me about this girl you say you're in love with but that you aren't actually." She wiped her face with her sleeve and seemed to have completely washed herself clean from the crying.

"Actually, it's a guy."

"Oh, well, fuck me. You certainly don't seem—"

"Yeah. I get that a lot. It's a blessing and a curse."

"Makes no difference to me," she said with a shrug.

"I appreciate that."

"So," dragging out the word for several seconds. "Are you going to tell me?"

"Right. Yeah . . ."

I told her about Evan. She watched me intently as a replayed the details of who he was, what our story was, and, recently, what the events of the wedding had been. The speech was more in line with how I envisioned telling Daniel but without the theatrics.

"Sounds like a flight risk," Murph eventually said.

"Why do you say that?"

"Telling you directly he is looking for other jobs outside the city without consulting you. In his defense, y'all aren't married or dating for too long, but still, a bit of a red flag for me."

I nodded. Not really wanting to continue down that path of conversation, I changed course. "You mentioned that your boyfriend got an opportunity.

Have you found something to do once you get out there?"

"Not yet. My boyfriend will be making enough to support us while I find something. I have a degree in Human Resources that is collecting dust, so maybe I will try to go down that path again."

"Finding a new job is never fun, so may the odds be ever in your favor."

"Thanks Katniss or whoever the fuck said that." She pulled up her knees and wrapped her arms around them.

"I never liked this city. It's boring and stale for something this large, but I do like the skyline. I find myself staring at it during drives back to the city at night," I confessed.

"I'm sorry you don't like Dallas. Sounds like you should be the one leaving. This has always been home for me. I still get lost around here more often than I'd care to admit. For me, there is always something new to see, but maybe I'm a glass-half-full type person," she suggested with another shrug.

"You were crying an awful lot for someone who was only saying goodbye to this city."

"Are you judging me?" she asked, quite seriously.

"No."

"And who said I was saying goodbye to this city? I only told you I was saying goodbye."

"Ah, you're right," I conceded.

"My dad died a week ago," Murph said without warning. "Stage 3 lung cancer. That motherfucker never even smoked a cigarette in his life and he has the audacity to go off and die like that." My mom smoked for a really long time, so that fear of cancer was always hiding in the shadows for me. I couldn't/didn't want to imagine that happening. Things were going to become hard enough already.

She continued: "Have you ever seen someone die from cancer? They look pathetic at the end, but through no fault of their own. And now, I'm leaving behind my mom and two younger brothers. I cried. I am still crying—not in this very moment, thanks to you—but I have been torn about whether I should go. I keep reminding myself of the last thing my dad said to me. Classic, right? Everyone gets their parting words. Luckily I was there to hear his."

"What did he say?" the words were barely audible.

"'Follow it.'"

A chill ran through me.

"Follow what?"

"Vincent, I haven't the slightest clue, but I will never forget those words. I imagine they will have meaning someday."

"I—"

"Don't bother. I know you are. Everyone is. Try to be a bit more original than that. At least you didn't make a Murphy's Law joke," she said, rolling her eyes.

I was expecting tears from her again as she told me about her tragedy, but there were none. She must have been sucked into my bubble of no emotion.

"I was going to say—" I stopped myself.

*I'm dying. Say it. Be dramatic. Ruin her moment for your own selfish gain. Tell a complete stranger about your trauma. It'll make you feel big and strong. Go ahead. Do it! DO IT! DOITDOITDOITDOIT . . .*

"Going to say what?" she asked.

"Maybe another time."

She peered over at me briefly and looked as if she would pursue my lack of an answer further, but Murph never did. Instead, she slapped me on the back and said, "Vincent, I don't believe there will be another time."

"You don't believe in fate?" I questioned with a smirk.

"No, Vincent, I certainly do not." She hopped off the side of the car suddenly. "I better get back to it. Lots more packing to do and such."

"I don't envy you."

"Oh, but you should! Think about all the tedious bullshit you are missing out on!"

"I'll pass."

"Maybe another time then," she smirked and turned in the direction of the elevator. "It was nice meeting you Vincent. Good luck with your situation. It'll work itself out the way it should. And thanks."

"For what?"

"For being in my hiding spot." She clicked the button and within moments the *ding* could be heard as the elevator doors opened.

"Murph?" I called out.

"Yeah?" she asked from inside the elevator.

"You're making the right choice."

"I already knew that, stupid," she quipped as the doors closed.

It was completely dark out now. The sounds of traffic returned, and I heard the audience standing up to leave their seats. The show was over. Nothing left to see that night.

I stayed up there long after the credits stopped rolling.

# forty

## MY WAY

I was ecstatic to get away from Dallas and Evan for my sister's wedding. Things were still raw, and I couldn't survive a whole weekend of stale air between us.

The wedding was three years in the making. They had been engaged for FOREVER because her fiancé was down in Miami getting his doctorate. Once he figured out when he was graduating, they set a date. Everyone was thrilled that it was finally happening. You knew all that already though.

The best part?

To my knowledge, my mom and sister did not have any blowouts over the details of the wedding. It was an unexpected twist. My mom could be demanding and controlling, but in a way where she only wanted what was best. My sister was headstrong and refused to believe anyone could have her best interests at heart. I gave up a long time ago to mend the divide between the two of them. My mom loved her fiercely; my sister also loved my parents, but she happened to be an emotionless git which make it difficult to understand her intentions.

Nothing of note happened on Thursday when I arrived back home in my rental car. My parents were in slight panic mode, so I tried to dodge, duck, dip, dive, and dodge any of the incoming fallout from that.

I gave Rigby all the hugs she deserved, which was a ludicrous amount. Don't judge me. I love that Buhl.

Thursday morphed into Friday. It would be a busy day of travel. My parents would take two cars down to the beach house they were renting for the weekend in some upscale part of the Jersey Shore. It was my first time heading down there since the hurricane back when I was in college. Within their two cars, they would be lugging an excess of supplies for the wedding and the three dogs. Quite the chore.

I, on the other hand, had the wonderful task of snatching up my grandma and Walter. Every time I picked them up from their abode, I felt as if I was a part of an elaborate breakout. We would always scurry out the building with all eyes upon us. In one sense it made me sad to think some of the folks who lived there never saw visitors, but I tried to push that thought aside. It was meant to be a joyful weekend with nothing but happy thoughts!

I drove at a leisurely pace, listening to the stories of old from my two passengers. In-between their stories, they peppered me with the usual questions of how my life was going. I told them that everything was fine because what else was I supposed to say?

I dropped them off at the hotel. They weren't staying at the house due to the lack of enough bedrooms on the first floor. Navigating stairs became the arch nemesis for the older generation.

I helped them with their luggage and before leaving, confirmed I'd be over in a few hours to pick them up for the rehearsal dinner.

The drive over to the house from the hotel was through a series of dilapidated neighborhoods that were clearly not seeing the prosperity of the area we were staying in. After crossing over a major roadway, I was greeted by the mansions. The sprawling houses of various styles and sizes lined the streets. Some were painted outlandish colors to stick out from the crowd, while others were hidden behind a thick layer of foliage.

The GeePuS brought me to the house without issue, but it would have been easy to spot from a block away. There were cars stacked in the driveway and on the front curb. It was evident I was one of the last to arrive.

I squeezed in behind the massive truck that took up a third of the driveway. I snagged my luggage from the car and walked into the house from the entrance in the garage.

As if they knew my exact arrival time, I was greeted by three faces when I opened the door. Their tails wagged furiously as they seemingly forgot I had seen them a few hours earlier. I gave them attention until they wandered off to busy themselves with exploring the house more.

It was quite the sight. Once beyond the hallway that led away from the garage, you were greeted with a massive open space that vaulted up three stories to the roof. Oak paneling lined the walls with oak beams jutting in several directions across the ceiling. The chatter of numerous voices echoed throughout the open space. One bedroom sat next to the front door on my right. Straight ahead was the kitchen and dining room. Between the two was the staircase that brought you up to a small landing before you could hop up a couple steps to get to the second floor. A bedroom stood immediately to your left. Walking down the hallway that overlooked the first floor brought you to the remaining bedrooms on the second floor. Up the spiral staircase you could go to find the last bedroom with a set of bay doors that opened up to a balcony in case you wanted to see what was happening outside. The space wasn't overly lavish like you may be expecting; it was massive though. It felt as if there was enough room to sleep a hundred people easily and that's before utilizing the backyard.

My mom was super excited to get the house for the weekend and showed me a dizzying number of pictures beforehand, so I had a solid idea of the layout by the time I reached the living room.

The commotion from the dogs gained the attention of everyone and I was greeted with hugs. My mom, dad, sister, and several of her bridesmaids were lounging on the couches and talking about the day's activities.

The next day passed at a lightening pace. There seemed to be things happening at every moment. None of them are worth rehashing to you. If you have been a part of one wedding, you understand the gist of what went down. Instead, we rejoin each other on the trolley ride from the park, where a majority of the wedding pictures were taken, to the venue.

It was as if I had awoken from a coma and had just become familiar with my surroundings. I sat in the back of the trolley and surveyed the scene while occasionally making a fist. *Am I already losing strength? No. The doctor said that wouldn't happen for—*

"Vin," a tap on my shoulder, "time for a shot."

"Yeah . . . yeah, let's do it," I said, ripping myself from my own thought.

Lorenzo presented me with a red solo cup that was filled with a tiny amount of liquid. We slammed the cups together, gave a nod to each other, and flung back the drink.

He was wearing a light gray tux with a pink bowtie. I looked around and spotted the others with the identical get-up. I had never worn a tux before, so I was thrown off by how you don't need to wear a belt. Seemed like an odd thing not to include, but I guess it was standard.

He looked happy as he talked excitedly with the other groomsmen. I had met them back in July at the bachelor party. They were a solid group of friends who welcomed me into the fold without any awkwardness. It had been a fun weekend of drinking and general debauchery.

The trolley came to a stop in front of the venue and we all filtered out into the parking lot. I swayed slightly as the alcohol worked its way through my system.

"You look great," a voice said in my direction.

I turned to locate the source and found my mom in a purple dress. She had slimmed down significantly for the wedding, which restored any lost confidence for her.

"So do you," I called over.

We were ushered over to an area behind the altar to take a series of family photos. It was an arduous affair that lasted longer than expected, but there were some good pictures that came out of it.

Following the last batch of pictures, my sister, Lorenzo, and myself rejoined the wedding party in the back room.

The maître d' strolled into the room a few minutes later to let us all know that the first guests had arrived and we should start to get ready.

One of the bridesmaids snatched the bottle of champagne from its perch and took a long gulp from it. "Any other takers?" she asked. "I'm trying to get rid of any pre-wedding jitters."

Naturally, everyone took a healthy amount from the bottle. Ya know, just to loosen up for the walk down the aisle.

I took one last bathroom break and stared into the mirror as I tucked my shirt back into my pants. My face looked more defined do to the excess weight I had lost over the previous couple of months. Light stubble covered my face and the haircut from that morning was still holding my jumble of hair in proper order. I took a deep breath and continued to stare, waiting for the image in the mirror to move. Eventually it did, and I walked back out into the holding room.

"Okay! It's go time!" the maître d' said as he came back into the room.

We all pushed out the doorway and formed into two rows. I walked up toward the front and stood next to my mom.

"Remember: there's no rush. Take your time walking back. We won't send anyone else down until you come back," the maître d' told me as he walked by. I nodded in his direction.

"It's finally happening," my mom said while squeezing my hand.

The next thing I remember was standing up at the altar, off to the side, with a leash held tight in my hand. I looked down and saw how I was making sure Gunner didn't bolt off. *That's right. He brought the rings*, I reminded myself.

The vows were exchanged and then I recall walking back down the aisle with the dog in tow. He wanted to sniff and greet every person we passed by, so I held on tightly to the leash.

Back into the holding room. Everyone was celebrating. They were officially married.

Next, I was walking around cocktail hour and saying hi to all the family and friends I passed by. Conversations were brief and impossible to recall in hindsight.

The hour passed in a blink and we were shuffled back into the holding room as all the guests were brought upstairs and sat at the appropriate tables.

The wedding party snuck around back and up a secret set of stairs that put us near the kitchen. We were gearing up for our entrance and I was hit with a devastating bout of stage fright. People were expecting each couple of the wedding party to do something witty and I just didn't have the aptitude to pull something like that off.

Next, I was at my seat. *What happened*, I wondered. The afternoon was passing by in chunks of time I could barely recall. I just hoped I hadn't done anything stupid.

My mom leaned over to me and said, "Vin, your dad said that he won't be able to give the speech. Will you be able to do it? Do you have anything prepared?"

For months, my dad had been waffling on giving the Father of the Bride speech in front of everyone. Whenever he would talk about it, he would start to clam up and get extremely anxious. My mom warned that I had to step in if he wasn't able to do it. I promised her I would think about what to say if I had to give the speech myself, but, of course, I did not.

"Yeah, I can do it," I answered back.

Everything slowed. The rest of the night played out at normal speed—as I wished the whole day would have.

My mom called over the emcee and whispered something to him. He looked over at me and mouthed the word *Vin?* and I nodded.

Several minutes later, he spoke into the microphone: "Let's give it up for the bride and groom! As you get settled in, we would like to start with the speeches. First up, we have Vin Besser, the brother of the bride."

I hesitated a moment and the emcee raised his eyebrows. My brain clicked that it was my signal to stand up, so I did. I moved out into the middle of the dance floor that separated the two sides of the room and grabbed the microphone.

*Do not fuck this up!*

"Instead of doing the Father of the Bride speech, my family decided to do a *Family* of the Bride speech. For those that know us—which I assume is a lot of you in this room—you know that we are anything but traditional . . ."

Slight laughter from the audience. It was more of a sympathy laugh than anything, but it gave me enough courage to keep going.

"First of all, I'd like to thank Lorenzo's family and friends for being here. I don't know too many of you yet, but I am excited to meet you all and spend time together in the years to come. Secondly, I'd like to thank our family and friends for being here. I was lucky enough to grow up in a neighborhood surrounded by amazing people and it's great to see you all here tonight as well. Okay"—turning my attention to the small table behind me—"finally, for the bride and groom." A rip of applause from both sides of the room. "I'm not the first to say it tonight and I probably won't be the last, but you two have been through an incredible journey together so far. Spending as much time apart as you did would challenge any relationship and yet you managed to overcome it. I have been fortunate to watch it from afar. From me, my parents, and everyone else in this room, we look forward to seeing you two grow in the many years ahead. Now if everyone could, I'd like to do a toast to the bride and groom. Congratulations!"

The clinking of glasses could be heard all around.

Understanding that I was done, the emcee came back over and grabbed the microphone and freeing me up to move back to my seat. My mom gave me a hug and my dad leaned over to give my shoulder a squeeze.

I'd never claim the speech was revolutionary, but I refrained from any sort of self-deprecating humor which was a step in the right direction.

Several more speeches followed, but I hardly paid attention to them. When those were out of the way, the first batch of food was delivered to the tables. Music played softly in the background as not to disturb the conversations happening.

After gnawing on a piece of beard like a Neanderthal, I finally took notice of the song that was playing.

"My Way" by Frank Sinatra. The happiest song about death.

I stood up and walked over to my grandma on the opposite side of the round table.

"Time to dance," I said. "This is your favorite song!"

"No. No. I can't dance," she stressed back to me. She had some misfortune recently and her balance wasn't what it used to be, so she was nervous to walk anywhere without her walker.

"It's okay. I'll be dancing with you the whole time," I said, attempting to squash any fear.

My mom chimed in. "Go ahead, Mom!"

She finally nodded and began to push back her chair. I grabbed her hand and led her the short distance out to the deserted dance floor. We took up residence near our table and started to do a slight sway back and forth.

After two minutes of dancing, I leaned down and said, "I forgot how long this song is. And everyone is staring at us too."

She laughed. "They're just jealous."

I didn't mind it though. Everyone could stare if they wanted though I seemed to think they were admiring us more than anything. There was no place else I wanted to be in that moment. I was guilty of taking advantage of assuming my grandma would always be there. For twenty-five years she was, but it was naïve to think it would always be the case. I reminded myself it was moments like this that I'd remember. Not the hook ups, not the fights with Evan, not the laborious days at work, but the quiet moments with the ones you loved.

For once, the audience that followed me around was one that was filled with familiar faces of people who knew me, of people that cared about me. It was refreshing, and I had to remind myself that a majority of them knew I was gay, which spared me from awkward conversation.

The song did eventually end, and I brought her back to the table. Some say that the smile on her face is still there to this day.

Much of the remaining time at the wedding consisted of trips to the bar, trips to the bathroom, or trips to the dance floor.

Each time one of those events happened, I had a conversation with a different person.

One time, I ran into my cousin and walked over together to get a drink. He filled me in on how being an FBI agent was going. I'd tell you his name, but I'd probably get put on some Most Wanted list.

Another time, I started talking with Ralph, my old neighbor. He was the Vietnam vet I spoke of at the end of the previous book.

"Hey Vinny! How about those Eagles? They are going for two straight! You just watch!"

"As long as the Giants beat them, I could care less how they end up doing," I said with a pat on the back.

He turned back to the music and continued to dance like he had no aches.

At one point, the entire neighborhood (and others) were gathered in a circle and sang "Sweet Caroline" as was decreed to be done at every social event that involved the neighborhood for as long as I could remember.

During another trip to the bar, I ran into Ellie.

"Vinny Boy! Long time no see."

"Ellie! Glad you could make it. How is everything going?"

"About as well as it could be. I am moving out to California soon to move in with Lorenzo," she said, motioning to the guy walking toward us.

(The more I write, the more I realize how I know a bunch of people with the same names. It is sort of freaky once you come to terms with that.)

"Wait?! The guy from Coachella you kept meeting up with?"

"Yeah. We have been dating ever since then. Ren—you remember Vinny?"

"Of course. What's up, man?" he said all suave-like.

We shook hands.

He seemed like a nice enough guy and obviously they cared about each other enough if they kept a long-distance relationship running for over a year before moving in together, so he got my seal of approval as if that meant anything.

"Let's do a shot," she commanded.

The bartender stressed they weren't supposed to give away shots unless the maître d' said it was alright, but after a minute of pleading, Ellie walked away with three.

"To new beginnings," she said.

I threw back the shot without hesitation, numb to the sensation of alcohol burning down my throat.

I excused myself from the duo and went to the bathroom. Nothing eventful happened in there. Following my excursion, I returned to the bar since the gravitational pull was way too strong to ignore and I ran into the mother of my former friend.

"Hey Cindy! How are you?" I asked, giving her a hug.

"I'm doing great! This is an amazing wedding and you look great!"

"Thanks. So do you." She looked the same as when I met her for the first time twenty years ago.

"How is everything down in Dallas?"

I told her. For an idea of what I may have said, I will refer you to the previous eighty thousand words you have read, only with slightly more optimism.

She nodded and absorbed the information. "Nate misses you," she said suddenly. (I forgot to mention that Nate's mom was very good friends with my mom still. For a refresher on who Nate is and why the name sounds familiar, please refer to Chapter 13 of *I Wanna Get Better*, which can be found in your local trashcan.)

"I . . . I miss him too. I haven't talked to him since I visited him in Vegas," I said, taken off guard by her comment. "He moved back home, right?"

"Well, he moved closer. He is living outside of Washington D.C. at the moment. Still dating the same girl from college. It's amazing to me they have made it this far," she mumbled the last part mostly to herself.

"I'm glad he is doing well. It's not surprising to hear. He was always driven and talked about the idea of leaving Easton."

"Yeah, it's hard though. One part of me wishes that he was closer. I'm sure you understand that though with being so far away."

"For sure. I will make my way back to the East Coast at some point."

We stood idle for a few seconds, unsure where to go from there.

Cindy eventually said, "So, I just wanted to tell you that your mom told me—"

"I figured as much."

"You know this doesn't change how I see you. You will always be the little kid that came over to the house. So polite," she said, attempting half-heartedly to hold back the tears. "I know that Nate feels the same way. You two were such good friends. Such good friends . . ." she trailed off.

I pulled her in for a hug.

There was a part of me that wanted to cry with her because I missed those days too. I missed being friends with Nate and always going over to hang out in their basement. It was never about anything more than two kids just trying to keep each other company. Things were easier. There was another part of me that wanted to cry because the booze told me to do so.

But I was too emotionally damaged to actually show any emotion. The years of useless shit I had put myself through closed me off from ever being normal again, from ever being that carefree kid.

I had been through the motions of this conversations enough times to understand how it would end. She would walk away feeling as if she did a good service by telling me I was accepted and nothing would change. I no longer needed the validation. This coming-out story had dragged on for long enough. I was ready to move on. They could find another trauma somewhere else.

We talked for a bit longer before I walked back to the dance floor.

My sister was in the middle of a large group, hopping up and down, and enjoying every second she had left. I was thrilled for her.

The time remaining for the wedding seeped out like sand from an hourglass—slowly and then all in one final push.

The DJ played one final song and the lights came back on within the venue. People began to grab their coats and head for the exit.

There were so many people I didn't get a chance to speak to and I wasn't sure when I would see them again, but hopefully it would be sometime soon.

# forty-one

## TIME

After a morning spent at the hotel saying goodbye to my sister, her husband, and most of the wedding party, I returned to the house.

It was eerily quiet compared to the day before. I came in through the garage and the dogs didn't even get up to see me; they just picked up their heads, saw the familiar face, and returned to their nap.

My mom was cleaning absentmindedly around the house. She insisted she had to even though part of the cost for the rental was a cleaning fee. I could hear the sounds of a crowd and sporadically spaced whistles coming from a television somewhere in the house, which meant my dad was watching football.

"Why are you cleaning?" I walked into the kitchen and asked.

"You know me. I couldn't leave this place a mess."

I grabbed a donut from the box and took a chunk out of it. "We should do something today. No sense in just sitting around here when it's so nice out," pieces of donut fell out of my mouth and onto the counter. I quickly wiped it up before she saw.

"That's a good idea. We could take the dogs for a walk and drive over to Point Pleasant."

"Works for me. So, what did you think of yesterday?"

"I think it went perfectly. It seemed like everyone had a great time. The food was good. My only complaint was that they kept switching the songs before they would end, and you always missed the best part! But that is such a silly thing to be upset about."

"It really was the most ideal wedding you could have wanted. I'm glad it worked out so well. I don't know what you will have to look forward to now."

"Grandkids."

"You will have a while for that unless you know something I don't."

"If they were smart, they would enjoy a few years together before having kids."

"I'm sure they will. They don't even have their own place yet." Lorenzo was still having trouble finding a job, so they would continue to live at my parent's house once they got back from their honeymoon. The tension would continue to rise between my mom and my sister. It was an inevitable explosion, and someone was going to say something regretful.

"By the way," she stopped cleaning and turned to me, "thanks for all your help this weekend. We couldn't have done it without you."

"Of course. That's what I'm here for."

"I didn't even get to spend any time with you. I was so busy running around the whole time and now you have to go back tomorrow," she said mainly to herself. "It never gets any easier."

"Who knows. I could be back on the East Coast one day." *I wouldn't be.*

"You won't come back here. I know you." Damn, she called me on my bluff.

*Tell her. She needs to know. If not now, when?*

I wanted to, but how could you ever find the right words? So I stayed quiet until she spoke again.

"How are things with you and Evan?"

"Not good. We just don't have any interests that intersect with each other and our demeanors are so opposite. I really don't understand how people say that opposites attract because while that was initially the case with us, it has been pulling us apart." I felt like I had repeated that same answer a dozen times to people.

"You two should still be in the honeymoon phase. This is the easy part, so I'm not sure that is a good sign."

"Yeah, honestly, I don't feel like talking about it. It makes me anxious and I spend way too much time thinking about it already."

"Okay. Well, I'm here if you need to talk about anything."

*TELL HER!*

"Thanks."

*You stupid motherfucker.*

"Let me get your dad and tell him to get ready," she said while walking towards the stairs.

Half an hour later, the three dogs were all harnessed up and moving about wildly at the idea of going on a walk. Unfortunately for them, it didn't last long once we realized dogs weren't even allowed on the boardwalk.

With them stowed back in the house, we took the car and drove along the coast. We passed through towns I had never heard of. The same style of mansions permeated for miles until we crossed over the bridge into Point Pleasant. We tossed around stopping at the boardwalk, but no one seemed too keen on the idea, so we kept going down Route 35.

"Jesus . . . look at all the empty lots," I said as I slid across the backseat to get a better view out the window. In the usual spots of the multi-million-dollar homes were vacant lots—just large patches of sand where the foundation of the house once stood. The devastation of the storm was still apparent.

"Why do you think some of the area is still empty?" I asked.

"People are probably scared to rebuild. Worried it'll happen again," my dad said from the passenger seat.

It was naïve to think any of those houses were someone's first home, but it was strange nonetheless to see so much nothingness in a place where I distinctly remembered passing by each year growing up and admiring all the houses.

We continued ahead until we hit Seaside Heights. There wasn't much to see, so we turned around and went back the direction we came.

Ten minutes up the road, my mom made a detour and passed by the house we used to rent. It was largely different. It was now propped up on pylons to avoid any flooding. The pink color was exchanged for a more modest grey that allowed it to fade into every other house on the block. The memories from that place were abundant, too many to ever recall.

It was the second time that weekend my heart ached to be back to a younger age when everything was mellow. But it was foolish to think I didn't have worries back then—they were just a different beast. The spirals always led to the same place.

We stopped for dinner at some generic restaurant and got a generic round of burgers. Needless to say, nothing more eventful happened that day.

I helped pack the cars the next day with almost as much stuff as they came down with. As my mom went to wrangle the dogs and do one last walkthrough of the house, my dad and I stood aimlessly waiting for one of us to speak.

He decided to.

"We're glad you came for the whole weekend."

"Of course. I was happy to take off as much time as needed."

"You know, I never thanked you for giving the speech. I know it wasn't a big deal for you, but it meant a lot that you went up there and did that."

He stepped closer, gave me a hug, and continued, "You're a great kid. We are lucky to have you. I'm sure I don't tell you enough. I love you very much."

"Love you too," I managed to say.

We stepped back from each other and I saw he was trying to hold himself together. He cried several times throughout the wedding, so it was just an emotionally draining weekend for him.

In that moment, I felt like the biggest idiot. A simple gesture and kind words were enough to throw me from the funk where I actually believed my dad didn't love me anymore. He would never be the type to sit down and openly talk about my sexuality or any of the details regarding my half-sister, but it was undeniable that he loved his children very much. I was extremely foolish to think anything otherwise.

My mom came out with the three dogs and we herded them into the car. I gave them each one more hug.

"You'll be home for Christmas, right?"

"Yeah, I should be."

"Okay. We are going to miss you," she said.

"You always do. I wouldn't expect anything different."

"Drive safe and let me know when you make it to the airport—"

"Okay."

"—and text me your flight information too."

"Okay."

"I love you Vin. Very much."

"Love you too."

I took once last look at my parents and the dogs staring curiously back at me through the window.

I never wanted that scene to change. Three weird dogs, two healthy parents, and one fucked up son who was decaying.

Time changes everything though. The bubble always pops and reality saunters in with a drunken sway to destroy it all.

All you can do is live a great story and try not to get caught up in the chapters that sucked. There's no such thing as a perfect story in my experience.

# forty-two

## HIGH **HOPES**

This story ends in a similar vein to how it started . . .
I was high.
I was high and gazing into the nearly cloudless sky through the scattered branches on the tree. Evan was snoring next to me. It amazed me how he was able to fall asleep while so many people moved around us.

I was paranoid again. Paranoid that someone was going to step on me or try to steal my phone. Sleep clawed at me, begging for an escape but I continued to deny it and laid there.

It was Saturday and we were at Austin City Limits.

We managed to walk from the beer tent to a patch of grass in the shade that was unoccupied. We collapsed into a heap and Evan fell asleep immediately.

I decided to sit up and watch the crowds as they passed by. It was a muted music festival compared to Coachella, but I didn't mind. The crowds quickly became uninteresting as none of the truly eclectic people were milling around yet.

The high was wearing off and I figured the same must be true for Evan. I continued to underestimate the power of edibles.

"Evan," I said, nudging him. "Wake up."

He stirred briefly and muttered something unintelligible.

"You wanted to see Hozier, right?"

"No. Not really."

"Well, I do. They are performing soon. You can stay here if you don't want to go."

"Fine. I'll get up," he said. He pushed myself up onto his elbows and looked over at me. "Happy?"

*No.*

"Of course. Aren't I always?" I pleaded.

"Hardly."

It took several more minutes for Evan to compose himself. We wandered over to the stage and had a decent spot that was off-centered and fifteen rows back. We stood there for quite a long time before the band came out.

The set wasn't very good. It was overly chaotic, and the singer seemed aloof.

Oh well, onto the next one.

"Where to?" I asked.

"ODESZA for me."

"I wanted to see Paul McCartney."

"I have no interest in that," he said flatly.

"Uh, alright. Well, I have no interest in ODESZA so I won't be going to that."

"Fine."

"What's wrong?"

"Nothing is wrong."

"Okay . . . where should we meet after the shows?" I looked over at a series of flagpoles and pointed in that direction. "How about over there?"

"Fine. I'll see you after the show," he said and gave me a hug.

I forced my way through the forming crowd in front of the main stage until I was unable to inch forward any closer.

I had an hour until the show started, which meant a lot of time for my brain to run rampant.

It seemed like an amazing opportunity to reflect on the state of my life and my present situation, so I did just that.

I never expected to meet anyone significant in Dallas. That's not to say anyone before Evan wasn't, but I found it hard to visualize myself in a relationship. Obviously, that became a reality and now I had a hard time picturing myself single again. The idea of having to start over and open yourself up to someone new was daunting. Had I ever opened up to Evan though? I continued to keep him at arm's length because it was easier than letting him in fully. I didn't want him to see that my façade was paper thin and once he discovered my true nature, he would run to the nearest gay bar. After months and months of being so distant, Evan had finally caught on and peeked behind the curtain. What did he think of me now? I didn't have the slightest idea.

*Liar. Cheater. That's what he thinks.*

I wanted it to work out, but now, more so than ever before, things would change. They had to. There was no other way to receive the news I did and not have things shift. And still, after all the times I've teased it, I continue to be afraid in telling you. I can't even write the words.

*Who's going to get the good side?*

The lights on the stage dimmed and a roar rippled through the crowd. You know what happened next. We have been through this enough times before.

Paul McCartney played for over two hours and by the time I freed myself from the crowd and regained cell service, I had several messages from an impatient Evan.

I found him quite easily underneath the flagpoles considering he was one of the few people not heading to the exits. He was laying down, staring into oblivion.

"Hi," I said as I towered over him. "How was the show?"

"It was good. I smoked again," he said with a chuckle.

"How'd you manage to do that?"

"Someone offered me a blunt and I took it," he responded with slight confusion.

"Oh. Makes sense."

"Can we lay here a bit? I don't really feel like walking."

"Probably. Until someone walks by and tells us to leave."

I took a seat next to him and couldn't see him very well through the minimal lighting.

"I got a job," he said suddenly.

"How high are you? You already have a job."

"No," he shook his head. "A new one."

"Oh." There was a chance it would be a new job in Dallas, right?

"It's in Denver."

My heart sank deeper than the Mariana Trench. I had been anticipating some sort of news for weeks, but after a while I figured he gave up his search since he never talked about it.

"Are—uh—are you going to take it?"

"Well, yeah. I accepted it last week."

"Why are you telling me this now?"

"Did you want me to just move away and never mention anything?"

"No."

"There wasn't a good time to tell you and quite frankly the weed gave me some courage to do so. I always feel so much lighter and free of worries."

"When are—"

"Vin, I wanted this to work. I desperately did. I love you a lot, but you never gave me anything. You never understood what I needed, and rarely did you actually care to ask. I didn't want Dallas to be a stepping-stone. I'm tired of moving and tired of assuming the next place I go will be permanent, but I really feel like Denver will be what I need. The job is an upgrade from my current one too, which was important.

"I am so grateful for the time we spent together and the people you introduced me to," he finished with.

"Was not expecting that. I mean, I was, but—shit dude—I was not expecting you to do it now."

"I'm sorry," he said. It was difficult to tell if he was crying through the noise of everyone passing by. Honestly, it wouldn't have changed anything if he was.

"When do you leave?" I asked. The relapse of emotion that briefly passed through me disappeared in an instant. I was back to the person who wanted to change but didn't know how.

Nah. Fuck that.

I was now the person who didn't care to change. I'd go back to the hook ups. I couldn't wait to get back on Grindr and spend my life having meaningless conversation with people who were just as pathetic as me. I couldn't wait to waste away with them.

"In a week," he said quietly.

"How long have you known?"

"I told you I was doing a recruiting event, but I actually flew out to Denver. They called me a week later with the offer. I guess that was about two weeks ago."

"I'm assuming we won't even attempt a long-distance relationship."

"I thought about it, but I know it wouldn't work. I'd rather end it now on a somewhat good note instead of watching it fade to nothing."

"I understand."

"That's it? Do you even care? You seem unbothered by all this."

"I care, but I'm not going to be a bitch about something I had no control over."

"You did have control over this! You could have changed. You could have if you really wanted to."

"Evan, you never told me anything about how you felt. All you did is bitch about your job, so I'm not surprised you are running off to go somewhere else. It's what you do. I'm not going to chase after you and convince you otherwise when you made your decision without even talking to me. That's fucked up. I hope you know that."

He didn't acknowledge my rant and instead said, "Are you upset?"

"Are you?" I asked, denying his request to answer the question.

"Yes."

"I'm numb to it so I apologize if I am not showing the emotion you were expecting."

"I didn't know what to expect . . ."

"Okay. Well, I'm ready to go now."

*This is perfect. You are sparing him. Let Evan have the good side. It's a consolation prize for his wasted time.*

He struggled, but eventually got to his feet. We headed for the exit and away from the piles of people until the Lyft was an acceptable rate.

Not a word passed between us for the duration of the walk and the ride back to the house.

Once inside, he moved quietly to the bedroom. I didn't even make it there and stayed on the couch.

I stared up at the Stucco ceiling and the nothingness beyond it. I lifted up my arm and caught a glimpse of the tattoo. Most days I forgot I even had it.

The funny thing about compasses is that they don't just point you forward.

Before turning over to try and find the sleep I knew I wouldn't get, I checked my phone. The brightness of the screen caused my eyes to water.

I didn't have any new messages. The time was the only thing my phone had to show me.

You already know what it was.

Nothing ever changed.

# EPILOGUE

## MOTORCYCLE DRIVE BY

It may be said by some that this epilogue is unnecessary. This could have easily been the final chapter of the book, but as I sit here weeks later, this feels like a necessary bookend. And obviously, since I wrote a prologue, it's mandatory I follow through with the epilogue. First rule of writing. Trust me.

Three days following The Breakup (as the event will be known), I found myself sitting in a booth at an El Fenix. It was a quaint chain of Tex-Mex restaurants that spanned the Dallas area. I munched contently on chips and salsa and absentmindedly scrolled through Grindr. The selection was limited and the ones who were nearby demanded to be ignored due to their ridiculous requests and inability to form even the most basic words. But we have already covered this topic way back when, right? Honestly, is there anything that hasn't been talked about multiple times in these damn books?

With virtually no sound at all, Dylan slid into the booth on the opposite side from me. I quickly put down my phone in the false hope he hadn't witnessed me being desperate.

"Hi," he decided to say.

"Hey. Thanks for coming."

He looked the same as the last time I saw him months earlier. Something told me he would look like a pre-pubescent teenager for the rest of his life.

Time undoubtedly erases many recollections of past conversations, so I firmly believed Dylan wouldn't be bringing up anything from our last face to face encounter. I didn't intend to either.

"What happened?" he asked me.

Earlier that day, I had texted him on the off-chance he would respond. Obviously, he did, and I told him I needed to not sit around my apartment for the entire night or else I'd likely do something regrettable.

"He got a job and is moving to Denver. Nothing much more to it than that."
"I don't believe that."
"Don't worry. It's how it was supposed to be. He got the good side."
"What does th—"

The waiter came over, grabbed our drink orders, and since we were seasoned professionals, we ordered food as well.

"How are you feeling?" he continued, abandoning the previous thread. He seemed genuinely concerned.

"This is going to sound terrible, but I feel relieved."

He bit into a chip right as I said that, and a look of confusion appeared on his face. "What?" he asked, spraying crumbs in my direction.

"For months it felt like he had been dangling this notion of him getting a job in another city. We didn't talk about it much, but it felt like a threat. As in, if I didn't get my shit together he would leave. While all that was happening, I just couldn't move past that we weren't right for each other. I began to think we were wasting each other's time. I was so anxious and constantly bogged down that while I was definitely upset when it happened, I didn't fight too hard for him."

"Wow. That's kind of fucked up."

I shrugged. "We hadn't even been dating a year. Would you have done it differently?"

"Yes."

"Does it matter?"

"Well, it's not like it would change anything at this point."

"You gotta understand that I was gluttonous for Alex. No matter how much he hurt me, I always went back for more, which is why I would have tried to persuade him more to stay."

"What is the deal with you and Alex now? The last time I saw you—months and months ago, dickhead—he had moved back in with you."

"He is essentially a full-blown heroin addict and needs rehab. I couldn't take it anymore and kicked me out. I have tried to tell his family that he needs help, but they refuse to believe it. Sometimes I have dreams about him overdosing and I . . . I just—I don't really want to talk about it. I'm trying to move past it all."

"You know I'm here to talk if you ever need someone to listen."

"Yeah."

"There is one thing that fucked me up more than anything about The Breakup."

"What's that?" he said as he inhaled a large portion of his drink. He was finally twenty-one and could live a normal life like every other adult.

"He came home with me to Pennsylvania back in September—"

"He met your family?" he asked incredulously.

"Well, yeah."

"Wow. Continue," he said, moving his finger in a rolling motion.

"He came to Pennsylvania in September and the weekend went fine. It seemed like everyone liked him and my dad was surprisingly chill about the situation. There was something off though. This intangible issue hung in the air between us. It wasn't until the flight back home that I realized it . . . he was the thing before the thing. For a long time, I figured that the hook ups, the pain, the anger, the lies, the cheating, and all the other emotions were the things before the thing and that Evan would be the turning point, but it wasn't the case. The worst part is that now I really believe Evan is going to get it right next time. Whoever he dates next will be the one that lasts a lifetime, so, in reality, I was the thing before the thing for him. It's a shitty conclusion to jump to and considering I don't have any facts to back that up, it's all just useless conjecture."

"That is way too deep, but I'll indulge you for a second. If he *was* the thing before the thing, what is the thing now? Christ, how many times can the word *thing* be said in this conversation?" he wondered aloud.

"It's funny you ask because The Breakup wasn't the real reason I asked you to dinner. There's been this *thing* that happened not too long ago now that I haven't told anyone about."

He sat up in the booth and stared intently at me.

I continued: "Since the end of last year, I have been getting random headaches that would pop up and ruin my whole day. It felt like I was standing in front of a pitching machine and getting repeatedly smacked in the head with baseballs. I held off on going to the doctor for such a long time because it felt miniscule. My mom has a history of headaches—she'd call them migraines—so I figured it was hereditary. Eventually, I decided to go. I had run out of excuses I made up for myself. The doctor asked me how I was feeling besides the headaches and I said I was fine except for this strange twitching in my thumb. It was difficult to recall when it started, but it was around for long enough that I was slightly concerned about it. He asked me to make a fist and I did. It felt like someone was trying to hold my hand from closing, like there was some unseen resistance. He told me I shouldn't worry, but he figured it would a good idea to run some tests to see if the twitching had any underlying issues. It brought back memories of the time with my heart."

"You had issues with your heart?"

"Yes, but no. That's a different story for another time."

Our food sat untouched.

I fished Evan's apartment key out of my pocket and fiddled with it in my hands, thinking briefly about a different time.

"I'll spare you the middle part of the story where various tests happened, and second opinions were gathered."

For too long—far too long—I had kept the next bit of information to myself. I shocked myself a bit because I generally told people I was close with practically everything. I was so afraid of being a burden and being fearful for how the information would change things that I ran away from it. I hid behind the books and the video games and the carrot of attempting to fix my relationship with Evan that sometimes I completely forgot I was slowly dying.

"Have you ever heard of ALS?"

He shook his head.

"It's also called Lou Gehrig's Disease. Maybe that rings a bell?"

"I have no clue who that is."

"Oh. Wow. Uh, okay, we will work on your knowledge of sports."

"Wait. Isn't this the thing that everyone was doing that bucket challenge for a few years ago?"

"Exactly. The ice bucket challenge was to raise money to research a cure."

He nodded.

"Anyways, ALS is a neurological disease that essentially destroys your nerve cells. When I was younger, my best friend's dad was diagnosed with ALS. For several years, it was impossible to tell he was sick. It wasn't until the muscle started to fade away and the breathing became more difficult and he wasn't able to walk anymore that you realized how savagely the disease could ravage someone. Essentially, over the next five years, I am going to waste away to practically nothing. I'm the youngest case my doctors have ever seen. Imagine that," I finished with a nervous chuckle.

The tears were building up, but I attempted to keep them locked away. I didn't want to get tears on my cold food.

Dylan's eyes widened, and he leaned back in the booth.

"I—what the fuck? I . . . uh, don't know what to say," he continued.

"It's okay. I'm sorry. It's a heavy burden to throw on someone."

"You haven't told anyone else yet?"

"No, it just hasn't felt right. But after Evan and I broke up, I knew I couldn't run from it anymore. I don't think I can tell my family though. I just—how do you even tell them that?"

"How are you feeling?" he asked, each syllable stressed as tears flooded into his eyes too.

"I feel fine! That's the crazy part. I am taking medication that will hopefully slow down the symptoms for a while, but there isn't a cure for this, so I technically have an expiration date sometime in the near future.

"I do find this funny though," I said.

"Why?" he asked with hesitation.

"Because I have wanted this. I joked so many times about dropping dead and how I would die at a young age. I finally got my wish! The only drawback is that it's going to be a slow, debilitating end where I will be dependent on others to help me survive for just a bit longer. It feels like I got all but one number correct in the lottery."

"We can go and get other opinions. I know doctors in other cities. I have friends who mus—"

"Dylan, I just need a friend right now. There will come a time when I severely contemplate my morality, but I am healthy right now. I don't have this magical list of items I want to complete before I die. I just want to live."

"We can do that. You need to tell your family though. They have to know."

"I'll tell them sometime after Christmas. I don't want to tell them beforehand and have that be the first time they see me. It will completely ruin the holiday. I have time. They will be angry I didn't tell them right away, but they will understand."

I thought momentarily and then resumed talking.

"Have you ever heard of Third Eye Blind?"

"Uhh, no. Not that I recall," he said

"They are a band from the nineties. Pretty famous. I stumbled upon their first album and listened to the whole thing. One of the last songs on the album is called 'Motorcycle Drive By.' It's a great song and I have really gravitated recently to the line that goes:

> *I've never been so alone*
> *And I've . . . never been so alive*

I'm scared. So fucking scared. I'm trying to run from the notion that I am dying, but I am having trouble. In that regard, I'm alone—"

"What is it with you and music lyrics?" he questioned. He grabbed the napkin and covered his face in an effort to wipe the tears away. After he composed himself again, he continued and said sternly, "You aren't alone though. You know that."

"**Yeah** . . . yeah. You're right. At the same time though, I finally have this clarity to my life. I'm recognizing right now because I certainly didn't feel this way three days ago when my relationship ended. My emotions ebb and flow, but I'm hoping this finally sticks. I don't need to beat myself up anymore for the past. I think I can finally unburden myself from the hook ups and hurtful things I have said and the countless times I have disappointed the people I love. Because at the end of the day, I didn't deserve to get ALS, just like no one deserves to get cancer or any other disease, but this is the path I'm on now. The first step for me is to forgive myself, to move on from all the things out of my control. I'm not a bad person, nor have I ever been. I made mistakes, but that is no different from anyone else. Dylan, I need to make the time I have left worthwhile. Will you help me?"

"Yes. Of course."

We didn't bother eating any of the main course, but we had the chip bowl refilled three times as we sat there and talked endlessly. He asked me a million questions, which was highly unusual of him, but I felt the conversation sparked an instant shift in him. He asked me about work and how long I'd continue with that. He asked me about the traveling I wanted to do. He asked me if I would move back home. I didn't have an answer to any of them. I would with time, but it could wait.

After three years down in Dallas, the thing that finally helped me to change my perspective was that I was dying. And I thought I was trying hard to avoid stupid clichés like that. It feels like a cop out to me too, so don't worry. I understand if you're rolling your eyes at how convenient all of this has turned out to be. If anything, I learned that you can only run from the clichés for a while. We all get put back in order eventually to follow the same path as everyone else. Who's to say I will follow through with my new outlook on life? That's a different contemplation for a different day. I guess we will just have to wait and see. There needs to be a third book, right?

He offered to come back to my apartment and talk more, but I declined. I had a feeling it would lead to something rash and if we did want to explore that avenue of being intimate again, I didn't want it to be because we were both emotionally charged and not thinking clearly. I wasn't in a rush. There would be a moment where we would figure it out together.

My drive back home was not very far. I drove slow enough to listen to the song twice. I rolled down all four windows and spun the volume dial up so loud that I couldn't even hear myself yelling the lyrics over the thumping sound of the melody.

Maybe there was someone out there who heard me pass by and wondered what jackass was blasting music so loud at such a late time.

I couldn't have cared less.

For once, I wasn't concerned about time.

For once, I had all the time I'd ever need.

To make friends and reconnect with old ones.

To create memories.

To actually get better.

To feel alive.

To be fucking happy.

And most of all . . .

To finally change.

Are you seriously that gullible? Do you honestly think I sat across from Dylan and poured out my heart with the newfound epiphany?

Listen:

That is the ending you want, but this isn't that kind of story.

I'm not here to hold your hand and whisper pleasant thoughts into your ear before bedtime. I couldn't help myself. I guess I read too many John Green books and couldn't pass up the opportunity to give you a sappy ending.

How about we back up a bit and give the people what they came here for?

I didn't lie to you the entire time. I went to dinner with Dylan and told him that I'm dying because that's my boring reality. I do have a debilitating disease that will make me spiral to the darkest depth I will ever see. I did quote him a line from a Third Eye Blind song because I really like music. I did hear him say how I wouldn't be alone. Everything after the bolded word is bullshit though. (I just wanted to make it easy for you to go back and see exactly where I deceived you. Didn't it strike you as odd that a random word was bolded, or did you just chalk it up to one of my silly mistakes?)

When our conversation finally ended, I sat in my car alone for a while. I watched as his BMW pulled out of the lot and whipped down the street toward home. He wanted to come back to the apartment and make sure I didn't kill myself or something, but I told him I was fresh out of razor blades, so I'd need to try another time.

I knew Dylan didn't want to help me. He didn't know how and didn't have the energy to do it, but much like me, he was a fixer—just one that was taking longer to discover it. I'd see him again because misery loves company.

One thought kept repeating in my head: *I never thought I'd meet so many meaningless people.*

I tried to line up all the faces and sort them out within the queue, but it was impossible. The faces stretched well beyond the confines of the fictional building and I didn't have the patience to step through each one to recall their purpose.

Most didn't. Most of the faces would be of those inconsequential people that slipped into my life for a month or a day or barely an hour and then fucked off back to their own spiral.

And for the people who weren't entirely meaningless, you've heard pieces of their story but never the full thing. What would have been the point?

I backed out the spot and rolled the windows down. My commute home was short with just enough time to cycle through the Third Eye Blind song twice.

I pulled up to the red light and slowly smacked my head off the headrest three times.

"Sir?"

I jumped at the sound.

"Sir?" the voice asked from outside the window.

I looked over and saw the homeless woman who was usually staked outside the death wafting from the hospitals (specifically the one where JFK was taken after his head was blown to bits) that I so swiftly avoided each day. She had migrated over to the other side of town where the stink of death was minute. Maybe she could smell it on me though. It was closer than five years if I knew anything about myself.

The woman looked worse up closely.

"Hi. You scared me," I told her.

"Sorry sir. Do you have anything to spare?" she asked, holding out the cup. Not much was in there.

"I . . ."

"Whatever you can spare."

"How long have you been homeless?" I reached down toward the center console and began to scoop up what I had.

"I don't remember anymore."

"It'll get better soon."

"No. It won't."

I stopped grabbing the loose nickels and stared back at her. "Why not?"

"The light's green, sir."

I looked up at the rearview mirror. There were no cars behind me. Actually, there was no traffic on either side of the road. It's like the world stopped for us. Just for a moment though.

"I have nowhere to be."

She shook her head and began to walk away.

"Where are you going?" I asked.

"I have somewhere to be."

Not the answer I was expecting. "Oh—take this then."

She wobbled back over, and I dumped what I had in the car into her cup. "Is this all the change you have?"

"It's all I got unfortunately." For years I had been throwing spare pennies and quarters into the center console of my car, assuming I would need it for some big expenditure. What was the point of keeping it around any longer? I didn't see a point to much anymore. "I don't carry cash with me or else I could have given you more."

"This is plenty. Thank you, sir."

"You're welcome."

The woman turned away from the car and sat down in the small strip of grass. She flipped over the cup and began to sift through what I'd given her.

The light was still green, and I still sat there. I watched her push the quarters into one pile while everything else stayed lumped together. She was another meaningless person. It's not that she didn't have meaning to the world, just not to me.

I stepped off the brake and rolled through the intersection. The song was repeating for the fourth time.

I didn't pass by any cars for the rest of the drive. The world was quiet.

I winded up through the parking garage until I reached the top and was greeted again by the darkness. I parked haphazardly across three spots and got out with the engine still running.

Third Eye Blind told me again how I wasn't alone and how I should feel so alive. I didn't believe them, so I pulled myself up onto the ledge and looked down. Five floors up would probably be enough. I dangled one foot over the edge and tried to keep my balance.

I looked out. The skyline radiated with each building seamlessly blending into the next one like a dying mirage. The unmistakable roar of a 737-engine rumbled overhead.

It was just enough.

I placed my foot back on the ledge and dug my hands into my pockets. I pulled out two dimes, a nickel, and two pennies. How did I . . .

Dylan.

He paid with cash, remember?

I lied. I did have more change, but this was it.

The change began to get warm and soggy in my clenched fist. In a quick motion, I tossed it out into the courtyard below. I listened for the impact, but the sound never reached me.

I had nothing left to give.

I stepped off the ledge and sat back in the car. I picked up my phone and navigated to Spotify. I typed in **Ble** and the top result gave me what I wanted. The song sat in the Popular section and I selected it.

There was no chance in hell I would ever get better, but that didn't mean I couldn't listen to the song that inspired my failed journey.

I twisted the knob on the stereo until the car rattled from the deafening blasts of the bass. I kept turning it until MAX VOLUME showed up on the LED screen. I rolled up the windows to contain the noise. There was no need to spare my hearing anymore. I wouldn't need it intact for much longer.

I sat up there listening to Jack Antonoff sing the false mantra over and over. Sometimes I switched over to Troye Sivan just to remind myself of the good side Evan was enjoying, wherever he was.

Will *you* be sad when I die? Will *you* even remember me?

I'm so scared of being forgotten.

But I'm just another dot after all—a meaningless person in the great stories others are living.

If I stepped off that ledge and plummeted into the courtyard below, would I be missed?

No, I didn't think I would be. Which was just enough of a pleasant thought to get me down.

I had more meaningless people to meet, but it could wait.

It was past midnight and I needed to go home.

As I winded back down through the parking garage, one thought echoed in my head:

I am so tired of it all.

Made in the USA
Middletown, DE
09 August 2021